I0761178

A RIDDLE OF THORNS

SARENA NANUA & SASHA NANUA

HOLIDAY HOUSE  NEW YORK

Printed and bound in August 2025 at Sheridan, Chelsea, MI, USA.
www.holidayhouse.com
First Edition
1 3 5 7 9 10 8 6 4 2

Library of Congress Cataloging-in-Publication Data is available.

ISBN: 978-0-8234-6042-7 (hardcover)

EU Authorized Representative: HackettFlynn Ltd, 36 Cloch Choirneal, Balrothery, Co. Dublin, K32 C942, Ireland. EU@walkerpublishinggroup.com

For our mom and dad, who have the green thumbs in the family.

We love you so much!

PART I: THE INVITATION

Paris, France

September 1913, Cycle of Light

One petal for wisdom,
Two for the muses
Three to affect the mind
And four to heal all bruises.

ONE

Every year on my birthday, my mother gifted me a riddle. It wasn't my entire gift, but until I solved it, I wouldn't receive my true birthday present: a bottle of her sweet, handcrafted lavender perfume; a bundle of freshly clipped wildflowers; or, on my eighth birthday, a swing set in the garden wrapped in long vines of wisteria.

I suppose she was preparing me, in a way, for the largest riddle of my life—why she disappeared without a trace seven years ago.

The horses jerked to a halt.

My coach driver poked a bald head through the curtain that separated us. "For gods' sake, young lady, I can't leave you here! Don't you know Razorthorn Manor is haunted?"

As a matter of fact, I did know.

I peeled my gaze away from my gold pocket watch to look out the open window. Now a shade of its former self, Razorthorn Manor looked dull and overgrown, with vines smothering the cracked windows and empty sills. The knocker attached to the front door, shaped like the estate's namesake plant, had rusted from copper to murky green. The bleached roof sloped elegantly on either side, held up by several columns, the ivory pillars engraved with Flora's abundant garlands.

And there: the wrought-iron gate to the garden stood ajar, exactly as I remembered it, its silver lock and chain puddled on the grass. I didn't need to look inside to know what was left behind—the garden where I played and laughed, cried and raged. Dead.

Autumn air blew through the coach's window, soaked with a haunting chill. But it wasn't the wind that made me shiver.

This was the last place I saw Maman.

I cleared the cobwebs from my memory and summoned the dregs of one recollection in particular: Maman and I standing in front of the garden gate, just two days before her disappearance.

"How about another round of Marbles and Riddles?" Maman asked. Despite the way the sun's rays poured over her, she looked like a faded version of herself, as though I were watching her move from within a creased sepia photograph.

"Shh!" I chided. My hair was tied up in a bun in a failed attempt to emulate my mother. "Don't let Marta hear us!"

Maman winked, her deep brown eyes alight with mischief. She pretended to lock her lips, then pressed a velvet pouch of marbles into my tiny palm like it was a secret she wanted me to protect. I dashed off, barely noticing the faint wrinkle of worry between her brows.

"You must have heard the rumors, I'm sure," the driver remarked at my silence. "Ghosts, strange sounds in the garden, ever since that woman drowned in the Seine—"

"Her name was Tara Gupta," I snapped, my voice as harsh as the tug of the reins that leashed the horses to the carriage. "And she's no phantom."

Not the physical sort, the kind that haunts a place past death. No, my mother was a ghost of a different kind; the kind that plagued my mind, my dreams, and my nightmares.

"Of course, mademoiselle," the driver said, beads of sweat dotting his brow. "But don't speak her name too loudly, lest Pluto hear us and think we wish for trouble."

I smiled thinly. Clearly this man had no clue who I was—but then, I liked it that way. People who did know always compared me to my mother: how I looked, how I dressed, how I acted. Like I wasn't a girl, a daughter, in my own right.

Worse yet, the ugliest, beastliest rumors about her also colored their views of me. One rumor implied my mother hadn't drowned but disappeared for a bit of fame, planning to return within a month. Another said she was secretly bankrupt, owing money to the government and running from her home in shame. And most laughable of all: she'd joined the circus to become the Disappearing Woman, teleporting twenty meters in a matter of seconds.

Maybe not quite so laughable for the latter. Maman had been a famous aerial artist, performing at the most talked-about theaters in Paris: the Cirque Molièr, the Cirque Fernando, the Nouveau Cirque. People would come from near and far to see her breathtaking act. After she became a household name, she would often put on her show right here at the gate to Razorthorn Manor. She was something of a scandalous woman that way.

On instinct, my left hand rose to the necklace hidden under my dress collar, thumbing the key-shaped pendant as if it might unlock the truth to Maman's fate. She had left it to me, after all.

"Thank you for the ride." I pressed a heavy coin into the driver's upturned palm. On it, Janus's two faces winked in the gray September light.

I exited the coach with my trunk. The horses trotted away, the driver shaking his head. I clutched my coat tight, turned to the house—and stopped cold.

A stranger was standing outside the door to the estate.

The boy looked my age. Where had he come from? When his eyes caught mine, he raised a bony hand in awkward greeting. I didn't return it, preferring to study him from toe to collar. He wore a black trench coat that even a hard-of-seeing seamstress would know needed hemming, and he was nervously adjusting a bronze pipe between his fingers as if it were a prop and he was about to enter stage left. Altogether, he affected a caricature of an eminent but decidedly fictional detective.

I crossed the uneven cobblestone path toward him. His skin was flushed from the biting morning air, fading the freckles on his nose. Dastardly strands of reddish-brown hair were covered by a burgundy cap, which he doffed in greeting.

"A Sherlock reader, monsieur?" My old nanny, Marta—who had raised me in this very manor—always told me it was important to start a conversation with a common interest.

"How could you tell?" the boy asked, his English accent thick. Like mine, his eyes were a deep, rich brown, and his skin held a tawny tint despite his pink ears and nose.

In answer, I pointed at the small book poking out of his right pocket: *A Guide on Holmes.*

"Ah, that," the boy said, tucking it deeper as if it were a shameful report card. "I'm a fan of detective stories. But Father prefers I focus on poetry. So I've dedicated four days a week to reading Rimbaud. You've heard of him, I assume? *Voyelles*?"

I narrowed my eyes. Certainly *everyone* in Paris knew Rimbaud.

"This is my family's property," I stated, painting on a cool smile that did little to hide the scowl underneath. "Are you here to deliver something? A parcel, perhaps?"

"Not a parcel, no." The boy removed his cap and extracted a small piece of folded paper. He unfurled it, revealing the street name, rue du Renard. "There was more to the message, but I ripped this part off as instructed."

"As instructed?" I echoed. What was going on?

"Richard Fox," the boy announced, replacing his cap and sticking out a hand. I shook it weakly, still turning his words over. "Well, technically Richard Fox the Second. But just Fox will do."

The boy *did* remind me of a fox, with those keen eyes, blushing cheeks, and fiery hair.

"Pleasure to meet you, Just Fox." I hadn't meant to make him laugh, but he snorted anyway. *Odd, this Richard Fox.*

He pinched his features back to neutrality. "So, your family owns the manor?"

"They do," I explained, "though it's been empty for ages. Well, seven years to be exact." I shook my head. "Where *are* my manners? I'm Sana Gupta."

At that name, the boy frowned slightly.

He must have caught a whiff of my reputation, then. The famous Tara Gupta's only child, a child whose displays of temper and lack of decorum—something I considered highly overrated—were whispered of even when I was very young. And since then? An absent heiress. My new guardians in Canada, whom I'd been staying with since my mother's death, had received word from my estranged aunt Neena to meet me for my homecoming.

Now that I was here, I could fulfill my dream: to claim my inheritance and restore the house to its original grandeur. It would awaken to its former glory, the way a perennial withers before returning to full bloom. And then I would sell it and make a life all my own.

This was my chance to say goodbye to the estate where I had crawled, walked, and eventually raced among poisonous thorns.

A chance to say goodbye to Maman. To the woman who had never said goodbye to me.

"Enchanté, Sana." The boy's frown had morphed into a look of curiosity. "Shall we explore the moor? This place must be *crawling* with ghosts. Even a spirit hound or two." He leaned in conspiratorially. "Even all the way out here in the twenty-first arrondissement, I am certain we'd be able to find something... *otherworldly*."

He was referring, obviously, to the inexplicable string of strange happenings that had plagued Paris: the Great Flood of 1910, the lightning storms of 1911, and so on. They were splashed all over the morning papers, even an ocean away. Signs of the gods and their displeasure. Some went so far as to say that Paris was cursed—by Neptune, most thought, given the tempests. Many prayed to him, to placate him, though they didn't understand what offense humanity had committed in the first place.

"This estate is quite safe, I assure you," I sniffed.

"Not even any ghosts on the property?"

"I think the real question you should be asking is if there are any *bodies*," I offered dispassionately. I couldn't help myself.

Fox paled; I grinned.

"Come now, Sherlock," I said. "Holmes never believed in ghosts."

At that, the door handle began to rattle as if possessed. Startled, Fox dropped his pipe, and I jerked back. The door swung open to reveal a woman with a shock of corn-silk hair streaked with silver, wearing a smock and carrying a tray of freshly filled lemon macarons.

"Marta?" I managed after a moment.

"Mademoiselle Gupta!" My old nanny twisted her lips into a grin. "If it isn't the girl with the rosy cheeks and sour smile. Some things never change."

My face burned. I glanced at the garden, memories stirring inside of me. My childhood was full of days spent memorizing the shapes of the clouds, of grazing waxy orchid petals that stained my fingertips violet. But Marta was right—not a day went by without a tantrum of some kind. And when I'd roared with anger, it was Marta who had rushed to soothe me, not Maman.

Long-buried feelings resurfaced. When my mother left to perform her act overseas, it was considered normal. I pretended I was fine while Marta kept the household together. And when my mother came back, as she always did except the last time, she slipped in like she'd gone for a mere walk about the gardens, regaling no tales of her performances or discoveries. Sometimes I wondered if she'd kept secret a whole life outside of the manor. In the time she did spend with me, playing games and riddles was all that mattered—not slipping my baby-blue Mary Janes onto my feet, nor twisting a velvet ribbon into my braided hair.

Speaking of.

"Your hair…"

Marta ran a hand over her graying locks. "Yes, raising children will do that to you." Her fair skin looked like it hadn't seen sunlight in weeks. "But I see I am not the only one ill-affected by time. Only seven years, yet you've already begun to sprout premature wrinkles." She tutted. "I thought you were past temper tantrums?"

I pressed a hand to my forehead, which I prayed was smooth enough. "I'm not as stubborn as I used to be."

"I would hope not."

I still couldn't quite fathom that she was here, or how much time had passed—time that had brought us to the same height.

"You made macarons?" My mouth salivated at the sight of my childhood favorite, one she reserved for special occasions. Had she remembered it was my birthday? And if so, why were we dancing around the subject with trivialities like *wrinkles*?

"Yes, I knew you would be arriving soon," she said. "Come in. And welcome, dear boy. You must be Monsieur Richard Fox."

"I simply go by Fox, madame. Are you the one who invited me here?"

"And where is Neena Massi?" I wondered aloud. "My aunt should be here. She's supposed to help me with the house." I had met my mother's sister at least once as a child but could barely remember her.

Marta's gaze skittered away from mine.

"Come inside, children," she said, evasive as ever. "We have a lot to discuss."

TWO

"How long does a flower have to live?" Maman asked me once, tapping the dimple at my chin.

"As long as the love of its owner," I replied.

She had grabbed my nose playfully, excited that I was a professional riddle solver. That one wasn't a riddle so much as a lesson. *Care for what is yours. Love thy garden, love thyself.*

The words hummed like honeybees in the back of my mind as I entered the house. Each time I had imagined stepping back into Razorthorn Manor, I had seen myself weeping. I never would have guessed no tears would arise. I must have shed them all when Maman disappeared without leaving a note behind.

Instead of feeling a swell of pleasure at seeing my old home, my heart fell like a heavy coin into the Seine. Even my memory couldn't paper over what I now witnessed. The floral wallpaper had begun to peel and fade. Some of the walls sagged inward, like a child clutching their knees. Dust motes circled through the air. The only light came from the old chandelier, which bathed the entrance chamber in a deep orange glow. I had suspected disrepair—it was what I hoped to reverse—but what I didn't expect was the frigidity of the house's embrace.

The cold, unfeeling emptiness.

The scent of lemon zest whisked through the air. Memory led my feet, carrying me all the way to the kitchens. How strange it was to walk the halls of my childhood, so similar and yet so…empty. So much taller was I now that the corridors seemed too narrow. As if I had outgrown the home before it outgrew me.

"Incredible," Fox said, following behind me. He gestured at the four additional trays of macarons on the kitchen's central wooden table. "Mother never bakes for me. She resents it just as much as the illness that's eating her away."

"I'm sorry," I said, startled, but Fox simply shrugged, like he'd heard the stiff apology too many times before. I knew the feeling; apologies didn't fill Maman's absence, or the emotions that came with it.

"On the other hand," Fox continued, "Father says baking is a science, so I should study genetics before I even attempt a sponge cake."

"Biology before baklava?" I suggested, trying to lighten the mood. He must not have thought it was clever, because he simply examined the macarons at eye level.

Marta's voice was oddly warm behind us. "I've made raspberry macarons as well. Go on. Try them."

If this were a talking picture, we'd reached the part where the boy tried the sweet old grandma's cake, smiled dumbfoundedly, and proceeded to drop to the floor, poisoned.

But this script went askew. Famished from the trip, I gave in and tried a lemon macaron, taking a careful bite before stuffing the rest into my mouth with sudden appetite.

Each mouthful of the slightly crunchy exterior and the soft middle was like a summer day in the garden, when Maman brought lemonade to my wicker swing set deep in the undergrowth. She had always told me that the garden was gargantuan, filled to the brim with plants: profusions of roses and privets; riots of foxglove, lupine, and hollyhock; pergolas overgrown with clematis and jasmine. I never knew my father, but it was certain from the love in Maman's eyes that she and the garden were the truest soulmates to ever have existed.

Envy gripped me at the thought of those same flowers. Maman cared for them so much—it was only natural that they died after she left. Sometimes I wondered if she would have paid me more mind if I were part flower, part girl.

Marta cleared her throat sharply.

"Now, Richard Fox," she said, "I am Marta LeBlanc, keeper of the estate and former nanny to Mademoiselle Sana Gupta. To answer your earlier question, I *did* invite you here by post, and you arrived quite promptly. Thank you for coming all this way."

Promptly? What was this boy invited for? And how far had he traveled? If his English accent was any indication, his trip had taken only a few hours. Meanwhile, my transatlantic flight was noisy and not at all smooth, but at least I had my cross-stitch to accompany me. (One might consider that a dangerous sport on a small, bumpy airplane.)

"I should call upon the others from the sitting room. Mademoiselle Flores—"

A girl appeared in the kitchen in a flash. "Isabelle, please. Those macarons were delicious, madame. You got the feet just right—a *feat* in itself."

My nanny brightened as she flapped a hand. "It's an old family recipe."

This girl had drawn a smile out of Marta quicker than I ever could.

Warily, I studied her from the bottom up. She wore black boots and an ivory-white day dress with stylish Italian sleeves. Her dark curls fell in long waves, her tan skin washed with a dewy glow. On her nose sat a wiry pair of glasses, which framed her midnight eyes. But I swore when those eyes met mine, her lips pursed as if to resist a frown, and she offered me an icy gaze.

Marta glanced behind me. "Ah, there he is. Our final guest…"

"Not a moment too late, I hope," a deep voice cut in.

I whirled toward—and nearly growled at—yet another stranger who had appeared in my home, this one a boy who had snuck up behind us. The suit he wore, unlike Fox's trench coat, fit his every edge perfectly, tailored precisely to his tall body. He looked a bit like a gentleman plucked straight from the pages of an Austen tome, and he appeared to know it: handsome, poised, and wearing a half smirk, he exuded an air of haughtiness, not unlike the rakish George Wickham.

It was a good thing I preferred stories with rogues.

"Let me guess," I began. "*You* aren't here to deliver a parcel, either."

The boy's thick black eyebrows knit. "And how would you know what it is that I have to offer?"

I wasn't used to someone being so level with me. I equipped myself with my sharpest retort. "I'm a good judge of character. Believe me, there's nothing you have that I need."

"Now, now, Sana," Marta clucked, "where is your courtesy? These are our honored guests, and our hallowed halls are more than happy to accommodate them."

Hallowed. I nearly snorted.

The estate's grounds were ancient, rumored for generations to be a sacred precinct of the goddess Flora. Once, people had flocked here from far and wide, believing her grandiose magic was imbued into the ground, and that these very gardens sprang forth of her beneficence. When I was a child, I foolishly thought that the garden's flowers were tethered to my *mother* instead of Flora, as though she was their lifeline, their sun, their water, their soil. And when she was gone, there was no more point in living.

Now I knew better than to believe in puerile fantasies. This half-forgotten history, likely imagined, was secondhand to gossip, and I didn't have the mind to pay much attention to either.

I was too busy studying the three strangers in the room. The Sherlockian boy; the well-dressed but standoffish girl; and the boy who'd yet to introduce himself. Who were they? And why was Marta dodging my questions, her gaze restive, an excess of macarons on the table...

Oh.

There was only one plausible explanation.

A birthday party. Of course.

I was here to collect my inheritance, my property—but it *was* also my eighteenth birthday. Were there going to be gifts, or performers, or more lemony confections? Perhaps a charlotte russe, as was tradition for my special day? Was Marta going to announce my majority before a crowd of well-to-do Parisians invited to the manor to witness the festivities? It was no wonder my old nanny hadn't uttered any birthday wishes or that my aunt hadn't shown herself. It was to be a surprise!

I could play along, for Marta's benefit at the very least.

"Indeed," Fox asked me, grinning, "where *are* those precious manners you offered to me earlier?"

Two could play at that game. I bowed stiffly at the boy who'd entered the kitchen behind me. "My *sincerest* apologies, Monsieur..."

"Kim Minho," he filled in. I recognized the naming system from my time practicing Korean with my governess overseas, who taught me that language was a key to locks often overlooked.

This boy, however, didn't seem very unlockable.

"I assume this is the correct residence?" He held up a slip of paper identical to Fox's. "I wasn't aware there would be... others."

"Oui, oui. Explanations will come soon," Marta said, her French accent coming out in thick waves. From my time spent in India, Canada, and France, I only shared a fraction of my nanny's accent, as if my tongue couldn't quite decide where I belonged. "Now that you're all here, we can begin."

The study was a miniature library, with books in all kinds of languages and subjects surrounding a stately desk that faced a half-moon window. Maman had spent much time here, affectionately naming it her "puzzle room." Not for playing games, but quite literally puzzling. She had taken her coffee black and marched here right at dawn, like clockwork, for two months straight before her disappearance. Sometimes she'd passed entire days here, thinking to herself and not speaking a word, so that when dinner came around, her voice was dry from disuse.

The room was entirely how I remembered it. My mother's chair even sat in the same spot, slouching with tired, aching legs. Instead of wide-plank flooring, the study was covered wall-to-wall with a carnation-patterned carpet imported from India. The warm oak desk, made from a tree that had fallen in the garden, held several knots I'd traced over and over as a child.

Instinctively, I approached it, feeling the years between eleven and eighteen melt away. I was a child again, watching Maman fiddle with her papers, sunlight streaming through the curtains and kissing her warm brown skin. Maman lowered her glasses and let them hang from a beaded chain around her neck, pressing her fingers against the sides of her nose in exhaustion. But when she turned to me, the corners of her lips tilted up in a knowing smile. That smile... It flickered like autumn weather: some days dampened with rain, some days bright with sunshine. But it was a smile no less.

I wondered, occasionally, if she was just a vision made up in my mind, a woman I'd designed from scraps of paper and glue to patch the holes in my memory.

"Thank you all for arriving on time. I worried myself, wondering whether you would all make it," Marta said with a weak laugh. She placed herself before the door, as if blocking the four of us from leaving. "Now, where were we... Ah, yes." Marta unfolded and read from a paper in her hands. " 'The four of you children will have twenty minutes to complete this game—' "

"A game, you say?" Fox repeated quizzically. "I'm not sure I follow."

"Apologies for my vagueness. I wish I could tell you more, but..." Marta glanced behind her, as if there could be someone listening. " 'You have twenty minutes exactly from the moment the door is closed to find the means to exit this room. If you fail, you will have no further need to stay on the premises. I hope none of you will come up against any... *issues*.' "

Marta focused her eyes on mine. She knew I didn't play well with others.

Minho started, "But what about the—"

"Twenty minutes," my nanny repeated, as if she were simply telling us the time until the next train left Paris. "Bonne chance."

With that, Marta slipped out of the room, shut the door, and, turning the outside lock, trapped us inside.

THREE

Minho tried to rattle the knob, but it wouldn't budge. "I suppose this is *one* way to entertain visitors."

My first thought wasn't the peculiarity of Marta's dramatic exit; it was the fact that I didn't recall the study having *had* a lock before. Ever.

Silence hung thick in the air.

The guests scrunched their brows in puzzlement, but I had an inkling of what was going on. Maman always gave me a riddle to solve the morning of my birthday; surely Marta was merely honoring that tradition with this little game, and inviting the party guests to play as well.

That was Maman: a woman who loved riddles so much, she made her life into one.

Maybe Marta was still preparing for the party and needed us out of the way. Once I escaped this study, she would have a table laden with sweets and cakes to eat, and the finest of Maman's jewels for me to wear. Now that I was officially to inherit her things, it was imperative I did so properly. Maman had always wanted me to be her puzzle protégée.

A stab of longing pierced my stomach at the thought of my mother. *No*—today was my birthday, and I wouldn't let anything sour the mood.

"Hurry," I said, "time is wasting."

Fox checked his pocket watch. "Thirty seconds elapsed." He

snapped the watch face shut. "I've always wanted to be in a locked-room mystery, but I have to admit, I'm a bit stumped!"

The three strangers gazed at me expectantly.

Maman always told me that people were like flowers. *If you were a flower, you would be a razorthorn. A girl with wits as sharp as a barb.*

Meanwhile, Fox was a playful, if a bit aloof, hyacinth. Isabelle seemed to be a white carnation, innocent and pure. And Minho's prickly demeanor reminded me of a lily of the valley—a beautiful flower that was toxic in every part of its anatomy.

The group was still looking at me as if I had an answer, so I gave them one. "If we divide ourselves, we will find an exit faster. Isabelle and Fox, you look at the desk. Minho and I will examine the room itself."

Isabelle nodded. To my right, Fox slipped something out of his inner breast pocket—a *magnifying glass*, how Sherlockian—with which he began inspecting every inch of Maman's desk. I would have taken offense to his snooping if it weren't for the game.

I started by looking at the books covering the shelves from wall to wall. A collection of poems by Dickinson, Stoker's *Dracula* for a rainy day, ten dense encyclopedias on the matter of the solar system . . . My fingers trailed over the spines, each covered in the finest layer of dust.

"Interesting door." Minho rapped on the wood twice. "Walnut is heavy and durable. There's no pattern, though—no sign of craftsmanship at all."

I spun around, amused. "Are *you* a craftsman?"

"No."

I observed his polished cuff links. "A man of enterprise? A young businessman?"

His jaw clenched. "Not exactly," he said, almost offended, but then his tone lightened. "See the crown molding? It's a specific design—a series of Roman numerals. Perhaps custom-made for this very room."

"And?" I asked, approaching him. He certainly had an eye for architectural detail.

"The rest of the manor doesn't appear to have the same molding, which indicates—"

"This might be a clue," I finished, breathless. Although I hardly knew the stranger before me, he tilted his lips into a small, satisfied smile—one that took me a long second to draw my eyes away from.

"*Over here!*"

Whatever bubble Minho and I were in popped. We moved swiftly to join Isabelle and Fox.

"I think we found something: a series of newspapers hidden in the drawers. They were behind a false panel. I felt the seam with my hand and pushed." Isabelle turned to me. "Any idea what these might mean?"

I glanced at the yellowed papers on my mother's desk. Maman had loved to pore over the morning edition of *The Paris Gazette*, the rings from her coffee cup staining the pages like a signature. I circled a finger over one of those rings, at a loss.

"I—I'm not sure." I looked up at the group, almost ashamed to let them down—but more terrified to let down Maman.

Look around you. Her voice was as clear as a crystal vase. *What do you see, ma petite papillon?*

Her nickname for me warmed my skin like candlelight on a long winter's evening. Although Maman rarely called me her *little butterfly*, and oftentimes left me for days or even weeks, I remembered our time together fondly. Beneath the shade of a vibrant magnolia tree, she told me stories of our ancestral home in Punjab, India.

"Over a century ago, our ancestors were farmers whose land grew arid and barren in the sudden heat of spring. No rain fell for weeks. They prayed and prayed, until a single seed fell from the sky. This they planted. And a spellbinding flower grew from the soil—the razorthorn."

Maman was fascinated by the legendary flower, by its very idea of its existence. She always spoke of it with a mixture of pride and terror. Like it was something too great, and too powerful, to have ever come into this world.

I thought of the razorthorn proverb my mother once recited to me like a lullaby; it explained how the flower's petals could be used, either alone or in combination, for four unique applications:

ONE PETAL FOR WISDOM,
TWO FOR THE MUSES
THREE TO AFFECT THE MIND
AND FOUR TO HEAL ALL BRUISES.

"Soon, my ancestors were no longer plowing the land under the sun's punishing rays, but cultivating the flower's power, and their fortune with it. They said the goddess of flowers, Flora, offered the razorthorn as a gift to the Guptas, a gift with godly abilities. Many of the Gupta women took to healing after discovering that brewing four razorthorn petals into a tincture could heal a bruise or reverse disease. My ancestors' fame grew, and anyone who married into the family took the Gupta name with pride."

"What if you combined all five petals? What power did that have?" I'd asked her.

"Unfortunately, it remains a mystery. Our ancestors felt such a combination might be too powerful, and they never attempted it. But I believe one day this power will be discovered, and it will be the key to unlocking the world of the gods."

She meant it metaphorically, of course. One could not enter Olympus.

But then I thought of the way Maman spoke of the flower—as if it were a deity. As powerful as Jupiter's thunderbolt, or Neptune's trident.

Jupiter and Neptune... I looked up at the Roman numerals on the ceiling, then back down at the newspapers. The pages had Roman numerals instead of Arabic numbers.

An idea sprang to mind. "Remember what Marta said? She hoped we wouldn't have any *issues*. She must have been talking about the issues of the paper!"

"*Aha!*" Fox cheered. He tilted the magnifying glass over his eye, enlarging it. "Which means... well, what does it mean?"

"It *means*," Isabelle huffed, "that we're finally getting somewhere. If we can figure out what's next."

"Deductive reasoning?" Fox tugged on his cap. "*That* I can do."

"There are too many issues here to sort through." Minho tapped the papers. "How do we know which one will give us a clue?"

"I'm guessing the Roman numerals might give us a start." I pointed at the crown molding. "They go around the room in a pattern: one to five, five to one. Let's look at those pages first."

I handed out issues to each of them, glad they all agreed with my reasoning. Precious minutes passed as we examined the papers, looking for anything relevant, but all I could spot were Maman's coffee stains.

"Is anyone missing a page?" Minho asked. "Page five is missing in this collection."

I double-checked my sheaf. "That's odd. I'm missing the fifth page in all of my issues, too."

The Roman numeral V was missing in Isabelle's and Fox's collections as well. But what could the number be pointing us toward?

"Five is a prime number," Minho supplied.

"We have five senses," Isabelle offered, "and there are five basic tastes to the culinary palette, including sweet, salty, bitter, sour, and—"

"Jupiter!"

Everyone faced me like I'd grown a third eye.

"Jupiter is the fifth planet in the solar system from the sun!"

"And one of the gods," Minho realized. My coach driver's words echoed in my eardrums. *Don't speak her name too loudly, lest Pluto hear us.*

The puzzle pieces snapped together in my mind. I scanned the shelves until I found the encyclopedias I'd spotted earlier and pulled each of them out. One in particular was stuck in place—the volume on Jupiter. I tried to pry it out. Even Minho tried, but it was no use.

Seconds slipped by like sand between my fingers. I needed to think the way Maman would. Every puzzle had a solution.

If the book wouldn't come *out*... it would have to go *in*.

I pushed the book back, relieved when a *click* emanated from the shelf. The bookcase swung open to reveal a small, bricked cavity—a hidden passageway, low enough that we would have to proceed on hands and knees. While the others gaped, I wore a proud grin as I dipped down and crawled. My mother had often hidden things around the house in little nooks and crannies for me to find, but this was something new. Were there more secrets like this waiting for me?

"Well?" I called back, already partway down the passage. The others stared after me in fascination. "Are you going to look at it, or are you going to come?"

To my surprise, Isabelle entered first, followed by Fox, then Minho. Once we made it about ten paces, we arrived at a blocked end. I noticed a small pinpoint of light in the wall, reached forward, and felt a latch. A small door opened into the parlor, and I stood up and dusted myself off.

Nothing Sana Gupta couldn't handle.

Minho, out last, slipped the door shut. It blended in perfectly with the wallpaper.

The parlor had several chaises, a piano, and a long, ornate table for tea and cakes. Portraits of philosophers hung on the wall (likely to incite stimulating conversation), but in practice, this had been more my playroom and less a salon. To my left, the lilting tune of Berlioz's *Symphonie fantastique* played from a phonograph. I recognized it as one I'd scuffed once when dodging Marta's scolds, which had earned me a harsh chiding and a spank on the legs.

"So? How much time do we have left?" I asked Marta, who stood by the door as she inspected the grandfather clock. Beside her, a butler I did not recognize waited with a tray of teacups and an ornate teapot.

No cakes or treats or birthday celebrations to be seen.

"Two minutes to spare. You children gave me a fright!"

"You really should have more faith in me," I said in jest, but something was off. *Where is my party? And my aunt?*

Marta paused the phonograph. "Looks like everyone is accounted for. Please, have a seat. I'm sorry for all the fuss, but I was following direct orders. Thankfully, you all passed the test. Monsieur Champlain, the refreshments, if you please?"

The butler immediately laid the teacups on the low cherrywood table and poured the floral jasmine concoction to the brim.

"Marta," I said, not even trying to hide the shade of bewilderment in my voice, "what is going on? I thought you were organizing some sort of surprise for me. For my *birthday*." I tried to wear something remotely close to a smile but failed. I never did learn how to smile like Maman. The old butler, Monsieur Boucher, thought I ate lemons for breakfast.

"Ah." Marta sat. "I'm sorry this isn't what you hoped for, Sana, and I do wish you well on your eighteenth birthday... but I'm afraid we're here for a much different reason. Now, I assume you all brought your slips?"

Each stranger obediently held out small, ripped papers, which the butler retrieved with pristine white gloves.

"One can never be too cleanly," he said to me at my look of curiosity.

As Monsieur Champlain left to dispose of the papers, tailcoats dragging behind him, Marta continued. "I asked all of you to burn your invitations except for the address in hopes that no one else would be informed of today's meeting."

"Meeting?" I echoed, my voice razorthorn-sharp. The only person I was meant to meet was my aunt—who clearly hadn't bothered to show up.

"I still don't understand, Marta. Why would you invite *them* to this estate?"

Marta chuckled grimly. "Why, Sana, that's where you're wrong. *I* didn't choose to invite anyone. Your mother did."

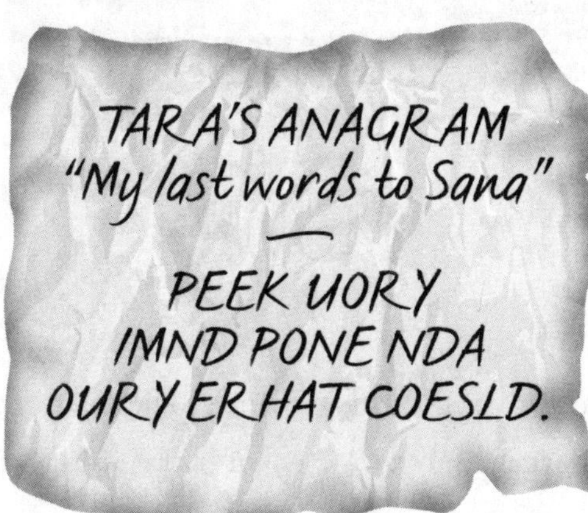

[Solution: Keep your mind open and your heart closed.]

FOUR

"Maman?" I gasped. My legs turned to liquid, forcing me to sit.

Marta calmly took a sip of tea, as if I hadn't just spoken. "She left me a letter in her will. In it, her instructions were clear, stating that you four were to be brought here on Sana's eighteenth birthday. The first test, in the study, was to ensure you would all be capable of the greater task ahead—and you have passed splendidly. It was imperative I kept this plan a secret until Sana's majority, in accordance with Madame Gupta's wishes. I have done only as instructed—nothing more, nothing less."

"You're saying *my mother* orchestrated all of this?"

Marta scolded me with her eyes. "Sana—"

"Excuse me, Madame LeBlanc," Isabelle began, "I don't mean to sound rude, but I believe there is a prize to be collected?"

"That is exactly the question I was about to ask." Fox nodded. "Good looking out for clues."

"It was written in the letter," Minho deadpanned.

Marta stood. "You are exactly right, Isabelle. And, Sana, before you have another outburst, let me show you the letter everyone else received."

My cheeks flamed. In my peripheral vision, Minho was looking at me with a certain satisfaction, as if he enjoyed knowing something I did not. Not very gentlemanly of him.

My nanny headed for a cabinet in the room's far corner. She opened it, unlatched a box, and removed a note before returning. Before she could even move to offer it to me, I rose from the chaise and rushed to take the paper from her with a hot hand.

Dear contestant,

You are cordially invited to Razorthorn Manor at nine o'clock in the morning on 22 September 1913. Please arrive on time to 129 rue du Renard, in the twenty-first arrondissement of Paris, to claim your chance at the inheritance of a lifetime.

Yours,
Marta LeBlanc

P.S. You must come alone, or else forfeit your chance at the aforementioned bequest. Details on what to bring are included below.

My eyes stopped reading, but my pulse raced faster.

Future. Inheritance. Each word coiled in my mind, ready to burst forth like springs.

"What is the meaning of this?" I asked, crumpling and tossing the letter on the table.

Marta sighed like she knew this was coming. Carefully, she set her teacup down on a bone-white saucer. "Put simply, you are here because one of you stands to inherit this estate."

"*What*?" I cried. It came out almost as a scream, one so forceful I fairly fell back into my seat.

Marta gave me a long, hard stare. Isabelle looked frightened, while Minho only gazed at me out of the corner of his eye, as if embarrassed to be seated beside such an unmannerly girl.

"Only a fool would believe Maman wanted a complete *stranger* to have the house," I spluttered, as if I'd just drunk a scalding cup of tea. "You all can't possibly tell me that you all believed such a cryptic letter and came all the way from— Where *did* you come from?"

"East London," Fox answered simply. "My father was a bit concerned at first, I admit, but I insisted on attending. An offer of an inheritance isn't to be taken lightly."

Minho clasped his hands together and said, a bit boastfully, "I've recently begun my second year of studies at the Sorbonne and am living with my uncle here in Paris. While I'd never been to the twenty-first arrondissement, I've heard Razorthorn Manor takes up quite a bit of the acreage. If the house itself is the inheritance, then . . ."

Isabelle adjusted her glasses. "Then we must have been invited here for a special reason."

Marta nodded. "According to Tara Gupta, each of your families' ancestors once possessed the razorthorn flower . . . and then lost it."

Four families.

Four flowers.

Of course—Maman had told me stories about the other three families who'd once possessed the razorthorn. Their names, formerly blurred in my memory, now stood out with sudden clarity: the Foxes, the Kims, and the Floreses.

I glanced at Fox, Isabelle, and Minho as understanding dawned on us.

Marta continued, "To understand the origins of the razorthorn flower, we must first speak of its creator: Flora, goddess of flowers, fertility, and youth. Since the dawn of the age of the gods, she often descended from the heavens to commune with and gift knowledge to humans. She and the other gods have had a special role to play in history, as you know."

Minho tucked his hands around his crossed knees studiously. "Some say Cupid brought together the great and terrible couple that was Louis XVI and Marie Antoinette."

"I was taught that the Great Fire of 1666 was Mars's doing," Fox tacked on. "Being the militant god of war, it's a wonder the fire didn't spark the flame of a revolution."

"Perhaps it did. A silent one, still growing—not *everyone* agrees with the gods' ways." Isabelle whispered these words, but all of us could hear her. She wasn't wrong. The gods' interest in our world wasn't always in our favor.

I broke the silence that followed. "And Flora gifted our four families the razorthorn flower."

Isabelle spoke again, only louder this time. "My mother says the flower came to her ancestors in a time of great need, and that the seed bloomed in just one day. They simply called it Bulaklak—the Flower. They used two of its five petals—which regrew in a matter of days—to call upon the muses and stir their creativity, infusing the petals into homespun recipes. Instead of traditional hibiscus or squash flower, the Flower became my family's most treasured ingredient. When eaten, its power allowed them to create shimmering paints, to bend clay into the finest pottery. My great-uncle swore the Flower enhanced his artistry, so his portraits looked almost alive. And my grandmother sold paintings so fine that they covered the cost of our house in the Philippines."

"Is that where you traveled from?" I asked.

The girl shook her head. "Actually, my family lives in America now. They hoped for a good life, a lucky life, in the West . . . even after the flower died."

Fox fiddled with his pipe. "Indeed. My ancestors discovered that just one petal could be used to extract knowledge from others: all they had to do was crush it, steep it, and offer it in a drink, like a cup of English tea. The one who drank it would tell you anything you asked. The Foxes learned many mercantile secrets, and our shoemaking factory has been thriving for generations.

"Rumor spread across the country," Fox continued. "My father says that famous men came knocking at our doors, believing the tea could improve their fortunes. My grandparents even put it on display at the Great Exhibition. However, despite the wealth and fame the razorthorn brought my family, it eventually perished when my father was young, just like Isabelle's."

"The Kims' is long dead, too, of course. Flora doesn't seem to be helping much on that front," Minho said, in a dry, accusatory fashion.

I supposed we had a dislike for the gods in common.

Isabelle's voice punctured the air. "When my family's razorthorn died, our art suffered. No one bought our paintings at the rate they used to. My elders quit all artistic endeavors. My mother warned me not to follow a creative pursuit, insisted that our family was practically *cursed* without the razorthorn's help, but I love to cook. Against her wishes, I came to France to audition for a full scholarship to Le Cordon Bleu. I've passed my first audition, but the next one won't be so easy." Her eyes glistened. "If only we still had the flower..."

A somber silence fell over the parlor.

Fox's eyes clouded over. "My ailing mother has never been much of a believer in the gods' benevolence. But Father is. I overheard him in his study, ages ago. He thought he could find another razorthorn—one that hadn't yet withered and died. He was so determined that there would be another seed, another flower, out there somewhere, so he could use it for Mother."

"Four petals are said to be enough to heal the body," I recalled.

Fox nodded. "With his connections across the globe, Father's spent the last few years visiting the most remote botanical gardens, scouring the largest rainforests, tracking down every location he could think of. Still, he's come up with nothing. He's obsessed, and certainly far more interested in those petals than in me."

"I suppose when magic was once at your fingertips," Isabelle offered, "you'll believe anything. *In* anything."

"Or anyone," I murmured. I no longer believed in magic but money. There was no other way to survive.

We all turned to Minho.

"I don't know anything about how my family used the plant," Minho said, quite indifferent. "Maybe they didn't use it at all."

My patience was thinning. What was the point of discussing a long-dead flower when the matter of my inheritance was on the table?

Fox burst up from his seat, triumphant. "I think I've cracked the meaning of all this! We all have a connection to the razorthorn, which means we all have a connection to each other—or, more to the point, to *you*, Sana. Don't you think this meeting is about something bigger than an inheritance? I sniff a mystery in the air."

I didn't enjoy the way Isabelle was examining me, or how Minho seemed to be deep in study of my face. It was like he was trying to memorize the heart-shaped bow of my lips, or the subtle droop of my left eyelid compared to my right.

Like he was trying to solve a puzzle.

"Flowers or no, this house was my mother's. It's *mine*." I stood and marched toward the window, where vines crept across the glass like tentacles. They were clawing their way up the house, across my skin, into my heart.

During our conversation, Marta had produced a box from a nearby cabinet. It was a music box of either Swiss or German origin, likely configured to play Chopin or one of his contemporaries.

"Music was one of Madame Gupta's great loves. She kept this precious music box for many decades, but it will not operate without the key. One which has gone missing...or rather, been misplaced." Her eyes flitted to us.

Unwillingly intrigued, I returned to the chaise aside Minho.

"You want me to find a key to a music box?" Isabelle asked.

"All four of you, actually. It is the start of the game. Tara requested that this task be done first."

"*First?*" Minho echoed. "We already played a game. I thought we would move on to a will reading of some sort."

"No. This is definitely the start of something larger." Dread pooled in my stomach. My life was not going back to order. I would not be restoring this estate anytime soon. This contest was real. Because everyone knew who Tara Gupta was. A woman who loved a good secret—and a good game.

But why this game? Why now?

I slipped the necklace from my neck and dangled it in the air from my pinkie. Maman had given it to me shortly before her disappearance, and I had tried it on every lock imaginable before I was sent to Canada. It opened, seemingly, nothing.

As if reading my mind, Marta set the music box on the table and pushed it closer to me. I hated the way my hand shook as I grasped the key and inserted it into the hole.

Turn, I begged.

The lock refused to give. I heard only the telltale scrape of metal against metal.

Frustration mounted inside me. I *knew* it couldn't have been that simple. But it had felt right. This competition, the mystery of my mother's disappearance, the key that symbolized a locked-away past—I hoped against hope that everything would line up like a set of freshly polished chess pieces.

Despondent, I placed the necklace back over my head and cleared my throat. Marta had the gall to wear a look of pity, but I pretended it was aimed elsewhere.

"So if we find the *right* key—and whatever else this game requires—hypothetically speaking, one of us will win the deed to the estate?" Minho asked. I could see the numbers running through his head. If he sold even a portion of the gardens, ravaged as they were, the land alone was well worth it.

"Not simply the estate," Marta said calmly. "A razorthorn seed itself."

Fox gasped, which sounded more like a choke. Isabelle clasped her hands around her thighs like she didn't know what to do with herself. Minho's eyes flickered like a freshly lit match.

Stunned, I curled my hands into fists. My throat locked with unanswered questions. Why had Maman created this game? Where did she find another seed? Why offer *my* inheritance to a group of strangers?

"Tara wanted you *all* to work together to find the key. The instructions say the game's first clue must be solved as a group; otherwise, you have no hope of opening the music box. The following clues may also be solved collectively, but the level of collaboration will be up to you to determine. Whoever solves the final riddle . . ." Marta trailed off, sliding the box back to the middle of the table. We eyed it like it was a grenade. "Here is where things become tricky. There is only one seed. Only one inheritance. The one to uncover the final clue will take the prize for themselves. This was Tara's final wish—for one of you to prove yourself worthy of this estate, and her dreams with it. You may do whatever you wish with the seed. Sell it. Use it. Bury it."

Marta's eyes landed on mine, sharp as an owl's, but deep enough to hold a trench of secrets.

"I know all of this may be hard to believe, but Tara left a note in her own hand. I'm sure Sana can verify it." Marta pulled a small piece of paper from her skirts and splayed it on the table.

Welcome to Razorthorn Manor. Complete my tasks, and you shall win my inheritance: one elusive razorthorn seed, and the manor itself. All competitors must swear their secrecy with blood.

When all is said and done, one victor will rise.

Let the game commence.

If it hadn't been clear that the house was not mine, it was now, sealed and inked with my mother's own handwriting.

For the first time today, the three strangers and I faced each other with alarm, realizing we each might do anything to win this twisted game.

FIVE

Let the game commence. It was one of Maman's favorite phrases, the one she used before we played Marbles and Riddles. She was highly competitive, like she wanted me to keep up with her wits. To train my mind alongside hers.

Perhaps for this very moment.

"'Swear their secrecy with blood'?" Isabelle's voice was thick with trepidation. "That can't be literal?"

"Well, it does have precedent," began Fox, crossing one leg over the other. "In the Middle Ages, blood was used for many rituals, especially to help with diseases, including—"

I shot up from the chaise, unable to take another moment of his jabbering, and headed straight for my nanny. "Marta," I said in lento, for if I spoke any faster, I might throw up, "can I speak to you privately?"

She obeyed swiftly, ordering Monsieur Champlain to keep an eye on the others. As she took me out to the hallway, I recited each of my competitors' names in my head, mind churning. *Isabelle Flores. Richard Fox. Minho Kim.*

Three strangers. Three people standing between me and my birthright.

"You can't really be serious about all this." My voice was small but demanding. "Tell me that my aunt is arriving and we'll have everything straightened out. That this house is mine."

"I can't tell you that, Sana." Her words held only a drop of sympathy. "Your mother's last wishes were these. And I executed them as she would have wanted."

Perhaps the driver was right. My mother truly *was* a phantom, one who had devised a game right before her untimely death.

Overcome by a surge of fury, I banged my fist on the wall. Unchecked emotion poured from my lips. "Last wishes? Her last words to me meant nothing. *Nothing*!" Maman's final words had been "to keep my heart closed." Was that her way of telling me not to grieve when she left?

"Sana," Marta chided. She took my quivering hands in hers.

"Did you know she was going to leave?"

"I knew something was amiss in the days leading up to her disappearance. But I had faith she would one day return."

"And what do you believe now?"

It hadn't taken long for the police to find Maman's bracelet on the banks of the Seine. A deadly fall for anyone. Closing the case, they declared her deceased not long after. But I always wondered how Maman slipped when she was such a nimble aerialist: light on her feet, each step intentional.

"She must be dead, Sana, or she would have come back to us. We can't dwell on the past. Your mother is gone."

Vaguely, I realized I was sniffling.

When I was a child, I'd considered a terrible thought—that Maman had taken her own life—but I refused to believe it. Before my move to Canada, I had scoured the house for any signs of trouble, financial or otherwise. I rifled through her study, ransacked her bedroom, tore through every newspaper I could find about her disappearance. I even raced through the gardens, hoping her face might reappear.

"But," Marta continued, "she's given you a gift."

"My inheritance has been ripped away. Do you call that a *gift*?"

"Call it an opportunity." Marta over-enunciated the final word. "An opportunity to understand her. I believe your mother organized this game because there is something she wanted you to know. Something she wanted to tell you. As for the other players—well, I know it's hard, but can't you try to be a bit more hospitable to our guests?"

Little did Marta know just how much I struggled with niceties while in Canada.

My family in the rapidly expanding outskirts of Toronto were distant cousins of my mother's—the Atwals, with high cheekbones and thin coal-black hair. They were amicable; they let me bathe, sleep, and read as long as I pleased. They filled my stomach and never reprimanded me for sleeping in.

But sometimes, deep down, I wished they would. It was almost like I was too much of an inconvenience to care for, so it suited them better to leave me alone. It didn't matter; at some point, I learned there was only one person looking out for myself anymore. Me.

Which only made me even more tempestuous as I stumbled into my adolescent years. Friendship did not come easily to me. Making companions was fickle as a foxglove. The garden's flowers—my only experience with friendship, besides a brief spell with a girl whose name I remembered as Belle—had been nothing like *real* children, who poked and prodded and questioned everything about me.

I quickly learned it was simpler to guard the walls of my heart like the walls of my once-favorite garden.

Without another word, Marta collected me into her arms, and I finally let out a harsh sob.

"Do you think they'll stay?" I asked when I finally released her.

Was Fox's father still looking for a seed to cure his wife's ailments?

Was Isabelle hoping to find a petal to help herself earn a life-changing scholarship?

"I don't think many would pass up this opportunity."

"Fox believes there's something connecting us," I told her slowly. "Something even greater than the flower."

"I'm not sure there's anything greater," Marta said softly.

She was right. In this house, gods and flowers were equally omnipotent, and equally dangerous.

When we returned to the front parlor, Minho was gone.

"Where did he go?" I demanded. Fox looked up from a book, startled. Isabelle, hands still tucked beneath her thighs, examined my face with a frown. I supposed it had gone puffy from crying, but I didn't care.

Without a word, Fox pointed to the window.

Outside, then. Perhaps Minho was the only sensible person here—the only one who would leave this game before it had even begun.

Or maybe he was simply like me: afraid.

"He said he was going to the gardens," Isabelle offered.

I brushed past Marta and exited the house, marching straight for the gardens' entrance. Minho had left the gate open. For a moment, I hesitated on the threshold. And then, for the first time in seven years, I stepped inside.

The place where my childhood spurted like a flower looked nothing like it had before my mother's departure. It had become a skeleton of what it once was: overgrown, disordered, a scentless void rather than an all-consuming tide of colors. If I closed my eyes, I could imagine what child-Sana once saw: labyrinthine hedges; ivory-white chrysanthemums; beastly snake plants; even bushels of Tahitian vanilla bean flowers. By the age of nine, I'd known the genus of every flower on our land and had even named them according to their personalities. Mr. Bloom was always told to stay put, so he did, not daring to shiver even in the wintriest breeze. A bunch of marigolds with strange purple stripes—cross-bred as per the Mendelian theory—were aptly named Gregor.

My eyes instinctively sought out those same marigolds. Instead, I found Minho perched on the nearest rock, a drooping rose in his hands. Behind him were my mother's old rosebushes, massively tangled.

"Are you leaving, then? The carriage ride to the Sorbonne shouldn't be long. Be sure to take something to eat before you leave." The least I could do before ushering him out was to offer *some* courtesy.

"I'm not leaving."

Those words. Cold fingers inching up my spine.

"I'm not sure you understood. I'll *pay* for your passage. Give you food to eat. Even a book or two for the ride." He seemed like the type to enjoy Stendhal—thankfully, Maman kept his works collected in the manor's library.

"I mean I don't want to go. I'm staying. For the house. For the razorthorn seed." He twisted the rose between his fingers, as if imagining the famous flower in his grasp.

"You know the seed is just a lie," I told him, even though I wasn't certain of that myself. But just like Maman's death, I made it real through speech. "It doesn't exist. Even if it did, people believe in things so much they *make* them come true. Luck is just that. *Luck.*"

"Are you going to try and force me to leave?" Minho's voice held a trace of anger. He approached me, holding firm. "It would increase your chances of winning this—this *game*—and what you *think* you deserve. Wouldn't it?"

He waited, expecting a response. But just as he was firm in his convictions, so was I. "I do want this house. It is what I'm owed. What I loved. If you really want to stay, the least you can do is provide me with a reason why."

"I think the answer is obvious," scoffed Minho.

I confiscated the rose from his hands. "Not to me." I thought of Fox and Isabelle's reasons. At least they'd admitted *something* about their wishes, their families. "The other invitees were quite open. Tell me, Minho. Why aren't you? What makes you different?"

"What makes the sun different from any other star?" he said. "Perspective."

"And you came outside for what, then? To exercise your *perspective*?"

"No. For oxygen." He stared at the rose in my hand. "Something a bit hard to find here." He reached out and thumbed the petals. Heat climbed my cheeks as his fingers softly brushed mine. With that, he headed back toward the manor, and I fought the urge to look after him.

Back inside the manor, Marta marched us through the corridors, her sleeves puffing like angry rain clouds. She took us up two flights of stairs and turned around at the top so sharply I almost bumped into her. Isabelle tripped and fell behind me, and Fox gently helped her up with a smiling, "All right there, chef?"

Isabelle didn't seem fazed by the nickname. I turned back toward Marta. "Where exactly are we headed?"

Marta kept her arms splayed out on either side of her, as though trying to block us from seeing what lay beyond the stairs.

"I must warn you," Marta said gravely, "the following might give you a bit of a fright."

While Marta's features were usually severe, they were never this much so. She took a deep breath, led us down a narrow hall, and slid aside the double doors ahead of her.

An empty ballroom greeted us. Sunlight filtered through the grimy windows, illuminating the wooden floorboards and the cobweb-laced chandeliers. Empty tables under yellowing tablecloths lined the walls, leaving the middle of the room open for an elegant dance or society event, where I would peep through the doors with young eyes and a mouthful of sugar cubes.

The thought unlocked a memory: Maman twirling around the ballroom like a princess, wearing an elegant sari and matching bindi suited for royalty. Men and women fawned over her, as if only she could satiate their curiosity. She fed them stories from her mother, and her mother before her, of the hypnotizing razorthorn flower that had given them their wealth. Her stories were as magnetic as her person, drawing you in close enough to prick you like a thorn.

The scene melted away like frost, but the chill in my bones remained. Now, the ballroom was empty save the five of us and a cat with matted gray fur. It scratched at a nearby wooden beam, removing the beam's bark-flesh and leaving raw wood peeling and curling off. The cat continued, seemingly unaware of our presence, to the point where it seemed almost grim in its obsession.

"You're right. That is frightening," Minho commented wryly, gazing at the cat.

"I've seen lots of strange cats in England." Fox laughed. "Once, my cousin's cat Dolly, rest her soul, tried to eat my father's best—"

"Unfortunately, that wasn't what I meant," Marta interrupted, showing no interest in hearing what happened with Dolly. "The stray comes and goes as she pleases. Follow me."

Deeper into the ballroom, four of the tables were laid out with writing supplies and a set of instructions written in precise script. *Maman's.*

"These are your contracts. Read carefully, for once you agree to the game, there is no going back."

The four of us each moved to a different table and held the paper up to the light streaming through the arched windows. The legal parchment was thick, expensive, the writing almost mechanical. The terms were simple. Isabelle read aloud: " 'Should a competitor choose to leave at any point after signing, or divulge the nature of the game to any persons beyond those in the manor, they will forfeit their ability to win the prize: a razorthorn seed, the only one of its kind left in existence, and the manor with it. Furthermore, anyone who withdraws from the competition or violates any terms of this contract will be penalized in the amount of…' " Isabelle sucked in a gasp. " 'One thousand francs or the equivalent currency thereof'!"

I reread the contract to be sure I'd heard correctly. One thousand francs wasn't anything to scoff at. Considering my inheritance had just been pulled from beneath my feet, and I had hardly anything to my name, this wasn't a choice to be made lightly.

Maman didn't want anyone leaving the game, that much was certain.

Which meant she had something very, very big in store.

I eyed the writing tool on the table, then lifted it. It was part of a branch, the tip a thorn akin to those on the razorthorn. I pressed the tip to the dotted line on the bottom of the contract.

It bled red.

Curious, I tapped the ink with my finger before realizing this substance was anything but. The smell, tinny and nauseating, was undeniable.

"What in the name of—" I glanced up at Marta. The others started, too, dropping their twigs.

Fox paled. "That isn't . . . *normal*."

I recalled the story Maman told me one night as I pulled the bedcovers up to my nose. Flora fashioned the razorthorn flower from her own blood. It was enough to stain the petals red and give it an ethereal air, a piece of nature like no other plant in the world.

A bloody flower with a bloody past, Maman had concluded.

"All competitors must swear their secrecy with blood," Isabelle remembered, shuddering. "But . . . why?"

I turned to Marta for an answer, or at least reassurance. Yet, in truth, I knew why. Blood was binding. Ink was not.

But whose blood was binding our contracts?

Marta mouthed, *Go on, Sana*. I quickly realized then what seven years in this house had done to her. She had been waiting for this day for so long that she was nearly begging me to sign. Begging with her eyes, round as a doe's during a hunt.

So I bit my lip and began etching my name with morbid fascination.

It wasn't until I put the twig down that I realized what I'd done. Before, this game was merely hypothetical. Now, it was real, and my actions couldn't be revoked.

Beside me, Isabelle shook with nerves as she signed her name. Fox put his pen to paper and lifted it so many times I wondered if he was training for some Olympic sport in calligraphy—but, finally, he signed.

Minho, however, rose from his crouch, shaking his head. "I can't."

Strange. I remembered our conversation outside. Minho seemed so confident then, so eager to play.

"You can," Marta told him firmly.

"I need a black ink bottle, please."

She shook her head. "I'm afraid this *must* be done as Madame Gupta intended. Otherwise, you're permitted to leave."

Fox, Isabelle, and I glanced over at Minho.

Slowly, he seemed to master his nerves, and he bent over the table, closed his eyes, and signed his name: 김 민호. When he was done, sweat beaded his forehead, and he forced the contract into Marta's hand with a quick bow, refusing to look at his signature.

I stood and faced him. "What's wrong?" Besides the obvious, something else seemed to be on Minho's mind.

"In Korea, there are a few very potent superstitions," he began, wiping the sweat off his clean-shaven upper lip. "Writing a name in red ink is one of the worst."

"Like an omen?"

Minho's eyes seared into mine. "Yes. An omen of death."

THE PARIS GAZETTE

16 May 1855

Yesterday marked the auspicious start of Paris's first Exposition Universelle, a world's fair held on the Avenue des Champs-Élysées in three newly erected buildings, as decreed by Napoleon III.

Most noteworthy is the Galerie des machines, which was the site of a unique and fascinating display—the much-rumored razorthorn flower. The flower was on display for just an hour but drew the attention of many local fascinators.

One viewer told the *Inquirer*, "It was a sight to behold. A flower that closed with a single touch... a flower that stole the very breath from my lungs." Another called it "a rare spectacle of the godly world."

Indeed, the origins of the flower are simple: the seeds, which could not be replanted or re-harvested, were a gift from the goddess Flora to her most cherished devotees. Acclaimed writer Alexandre Dumas went so far as to call the beauty of the razorthorn "a rival to the Black Tulip itself." But there is still speculation behind the reasoning for its bloodred petals. Some believe it to be Flora's blood; others, that the flower first appeared during the Revolution of 1789, transforming the blood from the guillotines into a living treasure.

Naturalists have observed the flower's otherworldly properties, and debate whether the flower could evolve in an evolutionary pattern. While there is no comment from Lamarckian fanatics, we expect to hear more about this infamous blossom in the days, or perhaps months, to come....

SIX

Marta's first set of instructions were these: "Settle into your rooms and get changed for supper. But don't get too comfortable. This isn't *your* house just yet."

Whose house was it, then? Marta wasn't its *technical* owner, merely its caretaker. Much like she was once mine.

The whole thing rattled me to no end. This house was supposed to be *mine* to restore, replant, rebuild. I loved my time alone in the gardens when I was younger. Enjoyed every second where my thoughts and words and voice could be bottled into a moment just for me, the flowers, and the trees.

Marta arranged for Monsieur Champlain to deliver the luggage to the rooms we'd be staying in. The second floor was filled with empty guest rooms, which had left us with far too many rooms stifled with old pillows and quilts.

Fox immediately took the room closest to the lavatory, while Isabelle claimed one with a better garden view. Minho, refusing the butler's services, lugged his own trunk up the stairs (one that looked far too heavy for one man's worldly possessions). He selected a room at the end of the hall and promptly shut the door.

The bloody red ink must still have been on his mind. For him to sign his name, he clearly wanted the razorthorn to a larger extent than he claimed.

For my part, I took my childhood bedroom. But when I first opened the door, I froze.

The first thing I saw was my bed, almost too small, with my trunk and carpetbag on top of the bedclothes. A candleholder covered in cobwebs sat on my armoire. The yellow wallpaper, with its ornate mirror print, made me dizzy.

Memories that once lingered like ghosts played through my head. Crying because Maman hadn't bought me the paper doll collection I wanted. Laughing when Maman tickled me in the spot behind my ear. Sighing as I dreamed of what I could be someday: perhaps an acrobat like her. Or maybe a chef, like Isabelle desired to be. I had loved cooking in India during my few short visits with Maman, making sweet kheer or spicy sabjis. (Even if I was just a lowly helper, too young to go near the coal-fire oven.)

Hit with a wave of exhaustion, I dropped my gaze to the bed. As badly as I wanted to feel the warm embrace of my sheets, there was little time between now and supper. Let the others settle into their rooms; I wouldn't let these hours pass me by.

My home wasn't all I remembered it to be, and it was time we were reacquainted.

The stairs to the third floor creaked unpleasantly beneath my heels. Once I reached the top, I was greeted by a series of doors. The hallway's walls could talk: Pencil marks documented how I'd grown from one foot to two, two to three, three to four. Maman loved capturing moments in time.

But oddly, we had taken hardly any pictures of us together. Maman never liked photographs. She didn't even enjoy looking at herself in the mirror, and I never dared ask why.

I snuck up to the next level, caressing the spindled handrail, and found a hallway dressed in a damask wallpaper of deep greens and golds. Portraits of Guptas greeted me all along the walls, their oil-painted eyes carefully regarding my every step. There was Avani Gupta, the first scientist of the family, caressing the razorthorn in her hand as if she were holding her own heart; Gurvir, my great-something uncle who had a monocle poised on his right eye and a sneaky lie on his tongue; and so many others whose names and accents were formed by years of travel, hardship, and regrettably, colonial rule.

The final oil painting was of Maman, capturing her in a state of intensity. Her brows dipped low, dimming her eyes, while the corners of her lips just barely tipped up in a poor excuse for a smile. I wasn't sure why Maman would commission an unhappy portrait like this—although she still looked beautiful, in a severe sort of way.

I had long put fantasies of Maman being alive to rest. I'd convinced myself that looking for answers meant I wasn't moving on. The Atwals told me that good girls didn't cling to grief the way I did, that it made them dreary rather than finished. Sharp tongues and dismissive tones slowly remade me in the desired mold.

But being back home after so many years, with so many days of mundane nothingness awaiting me in Canada if I lost—how could I *not* try to discover something in my time here? This manor, and my mother, were articulated puzzles, and I needed to sort through all the pieces. Pieces I had yet to find.

The portrait of Maman gently shook.

For a moment, I thought I had imagined it, but the same vibration came again not two seconds later. I pressed an ear against the wallpaper, but the tremor vanished.

Were those footsteps? Is someone else on this floor with me?

More urgently: *where*?

I made a painstaking search through all the rooms, examining every crevice, every inch of wallpaper, every inlaid cabinet, every chest of drawers, every card table. Soon, only one room remained, the door too heavy to open and too tall to even reach for the latch.

Through the arched window to my left, folds of twilight clouds hovered in the evening sky; somehow, hours had passed during my search, and I had found nothing. If someone had been on the floor with me, they were gone—or, I thought grimly, spectral. All I had learned was that my ancestors had a penchant for peering, and I no longer wished to embrace the weight of their heavy gazes.

I resigned to my room to prepare for supper; Marta would have a fit if she found out I hadn't changed yet. While I cleaned myself up at the washstand, an idea came to me. Maman's puzzles were never easy, but the solutions could be shockingly simple. Maybe to solve this riddle—this game—I should start with the basics.

I had to get to know my competitors.

Before I could fully make it out of my room, I slammed into someone headlong with all the grace of a flightless bird.

"*Oh.*" Minho's deep voice reverberated at my ear level. I rubbed my forehead, staring at his chest. And then I backed away.

"I wanted to see if you might accompany me into the dining room,"

Minho said, holding his arms behind his back. "But you seem to be in quite the hurry."

My cheeks flushed. Why did he desire me to accompany him? Such entrances were typically reserved for couples dining together. The thought made my cheeks flush deeper, until I was certain my skin flamed crimson.

"I wasn't in a hurry," I fibbed. "I was simply... eager to see what is being served. Perhaps a delicious rib roast? Or maybe some of my sanity? Because I fear that's all gone, too."

Minho's chuckle was almost a growl, unexpectedly alluring. "After the day we've had, a good heaping of sanity sounds like just the thing I need."

The last thing I was expecting was for Minho to agree with me. I couldn't help it as my gaze fell to his trousers and worked its way up, drinking in his put-together supper attire, including a cravat that accented his dark, smoky eyes.

By the gods' teeth, why was I thinking about his eyes? I grabbed my stole and forced myself to reject such frivolities.

"And perhaps there will be a glass of something special, fitting for an evening such as this." Before I could ask Minho what he meant, he pulled out a bottle from behind him, as if he were a magician pulling a rabbit out of a hat. "For your birthday."

My eyes narrowed. Why would he wish me a happy birthday with an entire bottle of champagne? I was nothing more than a competitor to him, after all. He had made that much clear after he'd rejected my kind offer of a book and a train ride home, free of cost.

"I'm guessing you didn't travel all the way to Champagne for this. Is the butler aware you took a little trip down to the liquor cabinet?"

Minho grinned, miming a locking-his-lips motion before throwing away an invisible key. "Monsieur Champlain won't notice."

My lips curled up of their own accord. I'd only known him for a handful of hours, but this playfulness sparked a warmth within me.

No. Charming or not, he's still your rival.

I don't know what persuaded me to accept the bottle, knowing that, but I did. It was quite the impropriety to accept such a gift from a boy my age. I could practically hear my governess screaming at me from overseas, the sound of her voice swelling with the tide. *Stay five steps back, Sana. Never touch, or linger.*

I never was one to follow the rules.

"Do you always offer gifts to those who stand in the way of your desires?"

"Only to those whom I might have offended earlier."

He was talking about his candor in the gardens. "If this is what you call an apology, then I begrudgingly accept. But only because of the bubbles." I turned into my room, placed the bottle in a drawer, then whirled around and steeled myself for my next words. "Perhaps I, too, should apologize. For trying to push you out of the game."

Minho looked pleased. "It seems your initial assessment of me was misguided. There *was* something I had that you needed."

Of course. Just as I'd apologized, there was that pompous attitude again. "Stolen from Monsieur Champlain's stores," I rebuked.

"I prefer the term *regifted*."

"How *do* you keep up such humility?"

Minho simply adjusted his collar. "Easily. I give off a modest aura."

I leaned in closer and sniffed. "Yes, and cheap cologne."

Minho feigned a look of hurt.

I took the opportunity to have the last word. "I don't require your company on the way to dinner. I can find my way down myself. This is my home, after all."

I didn't wait for his response as I marched off.

Everyone at the dinner table ate in silence, either impressed with Marta's sole meuniere or simply lacking the gall to speak, I wasn't certain. But as Monsieur Champlain brought out the final course, a fruit-filled vol-au-vent, we all eyed each other warily, as though the conclusion of the meal brought into sharp awareness the predicament we were in.

Four strangers breaking bread. Four strangers playing a game of riddles and risk.

"I think we all know what's on everyone's minds," Isabelle finally said as she finished the last of her pastry.

"Curiosity about each other?" Fox supplied, chewing. "I'll start. I've already told you a bit about my family, but there's more I can share. Shoreditch has been developing quickly, thanks to Father's newest shoemaking factory. He only makes the finest footwear. I can take mine off and show you right now if you'd like—"

"No," Isabelle, Minho, and I answered in unison.

Fox lapsed into awkward silence.

"I meant," Isabelle said, setting her fork on her plate, "we're all wondering about the legitimacy of this game. How do we compete with such an unfair advantage?"

"I'm not certain I know what you mean," I said, setting my fork down as well.

Isabelle's eyes darkened. "Sana knows all the ins-and-outs of this manor. That's not a fair playing field."

"I doubt any of us will cheat," Fox said quietly, as if trying to steer the conversation elsewhere. "We all signed the contracts. The penalties would be severe, monetary and otherwise."

Minho's face whitened, and he absentmindedly poked at his vol-au-vent with a knife. "It might be prudent for Sana to ensure us that the prizes *are* legitimate," he said, glancing at me sideways.

"And how? Shall I show you proof of this hidden seed my long-dead mother is offering? I've no clue where it is, or if it exists. I don't even believe it does." The words I leveled at Minho were brazen, but he seemed impressed by them, despite being the target.

Fox spoke next. "Allow me to take a page from Voltaire's book and be *candide*. Today has been both illuminating and perplexing. *Why* is any of this happening? Why a game? Would you tell us more about your mother, Sana? So we can understand."

I curled my hands into fists. "Fox, she simply disappeared. Now, please, no more questions."

"Should we go back to talking about my shoes instead?" Fox suggested lightly. At our silence, he shook his head. "Best I leave them on, then."

I turned to Minho, grudgingly. "No... Fox is right. Getting to know each other will help us. So tell us what you're *really* doing here."

"It's as I said," Minho answered, voice cold. "I'm studying architecture at the Sorbonne."

"It's quite a famous academy," I pressed. "Was it a difficult journey from Seoul? Expensive, perhaps?"

Minho took a spoonful of lacquered raspberries. "Not terribly." The food brought some color back to his cheeks. "After the Communal Railway Initiative was created to encourage more visitors between England and France, the rest of the world took notice. The Korean government began offering scholarships and bursaries to boost learning at universities across the globe, the Sorbonne included. I paid nothing to come here. Yet somehow, my coming here cost a fortune... in other ways."

His icy tone was clearly meant to end the discussion.

It was true that immigration and travel had been increasing exponentially worldwide. More women were enrolling at the Sorbonne at an incredible rate. France, under pressure from citizens inspired by the writings of the now-deceased political powerhouse Olympe de Gouges, had been signing treaties to ensure education for all genders and races.

I was no stranger to travel myself, nor was I immune to the consequences of stepping away from one's homeland. Maybe I was more like Minho than I care to admit. Or Isabelle, the girl with the cold demeanor. What would life be like if her family remained in the Philippines? What if *my* family had never made the move from India to France?

The question was too large to be answered over dessert.

We all left the dinner the way we came—silently. Minho went back to his room alone with a conflicted look on his face, not uttering so much as a good night. Was he thinking of those contracts again? It didn't escape me that signing them felt less like an opportunity and more like a death warrant. Especially with that monetary penalty hanging over our heads like a guillotine.

I took the long way to my room.

The house was so different at night. Eerie, even with the candlelight from my taper. My shadow loomed on the wall beside me, and my skin chilled as the driver's words came back to me. *You must have heard the rumors, I'm sure. Ghosts, strange haunting sounds in the garden, ever since that woman—*

A second shadow appeared on the wall, growing taller, taller. I raised a hand. "Don't come any closer!"

But my cries were for naught. A mewling cat appeared by my feet. The stray. She ran past me, altogether disinterested in my panic.

I dropped my shoulders. *Silly*, I told myself. But as I turned to continue upstairs to retire for the night, someone caught hold of my arm. I jumped as cold fingers clasped my skin.

"Isabelle, you scared me!" I cried.

"I know what you're up to," Isabelle said simply.

"What's that?"

"You want to learn our secrets. Want to get under our skin." Her eyes narrowed. Then she laughed. Suddenly, her pure, sensible appearance—the glasses, the white dress—felt like a costume. Up close, her lips were scarred from endless chewing. Her skin gleamed with sweat. Her teeth, so perfectly straight. But when she smiled wider, she bore fangs.

Like a wolf dressed as a rabbit.

She listed her head. "You seem to have disregarded me, Sana. But I *know* you. And I intend to win."

I stiffened as her voice filled the corridor like cold, clear water on a humid day.

I saw her face as it was years ago. Time had sculpted her rosy cheeks;

her once-short hair cascaded down her back like a silken waterfall. I remembered how pretty she was, even as a child during those sweltering summers when she'd visited me and Maman with her own mother.

Now I knew why she'd looked so familiar in Maman's study. *Belle.* She was Belle, from my childhood. I'd befriended her as a little girl.

We enjoyed playing jests on the manor's gruff and stubborn old landscaper, Ben Weatherstaff—who I nicknamed Old Ben—while Maman was busy with Isabelle's mother. They only ever came in the summers, and for no more than a week at a time. After my mother died, we had fallen out of contact, and the small comfort of a childhood friend withered away until it was hardly remembered.

I held onto the wall. "Belle. We . . . we knew each other as children, didn't we? I'm sorry I didn't recognize you earlier. I had forgotten. It's been so long. How are you?"

"Doing as well as I can," she answered, barring no pretense. "You think this makes us friends again, do you? No, not now. Not in this empty house." Her voice went gravelly, her eyes unfocused as she fell into her own memories. "There's something about this place that makes you want to spill your darkest secrets. And I won't."

Her eyes spun to meet mine. Knowing. Haunting.

My former friend darted down the hall and disappeared.

PART II: THE GAME

There are those who revere the gods and pray,
And those who speak their names with fear on their lips.
But few can articulate the truth—
that gifts from the gods are often not gifts at all.
They are curses.

—Extract from a pamphlet by Les Voyants, 1789,
Cycle of Light

SEVEN

After last night's interaction with Isabelle, the reasonable thing to do would be to stay away.

Instead, I knocked on her door first thing in the morning.

She greeted me with bleary eyes and a horribly unfashionable nightgown. The bottom of the gown looked soaked. "Good morning, Sana."

No sharp teeth to be seen. Something about the shadows and nature of the house at night must have put my imagination to work.

"Good morning," I offered back. "About yesterday—"

"I'm sorry." Isabelle wiped the crust from her eyes. "I think I said some things I shouldn't have."

No, you shouldn't have, I wanted to retort, but there was something about the innocence of her face, the morning sunlight sweeping past her curtains, that made me pause. Marta was right; I should be more amicable to my guests. Isabelle might be a useful ally to have—that was why I had come at all.

"It's fine," I said. "Although I still feel the house is mine, I understand this is a contest." I swallowed, trying to cope with the thought, but it refused to settle—much like a heaping spoonful of rotten eggs.

"Yes." Isabelle wore a tight smile, looking much more awake than a second ago. "And a contest always has a winner."

Isabelle, Minho, and I assembled at the breakfast table not an hour later. Monsieur Champlain served a platter of croissants and paper-thin crepes filled with strawberry jam, accompanied by tall glasses of orange juice.

It was only appropriate to wait for Fox, but by the time he got downstairs, wearing a corduroy jacket and matching suspenders, my crepes had gone cold.

I decided to forgo breakfast, focusing instead on Fox's flushed cheeks and strangely familiar smile.

"What a brilliant morning this is!" Fox slammed a notebook on the table.

"Indeed," Minho agreed coolly, using a fork to tear through his crepe.

"Did you rest well?" I asked Fox.

"Yes. I got a full three hours," Fox said, with a grin that did *not* belong to someone who got only three hours of sleep. Perhaps, like a real fox, our guest from London enjoyed nocturnal activity.

"I made a list." Fox opened his notebook to reveal barely legible handwriting. "It's everything we can work on together to get to know each other. Your mother clearly *wanted* us to become acquainted. The more time we spend together, the quicker we'll find that key."

"And how do you suppose we do that?" Isabelle, sporting a ribbon in her sleek black curls, squinted at the page. "Look for *knuckle sausages*?"

"That says *hidden passages*, silly!" Fox waved a hand in the air. "I am certain they will lead us to the secret knowledge we require to complete this trial. An estate like this is bound to have plenty of them. Am I correct in making that deduction, Sana?"

"I don't know of any hidden passages. But Maman did tell me some corridors were off-limits . . ."

He took that as a yes. "Perfect. I say we start searching immediately. I have conversation questions we can ask each other while we search and—"

Fox quieted as Marta entered the room in a snowflake-white uniform.

"Let's not waste any sunlight now," Marta said sweetly. It was the same voice she used to badger child-me into doing whatever she wanted. "Madame Gupta instructed me to offer you your first set of directions the morning after your arrival. Are you all ready to hear them?"

We leaned toward Marta, intent.

"For the competition's first test, you must find the key to the music box. You will locate this key by solving a trio of puzzles together. Heed my words: 'the *fruits* of your labor will *flower* into a *stable* thing.' " Marta grinned. "Once you've completed these three puzzles on the property, you will be left with a three-letter word that will help you uncover the key's whereabouts. Good luck!"

Fox's gaze volleyed from Marta to the three of us. "Do you mind repeating all of that at half speed? I can also understand Hog Latin—oh, go on, Madame LeBlanc, give it a try, it'll add to the cryptic atmosphere."

Marta's eyes sparkled. "Have a splendid day, children."

With that, Marta was off to do gods knew what. Isabelle blinked. Fox scribbled so hard I feared he'd rip a hole through the paper. And Minho simply scraped his chair back and said, "Well, we best not keep that razorthorn seed waiting."

Fox held up a finger as he continued writing. "Just a minute. I've got a few more ideas to note down..."

I scrubbed a hand across my face. Three hours of sleep. How joyous.

"Do you ever think about how windows are like mirrors?" Fox asked as he wiped, a bit too vigorously, at a speck of dirt on one of the windows we were passing on our way to the kitchen. The glass pane squeaked in agony.

"Not really," I answered with a sigh. It was Minho's idea that we head to the kitchen to look for the answer to the first puzzle—perhaps hidden among the *fruit*, he'd concluded.

"My brother Henry loves mirrors. He's *obsessed* with his good looks. Ever since that girl Marianne dropped by our house with his missing scarf, he thinks they're the key to winning her over. He looks at her like a lost dog searching for its owner. Father says he should start courting her before it's too late—"

"I'm sure he's very handsome," Isabelle cut in, if only to silence him.

"He seems to think so. He takes after our mother's side, and I take after my father's." He pointed at his pinkish cheeks, reddish-brown hair, and dark eyes.

I chimed in. "You said something yesterday about the razorthorn being able to cure your mother. Do you truly believe that?"

Fox's lips twisted into a frown. The atmosphere soured.

Immediately, I cursed myself for my stupidity. "I'm sorry. I shouldn't have brought it up."

"You make it sound like she's dead," Fox said as we stepped into the kitchen. "Worry not, Sana. This detective still has a mum. As for the razorthorn . . . well, if it doesn't help her, I don't know what will. I have to *try*. And I have to believe it's here. Now, shall we begin with the apples?" Fox suggested. "You know, apples are a symbol of suffering in Milton's *Paradise Lost*, which depicts the Titans and the genesis of Olympian gods—"

"Nothing in the bowl of apples," Minho observed.

I snuck a look at him. Underneath that irritatingly spotless and beguiling countenance was nothing more than a stranger who stood in the way of my inheritance. He had offered me a gift of liquid gold; he had offered to accompany me to dinner. It didn't matter. No distractions. I had to keep my distance. "So noted."

"Nothing in the pears, either." Isabelle lifted the fruit to her nose. "How divine would these taste in a tart? With a frangipane custard—"

"We're wasting time," I said flatly. "Perhaps the fruits we need aren't tangible. Or edible." Maman always liked to trick me that way. I should've known she wouldn't be so literal. "We should scour every wing. Let's start with the bedrooms."

Dutifully, my competitors followed me, aware of my knowledge of the house. We split up between the guest rooms, Minho and Isabelle taking the left side while Fox and I took the right. I slipped into the first room, curiosity pulling me toward the window. Not because of what lay outside, but because of what I saw *within*.

My face. The window was a mirror indeed.

For the first time, my features reminded me, startlingly, of Maman's. An oval face. Full lips. Sparkling brown-black eyes. A girl from the present and a woman from my past.

"Something wrong?" Fox asked. He'd crept up on me.

I shook my head, still staring blankly at my reflection before focusing on what lay below: a section of the gardens Maman called the Wildwood, which was difficult to navigate for those who didn't know it well. I had traversed the Wildwood on foot many times and knew its paths . . . at least I had before they had been mostly overgrown by bramble.

"The gardens mean a lot to you, don't they?"

I turned to Fox, wondering how he figured that out. I hadn't discussed them. Hadn't spent time in them. Considering we'd only met yesterday, he seemed to too-easily peel off the layers of protection I'd worked so hard to build these past seven years.

"Yes," I breathed, staring down at the gardens. I pictured pink flowers blooming in spurts across the Wildwood; trees whispering gently to one another, craning their curious branches to get a good look at you. Now those trees were twisted and scraggly, their branches mimicking thin, spindly claws, and the pink flowers were gone.

"At one point in time, the estate's gardens could put even the Jardin des Tuileries to shame. Maman was the best gardener I knew."

Fox stiffened. "Your mother . . . have you ever tried looking for her? What if she's not really gone? What if this game is some sort of precursor to her return?"

I'd asked myself the same question, but something about Fox's nosiness rankled me. Here I was, stuck with a detective know-it-all who seemed to think my mother's last wishes were his own personal sleuthing mission. If anyone was going to solve this case, it would be *me*.

"Why are *you* so interested in Tara Gupta?"

"No reason," Fox said lightly.

"Oh, I'm sure."

He turned and pointed at a frame on the wall. "Look here. There's something intriguing about this painting."

I gave it a glance. A monumental Italian still life darkened by age. Unusually, it didn't seem to Maman's taste.

"It's a fruit bowl." Not the most creative of paintings in the house. But then I started. "Oh, Fox, you're a genius!"

"I was actually admiring the short, thick brush strokes—but *gads*, you're right!"

"Help me lift it down?"

Fox's head bobbed eagerly as he moved to one side of the picture. I grabbed the other and pushed up, trying to detangle the thick wire from the nail. When it was finally unhooked, Fox and I scrambled to place the heavy painting on the bed.

"Jupiter's thunderbolt!" Fox exclaimed.

I spun around to find a hole in the wall. It was large—large enough to fit a human. I'd never seen it before, but it echoed the one in the study very closely.

Hidden fruit. A hidden passage. This must have been Maman's doing, a vestige of her curious mind.

Beneath the hole, a small insignia had been burned into the wallpaper—a crest of flowers.

Flora's symbol.

Fox stuck his head inside the secret passage and proceeded to cough. He stumbled back and swatted the air. "Ah, the dank smell of unused crawlspace is very refreshing in the morning."

"How deep?" I peered inside to find a soundless void. I couldn't tell. "I think we're meant to follow this."

I was struck by a Latin phrase Maman would always recite when I was younger: *Aut viam inveniam aut faciam. I shall either find a way or make one.*

Fox grinned. "Our first clue unlocked in the case! Well done, Watson."

I gestured into the shadow. "Lead the way, Sherlock."

Fox wasted no time, scrambling for purchase and pulling himself over and into the confined space. I went into the hall and shouted for Minho and Isabelle to join us, and we all watched Fox's rump as he squirmed into the channel, pushing with arms and legs until he was no longer visible.

"Fox?" I called. "Fox?"

No response. We waited a minute. Two. The clock on the Davenport ticked.

I peered deeper into the passage. The darkness was all-consuming. "Fox!" I cried. "Richard Fox, you get back here this—"

"*Look here!*"

Minho, Isabelle, and I almost fainted in relief at the sound of his voice.

I slipped into the passage, thankful I wasn't afraid of small spaces, and pushed myself to the end, Minho and Isabelle following just behind me. The tunnel opened up to an antechamber where Fox awaited, brass candlestick with lit taper in hand.

I pulled myself into the chamber, brushing dirt off my skirts. "Where did you get that?"

"The outfit? It's my school uniform—"

"The *candle*!"

"Oh. I found it here. And I never travel without a match. I keep them hidden in my father's pipe." He twirled it in front of me for extra measure. "Good thing, isn't it?"

I ground my teeth. "Yes. Good thing." Fox passed the candlestick to me. Behind me, heavy feet dropped on the ground.

"Apologies." Just a breath away from my ear, Minho's voice.

My skin warmed. All my traitorous head could remember was the way his fingers had brushed mine in the garden.

I eased myself away, grateful no one could see the flush in my cheeks.

Isabelle dropped out of the passage like a cat landing on all fours. When we were young, she was always the nimbler one. I just hoped she didn't have nine lives. "Ah, now we're getting somewhere."

The antechamber was nothing more than a closet between tunnels; it exited to another secret passage. We made our way, light-footed, into it.

"I've read all about old estates with secret escape routes. You know, in case enemies come into the house and catch you unawares." Fox flashed me a grin.

"This isn't the Revolution, mon petit renard," I told him.

We continued. Shadows crept up the walls from the candlestick's light. "Shadows are nothing to fear," Maman once told me. "They are our twins. Our darker reflections, but still a part of us."

I straightened my spine. "I shall either find a way," I whispered to myself, "or make one."

I pushed forward, determined to figure out where this path led. A howling wind blustered past us—and then we reached a dead end. No: we reached *a puzzle*, once again marked with Flora's symbol.

"It's here," I breathed.

"A word puzzle!" Isabelle traced her fingers over letters that had been painstakingly chiseled into the wall. "The first of three, just as the rules promised."

"But Marta told us we needed three *letters*. Not words."

"Then the answer to each puzzle should be a letter, to spell out a three-letter word." Minho reached an arm over my head and leaned a hand against the wall. I tried not to take notice of the heat from his frame. "If there's a letter hidden in this puzzle..."

"...then we'll find it," Isabelle finished, determined. We all examined the puzzle.

S N V Q A
U X C A S
P T I O S
D I P A W

"Any clever ideas?" I asked.

"No letters stick out to me," Minho admitted. "None of them appear to be written differently or stand out in any way. Then again, I spend more time tending animals than solving puzzles."

"I thought you were studying architecture?" I craned my neck just slightly to find him gazing down at me. I locked my eyes on his.

"I am." He cleared his throat, schooled his features, and leaned away before saying, "I suppose this isn't the first indecipherable writing we've encountered today."

"And what would the first be?"

"Fox's penmanship."

I smothered a laugh. Fox frowned.

"Now that we're finished discussing my poor handwriting," he said brusquely, "could we figure out this puzzle?"

"Wait—I think I know what to do!"

I turned to find Isabelle's face alight. "A painting was the first clue. Perhaps art is the key here, too. It's a word puzzle—look for names!"

"As in, the name of a famous painter, or artwork?" Fox surmised.

"Exactly." Isabelle was buzzing. Painting was in her family, after all.

I combed through my memory. We would often set up with easels and canvases in the garden, painting lazily under the midday sun. Marta did not enjoy scrubbing all that paint off my arms and legs during my evening wash. How had I ever forgotten?

We all re-examined the letters, trying to form words. I focused on vowels, as that would more likely help me string a word, or a name, together. Something was leaping out at me. *Suptios? Paosac?*

"I see it!" Isabelle drew out the shape with her fingers.

There. I followed the letters from the bottom *P* upward, to the *I*, up to *C*, then a sharp right—*A*, *S*, and below, another *S*, and to the left, *O*.

S N V Q A
U X **C A S**
P T **I O S**
D I **P** A W

"Picasso!" I cried.

"The cubist?" Minho sniffed.

"I'm more of a Monet fan myself."

"Fox," I warned, but my heart wasn't in it. Isabelle had been right, and I was elated. We'd solved one of Maman's puzzles!

"Picasso. *P.* And what shape does that name make?" Isabelle pointed at the puzzle. "A stick on the left. One turning right, then down, then left again."

"Also the letter *P*," Minho deduced. "We've found our first letter."

Now that we'd solved it, adrenaline coursed through my veins. My competitors and I were making progress, and that was all that mattered. "What was Marta's hint again?"

" 'May the *fruits* of your labor *flower* into a *stable* thing,' " Minho quoted. "We handled the 'fruit' part. So the next hint would be..."

"Flower," I answered.

We all knew what that meant. The next puzzle was in the gardens.

EIGHT

If the howling wind meant anything, we were close to an exit. The passage finally ended in a rotten door that led outside, unveiling a sky the color of iron. A storm was on its way, and quick. I imagined many shrines across the continent were preparing to propitiate Jupiter, each of them strewn with offerings to a god rarely seen—but always felt.

"Where are we?" Fox asked, shielding his face from the knifing wind. "Is this—"

"The Wildwood," I breathed, heart thudding. "It was once my mother's favorite place."

A memory crawled back to me: Maman, picking me up after I'd been slashed by a thorny hedge. She kissed every cut, not caring if blood touched her lips.

My blood was hers, after all.

The garden had begun to transform from lively greens to gilded yellows and burnished oranges. Autumnus had blown in with a vengeance, her voice the whistle of the wind and the chatter of the leaves.

Not a moment later, the wind raised some dead foliage from the ground and propelled it, rather unfortunately, into Fox's mouth. He spat it out.

"Any guesses on where the puzzle might be hidden?" Isabelle asked me.

"It could be anywhere," I admitted. "But Maman used to hide little trinkets for me to find in birdhouses. Perhaps the puzzle is hidden in one of them?"

"Birdhouses? Where?"

"Everywhere. They make a sort of trail through the tangle," I said. "Let's split up and check all of them."

Maman said the houses were for the birds, a home they could call their own. Now, I'd become one of those birds, desperately seeking a way to reclaim my home.

I found the first birdhouse with ease, which had begun to rot and chip away. Through the peephole, there was nothing but darkness. I swiveled my hand inside, but it was empty.

By the time we'd searched the Wildwood for clues, the home of nearly the entire northwest segment of the gardens, weaving between scraggly trees and branches, tiredness wrapped around me like a scratchy blanket I couldn't shrug off. It would take even longer to get to the east side of the gardens, which housed a maze Maman forbade me from entering, lest I become lost.

"The puzzle isn't here, at least not in the birdhouses," Minho panted as he approached me from the west. A cool wind picked up, slipping through the holes of my knit cardigan, and my teeth chattered violently in protest.

Fox appeared with Isabelle in tow. "Did your mother have an area of the garden she claimed for herself?"

It was clear they were still relying on me for answers, and for a flushed, embarrassed second, I worried I might not have one. What *did* Maman treasure most in the garden? What did she tend to with the fierce love of a mother?

My feet moved from memory, and I traveled south, out of the Wildwood and toward a small bridge. It once arched over a thin waterway that ran off into a river off the edge of the house's property. I took a tentative step onto the bridge, testing its weight—the view below was mostly dried mud—and crossed over. The others followed.

I approached a small, shriveled bush, where just a few lilac buds hung on for dear life.

"This was one of Maman's favorite things in the garden," I whispered.

"I can understand why," Minho offered quietly.

A silent tear fell down my cheek. "No, you can't," I said—not to be harsh, but frank. No one understood my mother. Not even me.

If I were being even more honest with myself, I didn't know my mother's favorite poem, or her favorite song, her favorite season—

Minho placed a warm hand on my back. "Breathe."

And I did, inhaling deeply and somehow smelling a plethora of lilacs, their scent strong and sweet. I couldn't tell if I was smelling a memory, or if this was the magic of the gardens I once so fiercely believed in.

A magic you could believe in again, a small voice rose up in my mind.

Bending forward, I swept away a slew of leaves that covered the ground below the bush. And laughed with little mirth.

Flora's insignia lay half-buried before me, entrenched in the ground and encased in dirt.

As I drew my hand over the symbol, letting my fingertips graze the surface, the insignia of the flower goddess let off a muted glow. Warmth diffused my fingertips.

"Be careful, Sana," I heard Maman saying, her voice coming from all directions. *"The magic of the garden is powerful, but yours is stronger. You cannot let it control you."*

Were those words something Maman had once told me, or merely a product of my overwrought imagination? Certain I was creating a scene in my head, I drew my hand back, and within a blink, the glow—and the heat in my fingertips—disappeared.

"Two puzzles discovered in a matter of an hour," Fox cheered. "We might be able to solve a mystery worthy of Doyle by noon!"

"Don't get ahead of yourself," Isabelle warned, inching toward the insignia of Flora. She leaned down and tapped it before it let out a small *pop*. The face lifted, revealing a hidden tray underneath. I pulled out the soiled tray—nay, the soiled *puzzle*—and held it before my competitors.

LSLHA I PRMCEOA TEEH OT A SEMSUMR'S DYA

"It looks to be another word scramble." The words *I*, *a*, and *to* were easy enough to pick out, but what of the rest?

"This calls for the notebook," Fox said, pulling it from his pocket. "The word before *to* looks like... *teeth*?"

"No, it's missing a letter." Minho leaned down to join me and Isabelle. "What about *thee*?"

"The last word is definitely *day*," I noted. "*Thee*... Hmm, what if this is a poem? Maman fancied poetry."

"Of course!" Fox looked like he was about to burst. "This is simply divine—a poem from the great bard himself!"

"Bard?" I pressed. "Shakespeare?"

"Yes! Old Will, Wicked Willard, Billy the Bard, *the* William Shakespeare himself! Come now, you haven't heard of Sonnet 18?"

The phrase was miraculously obvious, now that he'd pointed out the author. "Shall I compare thee to a summer's day!"

"Thou art more lovely and more temperate," Minho continued, his gaze moving up from the puzzle to meet mine. "Rough winds do shake the darling buds of May."

"Darling buds of September doesn't have the same ring to it," Fox snorted.

Isabelle chewed on her lower lip. "But what does any of this have to do with the letter we're supposed to find?"

"In our previous puzzle, the letters spelled out a word, and from there, the shape of the letter *P*," I said.

"There's no particular shape here, so I think we'll have to solve this differently," Minho said. "Shall we turn to mathematics? It's one of my many strong suits."

"Such modesty," I commented dryly. "But it seems Maman is referencing poetry here, so our answer will lie in the literary, not the mathematic."

"How can you be so sure?" Minho challenged.

"Because I've solved several puzzles on this property before. Have *you*?" I darted back.

"If I may—" Fox started, but Minho forged onward.

"No, but I have received plenty of awards for my arithmetic skills and other talents. Allow me to solve this *my* way, and we'll be done in a matter of moments."

His excessive boast of confidence jarred me, but I wasn't going to surrender.

"Fine. Since you seem so self-assured—what other talents are you hiding, Kim Minho? Most Irritating Competitor at the Manor? How about Most Hubristic to a Fault? List them out for me, in great detail."

The jibe hit Minho squarely in the chest like an arrow. I imagined him wrenching it from his chest, turning it around to face me. "I don't think we should be discussing those hidden talents of mine, but rather the manor's hidden *passages*. Were you truly unaware of them?"

"As I said before"—I didn't conceal the malice building in my tone—"I was *not* aware."

I knew that expression. He thought I was a liar. Cross at this unspoken accusation, I folded my arms and turned away from him.

Seconds later, clouds gathered directly overhead, as if drawn by my stormy mood.

"Sod off, Jupiter!" Isabelle shouted up at the heavens as rain assaulted the earth, a dark and challenging smile on her face. She wasn't afraid of his wrath, and that startled me—no, it fascinated me. Perhaps we had more in common yet.

"Come on!" Fox grabbed on to Isabelle and they ran for refuge.

"With your license," Minho gritted out as he shrugged off his suit jacket and offered it to me. "Here. For protection."

Rain slipped down his forehead, off the tips of his midnight hair, around the corners of his mouth. He was soaked in it, and yet he didn't seem to care.

"I didn't ask for your protection. It's only *water*," I said—just before the deluge intensified. Minho raised an eyebrow, as if I'd only proved his point, but I whirled around and stormed off for shelter. My feet squelched in the deepening mud.

I found safety under the branches of a nearby tree, shivering against the wind. Without asking for permission this time, Minho followed and slipped his jacket over me, creating a thin but welcoming buffer.

"Should we wait for the rain to die off, or make a run for it?" Minho's teeth chattered, the only sign he was the least bit uncomfortable. In fact, if not for his chattering, I would have thought he quite liked becoming one with the storm. Then again, I was tempest enough for the both of us. "We could hunker down here while the storm wanes... or we could dash. I say the latter."

"Sorcery," I mumbled.

"What's that?"

"You must be using sorcery, to make me agree with you."

"Persuasion or magic—call it what you want. Just don't hang me from the gallows."

Despite myself, I gave him the satisfaction of a smirk. We should have been running inside, seeking shelter in the manor, but instead he took a molasses-slow step closer to me. The rain had cast a spell over me and Minho, sealing us inside our own little illusion.

In the distance, a twig snapped. The spell over us broke; I cocked my head toward the sound, and, behind Minho, I swore a shape was watching me from deeper in the garden. The figure hovered by a tree, almost blending in with the bark...

...except for the face, a warm shade of brown matching my own, holding a familiar pair of coffee-colored eyes.

"Do you see that?" I wiped my eyes against the fierce rain and turned Minho around, but the stranger seemed to have vanished.

Minho's hesitation made my skin prickle over. "I don't see anything."

I cursed against the uneven drumbeat of rain. My hand began to throb where that golden light had touched it minutes earlier. "Never mind. Let's go."

Using Minho's jacket to cover my head, I trailed after him, his woodsy scent still clinging to the fabric, and into the safety of the manor.

"Nothing better than curling up with a mug of chocolat chaud to solve a mystery." Marta winked as she entered the sitting room, setting heavy cups down on their saucers. The frothy milk mixture had been topped with dollops of whipped cream.

After the four of us decided to pause on the puzzle, Minho and I retired to the chaises for the evening. I took the camelback sofa while he sat on the opposite couch, mug now clamped between his hands, the chess set in front of us battle-torn from Isabelle and Fox's unfinished game. (Those two were already upstairs, changing out of their supper attire into nightclothes after enjoying a simple soup du jour in the dining room.) Minho and I had decided to fare on nothing more than mugs of melted chocolate. Before us, the fire roared with wood chopped by Monsieur Champlain.

"I've got a surprise for you both." Marta headed back to the kitchen and reappeared with a tray of madeleines. The oblong seashell-shaped sponge cakes perfumed the room with their familiar almond scent. "I do hope this might help lift your spirits."

"Yes," Minho and I replied simultaneously.

I took one, then had a sip of the hot chocolate and sighed in contentment. Minho followed, gently smacking his lips together before going for a bigger gulp. Perhaps the drink truly was lifting my spirits, for I laughed as he lowered his mug.

"You've got a little something," I said, pointing at the tip of my nose. His was covered in whipped cream, which made him look like a child who'd been playing in the snow and finally resurfaced for air. Bashful, he wiped it away.

"I heard you all made a breakthrough today," Marta said, sounding impressed. "I knew it would only be a matter of time."

"Indeed, if you count a half-finished puzzle as a breakthrough." I tried not to think of those coffee-colored eyes in the bushes. Eyes that only belonged to one person...

"Give it time," Marta replied. "Time heals all things. Even heartbreak."

I examined my nanny, wondering where those words had come from, but she retreated to her evening duties. Thankfully, those no longer included giving me a bath.

Minho must have noticed my staring, because he said, "I hope you're not still thinking of our argument outside."

I turned toward him rigidly. "Of course not." It was only half a lie. "What are *you* thinking about?"

"The inventor of the madeleine." He broke the génoise sponge in half, dipped it into his mug, and devoured it. "I'd like to thank them. These are nothing short of *extraordinary*."

Relaxing from his tone, I leaned back in my chair. "I daresay you'd need a time travel machine—ones of Wells's, maybe. I prefer Verne."

"Ah, I adore Verne! I have always hoped to journey to the center of the earth," Minho commented, leaning back in kind, "just to get away from the *upper crust* of society."

It took me a moment to process. "That was—"

"Clever?" He smiled.

"Terrible," I finished.

Minho popped another madeleine in his mouth. "Then how about *you* tell me a joke, Sana?"

For some reason, my thoughts scattered. No pun arose in my memory. I was far too focused on the way Minho said my name—as warm as the first summer breeze, as clear as a raindrop.

Monsieur Champlain's staccato footsteps sounded. "Apologies, children. I don't mean to intrude, but I've been ordered to dust the sitting room, per Marta's instructions. You know how she can be." He went to work with a goose-feather duster. Held open in his other hand was *The Picture of Dorian Gray.* I didn't blame him for wanting the pleasure of a good book during his duties.

Still, his words gnawed at me. *You know how she can be.* Just how close were Marta and the butler? They *were* each other's only company. And how did Monsieur Champlain come to be in the manor's employment? Come to think of it, I didn't remember hearing that the old butler, Monsieur Boucher, had been removed. I didn't recall him being at my sendoff seven years ago, either. Had he resigned—or been *dismissed*—before I left? And when did Monsieur Champlain take his place?

"Oh, Monsieur Champlain?" I rose and approached him.

The butler turned. He resembled a telephone pole, utterly stiff and unmoving. "Yes, Mademoiselle Gupta?"

I eyed his shoes. The toecaps were dirty. Odd; he didn't seem like the disorderly sort. "You've dragged mud into the house. Why's that?"

Color drained from the butler's face as his eyes followed mine down. He snapped his book shut. "My deepest apologies. I must not have changed my attire before—"

"Don't apologize. Just inform me of where you were." The tone I used was the same one that scared away scores and scores of governesses in Canada. But I didn't intend to scare Monsieur Champlain. I intended to understand him.

"Well... at my favorite place in all the gardens—the stables."

I had started learning to ride when I was five, and while I'd become semi-accomplished, it'd been years since I rode. "I thought the horses were long gone."

"All but two. One was yours, and the other I brought over from my previous place of employment, Donne."

"You named your horse after a poet?" I didn't laugh. There was no greater language than a seasoned poem.

"No. Donne was my employer."

"I see." I leaned toward the butler, the following words whispering past my lips: "And when, exactly, did you gain employ at Razorthorn Manor?"

A thin sheen of sweat broke out across the butler's forehead. "Pardon?"

"I'm merely curious," I said, sweetening my tone. "Do you have family in the area?"

"I do have a cousin nearby. But, mademoiselle, why should I worry you with such trivial matters? Now if you'll excuse me..."

The butler tucked his book and duster under his arm, hastily collected the leftover mugs, and retreated without so much as a good-night. I moved sluggishly back to my seat.

Minho devoured another madeleine with impressive speed. "Maybe the other horse should be named after the Bard, in honor of our game," he said, seemingly unaware of Monsieur Champlain's discomfort. "How about Wicked Willard?"

"Brash Billy?" I offered.

"Wistful William?"

I pretended to think it over. "We'll have him dubbed in no time."

Minho's lips formed a half-smile.

His chivalry didn't escape me, nor did his wit, but his caginess wasn't all that appealing. Half of me wanted to peel back the layers of Minho Kim—to understand what made him tick—while the other half sensed that was the equivalent of opening Pandora's box.

"I think I've solved it!" Fox skidded inside the sitting room, his nightclothes rumpled and his stocking cap hanging askew. "Minho was right. We need mathematics to solve this puzzle! Well—sort of. We need to count!"

I could sense Minho's smug look without even glancing his way.

Isabelle followed behind Fox with heavy footsteps, clearly fighting fatigue. "You're certain this is correct, Fox? If you disturbed me for nothing..."

"Don't worry, I won't make you wait in suspense like chapter fourteen of *The Hound of the Baskervilles*—"

Isabelle cleared her throat in contempt.

"All right, no more dallying. I tried a few different variables." He waved his notebook. "Adding up how many letters are in each word, multiplying them . . . Nothing made sense. I realized we needed a number from one to twenty-six—to find a letter, you see. And then I thought, *what if it's even simpler*? If you read over the anagram—the phrase from the Bard—you'll notice only a certain number of letters were used. Let's count through them together."

I knew Fox wouldn't give us a straight answer, so we reread the anagram as a group.

LSLHA I PRMCEOA TEEH OT A SEMSUMR'S DYA

"One . . . five . . . ten . . ."

"Fifteen. Fifteen individual letters are used. And do you know what the fifteenth letter of the alphabet is?"

"*O*," Minho answered.

"So we have two letters then, *P* and *O*."

As if haunted by a ghost, the nearby wireless rattled to life. I caught snippets of the news reporter's story between the static.

"Les Voyants on the rise . . . have not been seen since the end of the Revolution . . ."

"Les Voyants?" Isabelle asked, turning up the volume, but there was only more static.

"I've learned about them from my governess," I explained quickly, unsettled by the transmission. "The story goes that Les Voyants, or 'the all-seeing,' formed during Le Grand Siècle. Under Louis XIV's rule, they began rioting against the monarchy, who were believed to have been hand-picked by the gods themselves. They craved revolution and spread sentiments of discontent with the gods and the heavens-touched Sun King."

Fox took up from there. "Indeed. And there *was* a small episode they fomented, the Revolt of the papier timbré. Some say they were behind the Revolution of 1789 as well; even the controversial Robespierre himself was said to have had ties with the group . . . but they haven't been heard from since the Napoleonic era. Until now, I suppose."

Isabelle and Minho exchanged uneasy glances.

I turned off the wireless altogether.

"*P. O.* It's all still nonsense. I'm going to retire." Isabelle parted ways with a limp wave, and Fox followed.

"We'll pick back up tomorrow after breakfast," I said.

"Breakfast," Minho agreed, but I stopped him on the way to the door, a hand curling over the muscles of his arm.

"Get on with it."

"With what?" Minho questioned with faux innocence.

"The *gloating*. Go on, tell me you were right about solving the clue."

"I don't boast *all* the time. And besides, I'd much rather hear it out of your mouth than mine." His voice bordered on playfulness and ruggedness, like he couldn't quite tell where he wanted to fall.

Ignoring his puzzling tone, I donned a mask of indifference. "I'll admit defeat as soon as the Underworld freezes over."

Minho smiled humorlessly. I stared down the barrel of his gaze, plowing onward. "Besides, *I* would much rather discuss what happened in the garden. I prefer not to owe favors, so don't bother coming to my rescue again."

"Is that so?" The cords in Minho's neck tightened. "Should a gentleman not offer a jacket to a lady in need?"

"He should. But I despise gentlemen." I had seen the way "gentlemen" spoke to Maman, and I didn't like an inch of it. "The courtesy they offer isn't out of kindness, but status. Behind closed doors, they are nothing but insufferable brutes."

His voice grew cold. "So you think me a brute."

"Not entirely," I admitted, but it was too late. This time, the arrow had landed true, and I could not take it back.

Minho removed himself from my grip. "If I didn't know any better, I might have thought you were enjoying my company this evening. But I suppose my conclusions were false. Any warmth I felt must have come from the chocolat chaud."

His words landed like a slap to the face.

Taciturn, he departed for his chambers.

My stomach churned. I plopped onto the couch, tucking my face into my hands. Had I just fallen into my old ways and made an enemy of Minho Kim? Once again, it troubled me, getting close to someone. I could only rely on the garden as my friend, and even then, the trees no longer spoke back.

I got up and eased open one of the curtains, staring outside to where I was certain I'd seen a figure in the Wildwood earlier today. The garden was eerily still, as if it were merely an Impressionist painting instead of grass and leaves and trees.

Too still.

Too quiet.

I didn't contemplate it a second longer and shut the curtains against the night.

NINE

I tossed in the cotton sheets until, mercifully, sleep claimed me. Such heavy sleep that, at first, I dreamed of nothing at all.

And then an image came to me—Maman in the garden, a bruised purple sky behind her. She wore the verdant gardening gloves she often sported while playing with me outdoors. She was bent down so we were eye level, and distantly, I understood that I was crying. My knee felt oddly warm, drip-drip-dripping...

Blood. Red as the razorthorn's petals.

Maman pressed me against her lavender-scented blouse, and then, kneeling, she kissed the open cut. I waited for it to heal, for the bleeding to stop, but it didn't. Pain pinched my skin, and all I could see was all that blood trickling—

down

down

down.

Maman leaned back and smiled at me, blood soaking her lips.

I shot up off my back.

Sweat clinging to my nightgown, I gazed out my window, where rain rapped fiercely against the glass like an unwanted visitor at the door. That nightmare—it was the same memory I'd recalled in the Wildwood.

But why *this* memory? Why couldn't I stop remembering Maman and all that blood?

I fluffed my pillow, ignoring the thunder roaring in the distance. I tried to fall asleep again, but it was no use. I hadn't yet become accustomed to the manor's sheets, or the way the floor creaked beneath my feet.

My stomach turned as a low moan traveled through the house, reaching my delicate ears and startling me upright once more. Had it come from the floor above?

"Enough, Sana," I berated myself. Flipping back the covers, I slid off the bed. "There's nothing out there. You're imagining things. I'll prove it to you."

I stood and lit the candle by my bed, lifted the candlestick, then padded to the door, my footsteps loud against the wood grain. For a beat, I hoped they would wake Marta as they used to when I was young and in a fuss. Then she could reassure me this was only a storm. I scolded myself for the thought, carrying my candlestick like a torch in front of me as I exited my room.

The hallway was dark and narrow, leading to Minho's chamber at the end.

Part of me was compelled to head there and ask him if he'd heard anything; the other half of me rejected this absurd notion. Minho wouldn't speak to me right now. Not when I'd called him such a horrible word, even indirectly.

I swiveled my feet so they carried me up a flight of stairs to the abandoned upper hall lined with portraits of my ancestors. I reached the final room once more, the door I hadn't been able to push open. The moan came from within; I sensed it.

I pressed a hand against the door, as if searching for answers within the fine veins of the wood, the scent of the lumber still powerful despite its age.

I set down my candlestick. Clamping hard on the doorknob, I inhaled heavily, then pushed against the door with my left shoulder. I bit back my own moan of pain when it merely budged half a step. *There is no pleasure without pain*, I remembered Maman telling me once in the gardens. I thought about the blood on her lips in my dream, changing the look of her features. The way she smiled at me, the single drop of blood falling onto her pristine blouse…

Steeling myself, I prepared to push my opposite shoulder against the door when a creak sounded from behind me. I grabbed my candle from the floor and whirled, waving it in front of me like a weapon. "Get back!" I whisper-shouted.

A girl stepped forward, no longer wearing a wolf's smile but a sheep's. Isabelle carried a similar candlestick in her hands. "Couldn't sleep, either?"

I shook my head. "I thought I heard a noise."

"As did I. Perhaps Fox was having a bad dream," she offered.

We both knew that sound hadn't come from Fox.

Isabelle set down her candlestick, and, wordlessly, we both shoved against the door in one great thrust.

It popped open, and we both spilled inside, landing face-first onto dust-ridden floorboards.

Isabelle coughed, swiping dust away from her face. "What *is* this place?"

I looked up at the plethora of dresses and gowns, saris and lehengas. "A boudoir," I breathed out, allowing Isabelle to help me off the floor.

We both scattered across the room, our fingers softly caressing the clothes, as if a too-harsh touch would rip the old garments in two. *This* was what Maman kept in here? Her clothes?

A thought heralded a rush of tears to my eyes—what if she wished to pass these onto me when I became of age? Wished for me to twirl around the ballroom the way she had with nameless men, the mistress of Razorthorn Manor?

No—Maman had left. A small, hateful part of me still hadn't forgiven her for it.

I felt Isabelle's gaze on me before I heard the words uttered from her lips. "You're probably wondering why I acted the way I did the first night. I was discourteous. But this game could change my life." Her eyes blazed as I turned to her. "I won't apologize for wanting to win."

"I am well aware of that," I answered, a bit too gratingly. "*Everyone* wants to win. And yet we need to work together. You see the predicament my mother has put us in?"

Isabelle's features darkened. "There's a reason Tara Gupta invited me here, and I'm going to discover what it was. She didn't do anything by halves, did she? Mama knew your mother well." She paused. "Until everything went wrong on your tenth birthday."

I was jolted back in time. The memory, once a foggy windowpane, was now wiped clean.

It was early autumn. Normally Isabelle only visited us during the summers, and her surprise arrival that day left me breathless. I wished for her to cling to my side the way a wallflower clings to a trellis.

"Come to the gardens," I had told Belle. "For a game of hide-and-seek."

The time in between was a blur. What had occurred that day? All

I recalled was that I was filled with such feckless jealousy over the way Isabelle's mother had gone after her. *Looked* for her, *found* her. Isabelle had come back to the manor in fitful tears, her clothes soaked. They had discovered her in the river just off the edge of the property.

She never spoke another word to me again.

A disruptive *pitter-patter* came from within the walls, heavy enough to belong to a human. Desperate, I pressed my ear against the source of the noise, but the movement had stopped.

"Perhaps there's a hidden room?" Isabelle surmised.

"Or a secret passage."

More closed doors, more hidden secrets.

"If only we had a map of the house," Isabelle sighed. She approached the small circular window that overlooked the twenty-first arrondissement.

From the front of the manor, a long, downward slope in the shape of a half-moon led to the main road. From up here, Paris felt so much smaller and cozier, its lights a collection of marbles I could grasp in my hands. But I knew that wasn't true. It was enormous, and our arrondissement—despite being on the outskirts—was just as bustling as the Champs-Élysées, filled with boisterous bars and a growing jumble of apartments.

It was only once you reached Razorthorn Manor that the glare of the city fell away. Not much lived on this land besides flowers and gossip, and the former seemed ever-waning.

"This may be a city of light," Isabelle breathed quietly to herself, "but it does not exist without darkness."

With that, she departed. I moved to follow her, but noticed a crumpled pamphlet had spilled out of the hump of Maman's dresses. I lifted it, curious.

École Botanique de Paris

Welcome to a haven for botanical savants, where science meets the natural world. Visit Blackthorn Hall to begin your studies; the library to sharpen your knowledge; and other dedicated spaces to draw your mind deeper into the study of flowers.

My head canted to the side. "Botany?" I muttered. I flipped over the pamphlet, finding information on classes at the esteemed academy. Why was this pamphlet among Maman's things?

I tucked it in my nightgown and thought of Isabelle's words. *Mama knew your mother well.*

Perhaps more than I ever did.

I awoke to beckoning sunlight, as if the sun itself implored me to rise from the bedclothes. I fought off the dregs of sleep and threw on a tea dress and a comfortable pair of shoes.

I meant to visit the stables and to make the acquaintance of the two horses. It wasn't difficult to decipher that the final part of Marta's phrase was meant to lead us there. I hoped to be the first one to arrive, so I might figure out the next clue alone—after all, what better way to prove to my competitors that I belonged here, and that I meant to win everything back?

Unfortunately, when I arrived, it seemed that someone else had beaten me.

"I knew we would meet here," said Minho.

Something eager burned in my belly before I realized he wasn't talking to me. Instead, he was turned away from me, brushing a chestnut mare he had brought out of her stall. Her mane was long and loose, save the two thick braids that wound down her back, and her coat glistened in the morning light. Minho worked with smooth, even strokes, finding all the grooves in the mare's powerful muscles. He moved both technically and passionately, assuredly and delicately.

"You're well-behaved, aren't you?" he asked the horse.

"I try."

Minho spun at the sound of my voice, blinking in disbelief and another emotion I couldn't quite decipher. Like the girl who stood in the doorway of her own stables was no girl at all, but a goddess.

I eased closer, enjoying the way he flushed red at his neck.

"Well, that's not entirely true," I said slowly. "I lied as a child quite a bit, had a temper, a stubborn streak..."

"I don't find that hard to imagine." Minho lifted a wet towel from a hook, wrung it, and turned back to work off the mud on the horse's muzzle. Once I was close enough to join him, I placed my fingers under the mare's chin groove, and she whinnied with pleasure.

Minho ignored me as he continued grooming the mare. I suppose he hadn't changed his comportment overnight. His pride had been wounded, and I needed to turn my voice into a salve to heal it.

"If you'd like to take the horse out, there's a great trail that wends up the perimeter of the grounds."

"That won't be necessary," he clipped.

"Don't tell me you fancy cleaning horses and not *riding* them? Are you afraid?"

I had hoped to rile him out of his unamenable mood, but I must have pressed a nerve instead, because Minho's throat bobbed. He gritted his teeth and resumed brushing the horse down in stubborn silence.

If my voice wouldn't work, I would have to let my actions speak for themselves. I got to work, plucking up my skirts and moving the hay bales for extra room. On my knees, I ran a hand down the horse's leg to let her know I was there. As I tended to the muck on the horse's hooves with a cloth, the mire had already begun to harden. I sought out the nearest grooming tool and leaned in close to the horse, ignoring the subtle stench of silt.

Minho peered over the horse's mane. "I don't think that's—"

"I know what I'm doing," I said, tossing the words over my shoulders. "I'm not precious enough to ride a horse and not care for her. I've done this plenty of times."

Minho didn't need to know how many *years* it had been since I'd cared for the mare. Unfortunately, my lack of experience showed, for the mud appeared entirely stuck. I grunted as I pried with the tool, and with a near-comical *flick*, a glob of mud splattered me on the face. I recoiled, reeling back with a gasp.

Now Minho had the gall to laugh. I wiped the offending sludge away, feeling *my* neck flush this time.

"I did try to warn you." Minho, clearly at ease now, retrieved a fresh wet towel and offered his free hand. I took it with as begrudging a look as I could muster.

On my feet, so close to Minho I could see the dimple on his chin, I cleared my throat. "Anks," I grumbled, glancing elsewhere.

"What was that?" Minho tugged on the side of his ear.

I huffed. "*Thank. You.*"

"So sincere, aren't you?" He held up the cloth in his hand. "Look up."

Too cross to say no, I tilted my chin skyward.

Minho cleaned my cheek in long, careful strokes, his other hand lightly holding the other side of my face to keep me still. Betraying me, my eyes slid down to find his face—lips open just a touch, eyelashes thick and full. His eyes met mine mid-swipe, and I glanced down, finding my shoes altogether too interesting.

"There." He stepped back once he was finished. "That wasn't so bad, was it?"

I wasn't about to agree with him. "Perhaps I should leave cleaning horses to the professionals."

"And not confuse a steel comb for a hoof pick." He tossed the towel into a bin. "Does the mare have a name?"

I reached into the recesses of my memory, plucking it out with sudden ease. "Misha. Chosen by my former trainer, a Russian woman whose stature was shorter than her temper."

"Misha. I like the sound of it. It's simple, but a bit uncommon here. Sort of like *Sana*."

"Maman wanted something akin to Tara for my name. Maybe she wanted me to emulate her and become a talented spectacle act." I was half joking, but I had started to feel a bit like one—the foolish jester whose own property had been stolen from under her nose. "But I'm assuming you didn't come here for the horse." I paused, training my gaze on him. "The next puzzle. Have you found it?"

"Yes. But I got caught up with Misha here. She needed grooming."

"You would prefer to be a stablehand? What happened to your passion for architecture?"

"Passion? Architecture is what my mother wants me to follow. It's in our blood; my ancestors used the razorthorn to build an architectural dynasty. But my uncle, the one who I came to live with here in Paris, is a veterinarian. I often help him instead of preparing for my studies. It feels more . . . purposeful. Caring for living things." He ran his fingers through the horse's mane. "You can build a structure, but it won't live and breathe."

His tone made the hairs on my arms stand on end, like his being forthright was not in my book of rules. No governess had taught me how to be vulnerable, but merely sensible.

"Yes, but it would *house* those who live and breathe. It would be their foundation. It's honorable work."

Minho stiffened at those words. "I don't think honor is in my vocabulary anymore," he whispered—to the horse or to me, I was uncertain.

"What are you saying?" I thought back to those words he'd said at the first dinner. *I paid nothing to come here. Yet somehow, my coming here cost a fortune . . . in other ways.* "What did you mean, that first night at dinner? About coming here costing a fortune?"

My words were too bold for a man I barely knew, a man who spoke little with words but volumes with his eyes.

Minho only said, "I thought you were good at solving riddles."

"Not every riddle wants to be solved," I countered, taking a step closer to him.

"You want the entire truth? It's not a pretty one."

"There's nothing pretty about our situation."

Minho seemed to steel himself. And then it came out, blunt and direct. "Two years ago, I cheated on my exams. My mother didn't take it well, and neither did my uncle."

Minho, a cheater? I hadn't known him long, and yet I sensed it was out of character.

With a flighty rub of his hands, he continued. "My uncle raised me after my father's death, when I was only a toddler. He became my father figure. Once I grew up, my uncle moved back to his other home in Paris, visiting Korea sporadically over the years. When news broke out about my cheating, his disappointment was... painful." Minho's face was pinched before flickering back to neutrality.

"Why did you cheat?"

"I thought it was my only way to get a scholarship at home. Mine is an old family, but no longer wealthy. We have lacked for money since the razorthorn died. Now I cannot even inherit the family business."

It seemed we had more in common yet. Heir and heiress, cast aside from our royal thrones.

"Thankfully, we still have influence, and the incident wasn't recorded by my professor after my uncle intervened. But he was furious—if word got out, it would stain our reputation."

"So when the Sorbonne began offering bursaries..."

Minho nodded. "My eomma sent me away to start anew. I received the letter from Marta at my uncle's home, forwarded from my family home address. But I didn't show it to him. I just told him I would be heading to Razorthorn Manor as part of an architectural study. He has no idea what is really going on. And when he finds out about this contest, which I've taken a leave from school for..."

"You'll have broken his trust again," I finished softly.

Minho swallowed. "Which is why I need to win this."

"If your uncle has influence, why do you *need* to win so badly?"

Minho clamped his mouth shut like a Venus flytrap. I supposed I wasn't getting *every* secret out of him that easily.

"You said you're attending the Sorbonne," I said, changing tack. "How long do you plan to stay in France?"

"My eomma expects me back once I've completed my studies. But to be honest, tending to animals with my uncle opened a whole new world for me. And coming here..."

Our gazes locked, and for a second, I wasn't certain if it was because he wanted to move toward me or away. His woodsy scent clung to me like a second skin, as if I couldn't rid myself of the mystifying Minho Kim even if I'd wanted to.

"So what do you want to do?" I asked him, taking another step closer. I didn't know if I was talking about his future, or this puzzling game, or something else entirely.

His mouth flattened in thought. I hated how smooth his lips were—or perhaps I hated myself for noticing them, and how full they looked in the morning sunlight slipping through the wooden slats of the stables.

"The puzzle," he said at last, and with that, he led Misha back into her stall, locked her door, and then guided me over to a lone calendar hanging on the wall. Flora's insignia had been stamped onto the paper, which curled inward from years of disuse.

"I think I know what month it is," I teased.

"Yes, but look. The dates are all jumbled. On the first three days of the first week, it's the third, fourth, and fifth. But after that, there's a zero. No date has a zero."

"Except ten, twenty, and thirty," I mused. But Minho was right. The calendar didn't even *have* numbers on each date, meaning only four columns had been filled out. I studied it closely, extracting all the numbers and forming a table in my brain:

3	**4**	**5**	**0**
8	**6**	**7**	**9**
3	**2**	**2**	**1**
1	**3**	**1**	**?**

A question mark. A number pattern.

Or perhaps no pattern at all.

"I would chalk this up to a simple equation. We add up the numbers in each column and see what we find." Minho dragged his eyes down each column, calculating.

"Fifteen," I replied.

"Exactly." Minho's features lightened. He seemed to enjoy arithmetic, or at the very least, numbers. It made sense; architecture was all about numbers, angles, and degrees, and he spoke that language fluently. "So the question mark would have to help us add up to fifteen."

"Exactly. Nine plus zero plus one is ten. Meaning our last number is—"

"Five." A rather simple brainteaser, but again, this was only a fraction of the greater puzzle. "Now we need a letter. So far we have *P* and *O*."

"The fifth letter of the alphabet is *E*."

We answered as one.

"Poe!"

Inside the sitting room, Fox trembled with delight, a gleam in his eye.

"Poe, you say! I'm assuming of the *Edgar Allan* variety?"

"He would be the most famous, so yes," I concurred. Minho and I had already assumed as much, but we decided to bring it to Isabelle and Fox for their approval. It was only fair; the first clue needed to be solved cooperatively, after all, despite my inner protests.

"Then let Poe guide the way," Isabelle announced. "Perhaps one of his works will hold the key we're looking for? Metaphorically speaking."

"We should parse the library," I suggested. "Maman had all his works in first edition. She loved him." Perhaps it was the way his words transcended printed ink to stir each dark emotion inside me, but I had always loved him, too.

We took off like a shot. In moments, my hands were set on the double-doored entrance to Razorthorn Manor's library, the cold brass of the knobs biting into my skin.

When I flung the doors open, the familiar enclosure of the library greeted me, each bookshelf tall and proud. I used to hide among these endless shelves for hours during games of cache-cache. I had loved the books—not only for reading, but for their company. Each crease of the spine told a story, every wrinkle of a page a tale. It was certainly a place that bent the rules of time; one could spend eons locked away in here and never come up for air or food, not when stories were the perfect sustenance.

Maman's collection of books rivaled that of the Library of Alexandria. To my chagrin, there was no rhyme or reason to the ordering of her collection. It would take us up to an hour, potentially, to find Poe's works. Unless I could remember where she kept them.

"We should divide ourselves and meet by the doors in twenty minutes," I told Fox, Isabelle, and Minho. From the looks in their eyes, it appeared each of them was as hungry as I to dig up the answers we sought.

"Agreed," Minho said, steering to the right. Isabelle jetted off without a word, while Fox whistled a staccato tune, pretending to search while always maintaining a five-foot distance from me.

I whirled on him. "Do you require directions?"

Fox startled. "I prefer to work in pairs. You know, my coachman told me there is a ghost walking these grounds. It could very well be the ghost of Tar—"

"There is no *ghost*. Can you please stop talking about ghosts?" My voice came out harsher than intended. Fox's whistling—and questioning—thankfully ceased.

Unnerved by his discussion of specters, I shook him off and then rounded a bend, leaving Fox's orbit to find Minho.

"What's your favorite work of Poe's?" Minho inquired. "Perhaps your mother intended for us to find one work of his in particular. One you fancy, maybe?"

"Well, I adore 'Annabel Lee,' Poe's last complete poem. But some days I think I prefer 'The Raven.' It unearths the deadly world of the macabre—the grief of losing a loved one."

I knew all too well what that meant, losing Maman. If I had one last chance to speak to her again . . . would I take it?

Yes. My heart pounded feverishly with the realization. *Yes, yes, yes.*

"I'm a fan of 'The Tell-Tale Heart.' The trauma, madness, guilt, a heart beating under the floorboards . . ." Minho trailed off, as if we had shared the same irrational thought.

"Under the floorboards."

Maman kept a rug in the center of the library so I wouldn't trip over a loose floorboard my foot used to catch on as a child. I raced toward it, flipping it over with Minho's assistance. I was sure Maman hadn't harvested a heart for us to find. Then again, perhaps I shouldn't put it past her, given the nightmares I'd been having.

I pried open the floorboard in question, finding a paper-wrapped package inside. I untied the twine; the package fell open, and two books slipped out, landing in a heap on the floor. The sound alerted Isabelle and Fox to our location.

"A pair of matching Poe collections!" Fox nearly did a giddy jump.

"The final hurdle," Isabelle corrected, reaching for one of the books as Minho collected the other.

"Perhaps we do work well as a team," he told me with a subtle smile. Something in my chest flipped.

Before I could reply, a flurry of *click*s and shuttering lights went off outside the library windows. I hurried to the nearest pane and saw a horde of dark-jacketed visitors gathered before the manor.

“They’re in there! In the house!” one shouted, gesturing up to the library window. I shrank back.

Fox let out a confused noise, and Minho and I swapped glances. Without a second thought, I turned on my heel and raced down to the front of the manor, throwing open the door. Shapes filled the front lawn: Men in derby hats and three-piece suits, heavy cameras grasped in their fingers. They swiveled toward me like vultures, fingers pointing as if in accusation.

I flinched at the first *click* of a camera. “Who are you?” I cried, even though the answer already choked my throat with unease.

Only breaths behind me, Isabelle replied gravely, “Reporters.”

TEN

Twenty pairs of eyes trained on me.

"Is it true the daughter of Tara Gupta has returned?" one man inquired, an eager gleam in his eye.

"She's her spitting image!" A different reporter shoved his way forward. "With your mother declared legally deceased, will you finally inherit the manor?"

"*The Paris Gazette* would like to know if you're open to an interview," called a man from the front, using a much smoother, more polished voice, sweet as honey but deadly as nightshade. "Many ache to see Razorthorn Manor as it once was. Last I recall, a ball hasn't been held here since 1905! No one would refuse an invitation to this cryptic estate!"

"Would you demystify what these *others* are doing here?"

Another *click* of the camera, and my vision spotted with purple.

I stumbled back, blinded, and was thankful for the two strong hands that gripped me, saving me from a fall. I didn't have to look back to know who it was, and I flared with heat, sensing the rapid rise and fall of his chest.

How had word of my arrival spread so quickly, and to so many reporters? I didn't know so many people still cared about the manor, about my mother's disappearance. Would the morning papers have my photo splashed on the front page? Would I look miserable and haphazard?

I almost laughed to myself. Now wasn't the time to worry about looks. I didn't truly fear the weight of the cameras' gaze, or the men hounding me. I didn't fear what Paris might think of me tomorrow. I feared what *my mother* would think if I didn't take command of this situation.

"They're not *others*. They're . . ." I faltered briefly. Minho, as well as Fox and Isabelle, who had emerged onto the front step, glanced at me with alarm, but my response was strong and sure. "They're my guests. And I very much resent this intrusion—no, this invasion—of a decent, private home. Can it really interest your readers to know there are visitors to an old house in the twenty-first arrondissement?"

My words struck the reporters with opposite intent—instead of allaying their questions, they only lobbed more at me, sharp as brambles.

"I'll tell what you want to hear," I interrupted. "My mother is gone. Her gardens have gone to seed. But this home should not be remembered as a place of death."

"Then what *should* it be remembered for?"

My throat closed up. *My mother*, I tried to say. *Remember her life, her legacy. Remember Tara Gupta.*

The reporters were silent, awaiting my response.

But even I didn't know what her legacy was. How would I, when all I could remember was a mother whose absence was deeper than the ocean? Whose heart was now locked as tight as a garden's gate, forever?

Shame clogged my windpipe, suffocating me like summer heat. I couldn't even defend my own mother to these loathsome reporters.

"Perhaps," Minho said, "you should stop throwing vulgar questions in Mademoiselle Gupta's face for the benefit of your employers. Civilized reporting shouldn't be so scarce in a city as advanced as Paris."

Gasps, clicks, whispers. Even I barely withheld a gape at Minho's boldness. Because it was clear that, despite all its advancements, this beautiful city was often only beautiful on the surface.

And then a new voice cut through the din. "No photography allowed, messieurs!"

Marta appeared from a side entrance of the house, red-faced. She stomped down the cobblestoned path ahead of us, shooing the pressmen away. But many of them wouldn't budge, too busy clicking their cameras and scribbling on their notepads, their eyes goading for quotes, details, a story.

To avoid these men and their questions, there was no shelter but the manor itself.

Minho seemed to know what I was thinking, for he grasped ahold of my arm and tugged me back into the house, Fox and Isabelle close at our heels. It wasn't until we'd shut the door and locked it thrice, rushing away from the entrance and safely into the heart of the manor, that I finally let out a protracted breath.

"How did they find us?" Isabelle's face was shadowed under the light of a single chandelier. "Do you think they know about the game?"

"No," I said, my voice nothing more than a croak. "Unless one of us has broken the rules."

"Nonsense," Fox deduced. "It's all very simple. Someone must have seen us rummaging around in the garden, and decided there was something interesting afoot."

"But who?" I asked. "The closest neighbors are down the hill, and the grounds are private…" I thought of the figure I thought I had seen in the garden and went cold.

Isabelle's voice took on an air of fright. "Is someone…spying on us? Perhaps the house was being watched *before* we arrived? Would anyone outside the manor know about the seed—"

"There's no time for speculation," Minho interjected. "Marta will handle the reporters. We should return to our labors if we ever want to figure out where this mysterious key is located."

"And if we ever want to win," I finished soberly.

Our newfound Poe books lay spread-eagled before us in the parlor. We had riffled through the books countless times, finding no hidden annotations or cryptic riddles.

Until Fox uprooted himself from the chaise with owl-wide eyes. "Wait! Look at the endpapers of both books. I *recognize* this paper. It's been glued on, see?"

We all nodded; even I had discovered that the peeling paper looked off from the rest of the well-bound books. The only indication they were a set was the "1 of 2" and "2 of 2" written hastily in the corners.

"I've used it before with my brother, to send coded messages. If you spill alcohol on the page, ink will appear."

"Ingenious," Isabelle whispered.

"Monsieur Champlain's stores," I said, already leaping up to the cabinets. I opened the nearest one and retrieved a bottle of merlot. Hastily, I uncorked the top and gently spilled the wine over the pages, silently promising to make up for it later.

White words appeared like fresh ink:

The key is not a key. The riddle is not a riddle.

On the second book: *Skip two and look both ways. My designs await you in the pages of this book.*

"What does that mean? Is there no physical key to be found?" Isabelle inquired.

"How else would we open the music box?" My voice verged on frustration.

"Skip two," Fox muttered to himself. "Skip two—meals? Baths? I am not giving up my worldly pleasures!"

"And there's nothing bound into the second book, either," I said, poring over the pages again to make sure. "We were so close."

"It's too bad we've hit a dead end," Minho said, dusting off his trousers. "But evening is approaching. A break would do us some good."

He left without another word. Isabelle huffed in frosty agreeance, citing that some time in the kitchens might clear her mind. I wished I had the same habits as she, because right now, preparing a meal might soften my mood. Not to mention eating one.

But the spilled wine—the new riddles—would have to satiate me. My mind was racing, and I wasn't going to lose momentum.

Fox said himself he preferred to work in pairs...

"Listen closely, Fox," I said once the two of us were alone.

"Yes?" Fox picked up on the gravity of my tone, looking serious.

An idea fluttered in my brain like a caged bird waiting to escape. It was impulsive. Daring, even. But I wouldn't win this contest without taking a few risks. Fox had singlehandedly helped us solve the wine clue, and I was beginning to think he might be more an asset than a hindrance.

"The game will become much harder soon. Even I'm not sure if I'll be able to decipher Maman's clues. But I know this house, and I knew her character . . . and you have a gift for deduction, as do I. Together, we can conquer her riddles. I'm absolutely sure of it."

"What are you saying?"

"Let's form an alliance. We'll help each other until the game's end, no matter what. Minho and Isabelle don't have to know," I said, voice lowered. I surprised even myself with my boldness—and, frankly, my duplicity.

Fox stared at my offered hand as if it belonged to an apparition.

"Did you hear me?" I asked.

He nodded, still staring. "That's quite the proposition." He produced his pipe from his vest and twirled it in contemplation. "But why me? Are you starting to believe my theories? Including my gothic notion about . . . ?"

"About Maman being a ghost?" I held back a smart comment, remembering those coffee-colored eyes in the garden: the color of Maman's eyes. Was I fantasizing? "That doesn't matter. Just think about my offer. Isn't this the perfect way to get what we both want?"

A grin lifted his face. "I see. So you've realized what a brilliant detective I am."

I smiled tightly. "Some might call you"—I scrounged for a compliment—"an improved Sherlock."

"I *have* always thought so." He stared up into the air, as if imagining solving a delicate case for the King of Bohemia.

I snapped a finger in front of him, and finally, he looked back at me. "So?"

Fox took my hand in his with a bona fide grin. "You have a deal, Watson."

ELEVEN

After an early dinner, I headed through the main corridor. As I passed a small linen closet, a pair of voices sounded, heated whispers coming from within.

"What if the children find out?" trilled a woman's voice. "Perhaps we should tell them."

"Hush now," a deep voice replied. "You needn't presuppose. You've done nothing wrong."

I leaned an ear toward the door, hoping to hear more, but a floorboard beneath me squeaked, giving me away. The voices ground to a halt. I froze, only stepping back an inch before the door swung open—and out spilled Marta and Monsieur Champlain.

"Ah, Mademoiselle Gupta," Monsieur Champlain said, pressing down the linens draped over his arm. "I hope puzzle-solving is going well?"

"It's a cryptic game," I said evenly, leveling my eyes with Marta's. "As cryptic as the conversation you were sharing."

Marta scoffed. "Don't let your imagination run away on those long legs of yours, Sana. I was merely here to ensure everything is in the proper order."

"Neat as a pin," Monsieur Champlain agreed, although his eyes appeared swollen with secrets. He turned to glance at his pocket watch as I inspected him, dubious. Maman often said my suspicious mind was both a gift and a curse.

"It's nearly time," the butler said to Marta lowly. "I must be off."

Monsieur Champlain replaced the linens expertly and, without another word, skirted around me for the front door.

A man poked his head out of 126 rue de Belleville. Rapid French reached my frost-touched ears, my head tucked low as I observed the scene from a distance. Beneath my eyelet parasol, a wide-brimmed hat shielded my eyes. There was no rain this evening, and despite the encroaching darkness, I would require cover still.

Then, a stranger's voice, low and unassuming. "Salut, Auguste. Ce n'est pas trop tôt."

I watched as the butler glanced both ways down the street and offered a tight smile to his receiver. The brownstone was tucked into the street like an olive in a jar, with little room to breathe. It mimicked just how breathless I was, slipping on my coat and taking Misha out of her stables to follow Monsieur Champlain.

I couldn't blame myself for thinking everyone at Razorthorn Manor had some sort of hidden agenda.

The butler had led me here. I'd ridden at a respectable distance from Monsieur Champlain's coach, noted the building he disembarked in front of, and continued a block further. I made sure to tie Misha securely to a hitching post and returned to the butler's destination on foot. I couldn't have him recognizing the mare so far out from the manor.

I could hardly recognize *myself*, with how easily I slipped into Fox's habit. Sleuth I would become to unfurl the mysteries of the butler who resided at Razorthorn Manor.

"Alain," Monsieur Champlain said as he entered the brownstone.

I fetched my courage and waltzed up to the façade, tucking myself into the shadows. Through an oriel window, I could see the butler speaking with fervor to the stranger, bowing his head low.

I needed to get closer. If I could perch under the sill, perhaps a few sneaky words might slip through the glass. I would have to tread carefully, so as not to flatten the flowers. They were living things, after all, and I had no right to disturb them.

I took one step forward. A second. My foot twisted on a garden rock, and I hissed from the pain, arms wheeling out for balance. From my peripheral vision, Monsieur Champlain cocked his head toward the disturbance.

The next thing I knew, someone grabbed me by the waist, slipping a hand over my mouth to muffle my cries until we were deep in the alley by the brownstone. I kicked against the aggressor with impassioned force, like I was drowning and kicking free of the ocean. The instant they let me go, I reached for a weapon—the hatpin I kept secured in my hair—and thrust it at them.

A man. He swooped low, missing my aim, but today I had come prepared. I closed my parasol and wielded it like a sword, swinging low to buckle him at the knees. I stopped just short, recognizing the woodsy scent that radiated off him in waves.

"Minho!" I gasped, cut to the quick.

"I would appreciate it if you dropped your weapons," he said, hands held up in defeat.

I did no such thing. "You *attacked* me!"

"Such a statement." Minho sounded relieved he was no longer about to be battered by my instruments of choice. "I *tailed* you. The coach was not cheap, mind you. And this time of night is no good for a lady to wander alone. I stopped you from almost getting caught, too."

"By grabbing me from behind like a disturbed highwayman," I corrected, not withholding my vitriol. I may not have skewered him with my pin, but I could skewer him just as well with a baleful look. Why had I ever thought we were warming up to each other? Working well together on *one puzzle* didn't mean we worked well in other ways. "You sound just like George Wickham, pretending to be the hero."

"One might take that as an insult, but I'll accept the comparison. Wickham was also known for his debonair looks." I despised how his smile could put the moon's brilliant light to shame.

I flushed at the insinuation. "His appearance was deceiving."

"And yet it seems I'm not the sole deceiver here, considering I wasn't the only one doing the tailing..."

"That's rich, coming from—" I started, but Minho placed a finger against my lips. That simple action sucked the breath from my lungs. With his other hand, he pointed up to an open window on the brownstone's alley side, out of which heated whispers escaped like coal smoke. But the hushed words split apart like curdled milk. Indistinct. I needed elevation.

"Quick. Hoist me up onto this crate," I ordered Minho, pointing at the box on the ground.

He raised a brow. "Are you certain—"

"Just do it."

Minho didn't waste any time. He took me by my waist, and despite the dress I was wearing, a searing heat radiated from his fingers and through the fabric as he heaved me onto the wooden box. I ignored the scurrilous sensation and pressed myself against the wall, turning an ear up to the windowsill.

"It's been six months. I want it to be known, Alain."

"In due time," came the stranger's voice, but I couldn't quite place his tone. It wasn't altogether defensive. "Donne threw us out on the streets. We must tread with care."

"I won't resign myself to standing still," came Monsieur Champlain delicately. "Now, the money?"

"I have it somewhere..."

The voices faded as they moved farther away. I grunted in frustration, rising up onto my tiptoes. Could I hear more? I needed to. Who was Alain? Clearly he had worked with Donne, Monsieur Champlain's former employer, which might make today's clandestine meeting about work-related matters.

Or were there other business dealings occurring beneath—or rather, above—my very nose?

"Do you not think this an intrusion of privacy?" Minho noted without inflection.

I looked down at him behind me. "I think we're well past being couth."

"I quite prefer being uncouth. Don't you?"

My spine pulled into a taut string. Something about his tone didn't sound like he was talking about intruding on Monsieur Champlain's privacy.

Distracted, my feet began to wobble on the unsteady crate, and my hands ungracefully relinquished hold of the windowsill. My skirts flew up as I stumbled backward, feeling nothing but air.

And then: two hands intervened, gripping my middle and effectively halting my fall.

I let out an involuntary noise as I grabbed onto his shoulders, steadying myself at the near blow to my behind. It was too bad the blow had gone to my ego instead.

My gaze caught on Minho's. His eyes were so intense, they rendered me silent. It was abundantly clear that he was a planet with an unknown atmosphere, and if I spent too much time in his gravitational pull, I would be smothered in its toxicity.

Minho released hold of me, and I stood on wobbly legs.

"What was that about *pretending* to be the hero?" he drawled good-naturedly.

"Har har. Now, shall we leave?"

"No—*restez ici.*"

A figure cut a slim shadow in the alleyway entrance. As if they were performing a magic trick, they raised their arms, holding out their cloak like a bat's wings. When they dropped the cloak, more shadows appeared, more figures dusted in the dark layers of night.

Robbers weren't unheard of in this part of the city. I should have known to bring more than my parasol tonight. I should have known to be less foolish than to leave the manor on a silly hunch.

I balked as the shadows took the shape of four women, prowling toward us like mountain cats, their cloaks susurrant underfoot. And then, with stunning speed, they had us entirely surrounded, moving around us clockwise.

Leagues away from home, I felt as though I were a deer standing in the middle of a forest, prey for the hunters.

I steeled myself to run, prepared myself for any possible attack. Minho backed closer into me, and I could practically feel his rabbit-quick heartbeat through his sack suit. Needing comfort, my hand jolted out, and Minho's hand was there, open and waiting. I grabbed onto it—or maybe he grabbed onto mine—surprised to feel a balm of safety in our shared touch.

"W-who are you?" I asked.

"We see what is unseen," one replied from beneath her hooded cloak.

"We hear what is unheard," another croaked.

"You're them," Minho said as the revelation dawned on the two of us. "Les Voyants."

"Don't speak of us with such *disdain*, young man. You must be one of those foolish sycophants who tosses prayers to the skies at the gods' every whim?" The woman's eyes slid, fastening onto mine. "And you... my, my, my. What is a pretty girl like you doing out so late?" She produced a knife from beneath her cloak, and it glimmered in the moonlight. "How shall we take your blood—a nick on the palm?"

"A cut on the cheek?"

"A prick of the throat?"

"Don't you lay a finger on her," Minho commanded with more bravery than I felt. The women collectively tittered.

"Our Great Sister was correct. She looks an awful lot like her," a different cloaked figure purred.

"And the boy—he must be descended from that other Keeper."

"This is no time to reminisce, sisters. Let us take what we came for."

A deep voice rang through the alley. In rapid French, he demanded, "Leave these children be, lest you wish to spend the night in a jailhouse."

"We do not fear the police, or the wrath of any god," snapped one of the women.

"Have you taken leave of your senses?" spat the knife-holding assailant. "Remember what our Great Sister said. No witnesses."

Silently seething, the women shrugged themselves deeper into their cloaks and fled on foot, leaving us alone with the man.

He stepped out of the shadows. A broom of a mustache. White-gloved hands.

"Mademoiselle Gupta," Monsieur Champlain began. He turned his stony gaze to my companion. "Monsieur Kim. You have some explaining to do."

TWELVE

The back of the enclosed carriage was lined with velvet and secrets. While Monsieur Champlain guided the horses—including Misha—toward the manor, Minho and I sat in relative silence, like children berated by their parents for sneaking sweets before dinner. Our bodies swayed as the carriage jostled along the cobblestone streets.

I turned to face Minho, my voice breaking the drum of clopping hooves. "Do you think Monsieur Champlain believed our story?"

"About needing air outside of the manor? It's not the most original," Minho snorted.

"A lady can go for a stroll, can't she?"

"Of course. But we *were* nearly cut to ribbons."

"That's quite the overexaggeration." Although the mention of those cloaked figures had me on edge. "I could have handled them. I'm not helpless."

"No, helpless you are not. But you are mulish to a fault."

"*Mulish*?" I shouted.

"Yes." Minho's eyes sparkled with a challenge as he barreled on. "Adjective, meaning *likened to a stubborn mule.* Synonyms: hardheaded, stiff-necked..."

"I didn't know I was sitting across from a dense thesaurus."

"Pig-headed, obstinate—" he continued.

I'd had enough. I stomped on the toe of his tightly laced shoe as we lurched onto new terrain. "*Pardon.* Must have been the carriage. I hope my *mulish* feet haven't hurt you."

Minho dug his nails into his thighs, hissing. His eyes were positively murderous. "Not a bit."

"Good."

Minho elongated his fingers one by one, then lounged back in his seat. "Look at us—bickering like an old married couple."

"Highly unlikely," I responded, although I despised how I couldn't help remembering the way we'd sought each other's hands in solace. I diplomatically erased the sensation from my memory. "No suitor of mine would drag me into an alley."

A muscle in his jaw twitched. "It's a good quality in a suitor to ensure his partner's safety. I was merely concerned for yours. Is that such a crime?"

Any of his previous provocation had dissolved, replaced by surprising sincerity.

I was too stunned to reply. *No,* I wanted to tell him, but the word was stuck to the roof of my mouth like a piece of old toffee. Why would Minho care about my personal safety? Unless he was interested in me out of more than mere curiosity…

My skin warmed at the thought, and I cooled it immediately by diverting my attention to the game. In seconds, my mental clarity returned like a rapid knock on the door. "'Skip two and look both ways,'" I recited. "What if it's referring to the house?"

"Skip two…tiles? Rooms?"

A beat of silence stretched between us. In unison, we reached our answer. "Floors."

At the house, my competitors and I skipped the first two flights of stairs and landed on the third floor. I hadn't given it as much scrutiny as the other floors. If I had, we might have reached our conclusion sooner.

But we still were missing another part of the puzzle. *The key is not a key.* I dragged my hand along the walls, closing my eyes to heighten my senses.

My eyes popped open. "Fox, do you have a pencil and—"

"Is that even a question?" In a flash, Fox produced his notepad and an array of writing utensils. I selected one, noticing he appeared rejuvenated from his "worldly pleasures" while Minho and I were gone.

I halted my pencil mid-sketch, letting the others examine the ballroom at the top of the drawing. "A circle."

I feathered out a slim rectangle beneath the circle. "A narrow hall."

Finally, I added two doors on the bottom right of the hall. The only doors in operation on this floor—the others were knob-less. "The bits of a key."

I presented the drawing with a flourish.

Fox gaped. "*The floor is a key!* What a find, Watson! It is a strange notion of architecture…but nothing our unstoppable duo couldn't deduce!"

"Duo?" Isabelle's voice was laced with accusation.

"Metaphorically," I hammered on. "Right, Fox?"

Fox nodded along vigorously, making me wonder just how limber his neck muscles were.

"So we've deciphered that the floor is the key we're looking for," Minho said. "But how, exactly, do we open the music box? There's still a keyhole."

"Unless there isn't." Gears were moving in Fox's head. "We need another look at that music box."

"Already a step ahead of you." I fetched the music box I'd kept on the ground and peered down at the keyhole. I imagined that whatever lay inside saw my large, black-brown iris and pupil, wide with anticipation. "Do any of you have something small enough to fit into this keyhole?"

"Would this work?" Isabelle drew out a needle-thin hairpin from her hair, capped with a pearl on the end.

"Yes," I said, grasping the hairpin between my forefinger and thumb. I pushed it into the keyhole. Instead of wiggling inside a contraption, it hit a wall. The backing was completely sealed.

"Closed," I confirmed.

"I was right! This *isn't* a keyhole." Fox bubbled with elation.

"The question remains: how do we open the box?" Minho asked.

"How about we break it with a mallet!" Fox proposed, a little too giddy at the prospect.

"That could damage whatever lies inside," Minho said. "We have to be methodical about this."

I set down the music box. "Let's scour the floor—that's the only key we have, after all."

Several doors awaited us, most of them ornamented in gold filigree... except four.

What made these doors special?

I closed my eyes. Shapes flashed beneath my lids, and I saw the puzzle pieces rearrange themselves until they clicked. I jolted my eyes open and really *looked*. The doors had visible brushstrokes in the lacquer, and in just the right light, I realized they were in the shapes of music notes.

Music notes. A music box.

"These notes were hidden here intentionally," I told the group.

"So what do we do?" Isabelle ran a hand over one of the doors, outlining a note. "We can't read these if we don't know the scale."

"Maybe we're not supposed to read them," Fox suggested. "If we need each other to accomplish this task, each of us should take a door. See if we discover anything else."

Promptly, we each chose a door.

"We should try pushing them," I said. "On my count: one... two..."

As I said *three*, we all pressed our body weight against the doors. Nothing.

Fox placed his arms akimbo. "Shall we break down the doors with a mallet—"

"No more talk of *mallets*," Isabelle interrupted.

"I knew it couldn't be that easy," I murmured to myself.

“There are no handles.” Minho ghosted a hand over where the doorknob should be. “There’s no way in, if pushing doesn’t work.”

I ran a hand along the hinges, then the point right where the door met the wall. A now-dried residue had been used to seal it. An idea sparked to life. “These hinges are *decorative*. Look.”

Fox, Isabelle, and Minho quickly checked their doors, then nodded in agreement. “The doors don’t open at all! They’re sealed shut,” Isabelle said.

“Unless they’re a different *kind* of door. Pocket doors! Maman only used sliding doors for larger spaces.”

“Like the ballroom,” Fox realized.

“Exactly. These are singular doors, but there’s still a possibility they might slide with a bit of effort…”

I pressed both hands against my door and tucked my fingers around whatever grooves I could find. The door creaked slightly. Minho rushed over to help. Fox and Isabelle eventually scampered to my corner of the hall, and with a great heave, we all pushed.

The seal began to dislodge. And as soon as it did, the door immediately slid to the left, disappearing into the wall and exposing beams at the top and bottom of the threshold. The room beyond was dim, more like a closet. I snuck inside, hands searching for something—anything—and grasped onto something cold and motionless. A lever.

I pulled it down. The other three doors immediately slid open, as if an invisible crank had reeled them into motion.

“How mysterious!” Fox rejoiced.

“Don’t get too giddy just yet, Sherlock,” Isabelle clucked. Then she and Fox dispersed to the other makeshift closets, each of them holding the same lever.

"Together!" Fox shouted. On the count of three, they engaged their levers. Instead of an open door, a small platform emerged from the wall between the doors. Shaped like a serving tray, it was just large enough for—

"The music box!" I cried.

I grabbed the music box from the floor. We were so close to making our first discovery—and opening the music box as Maman wanted. Something inside me felt alive, renewed. I was figuring out my mother's greatest puzzle moment by moment, and soon enough, I would finally crack the code.

Maybe I would discover what truly happened to make her disappear.

I gently placed the music box on the platform. The lid popped open a smidge and I gasped.

"Incredible! There must be some sort of magnetic repulsion on the platform," Fox rationalized.

"So . . . who's going to look inside?" Isabelle took an infinitesimal step backward, as if afraid a mouse might be lurking within. And yet something told me my former friend wasn't much afraid of anything.

"I will," Minho answered. He inched forward, tall enough to see over the platform. He placed both hands in the box, as if digging through a pile of mail.

I stepped closer to him, heart pounding. "What's inside?"

Minho's expression was unreadable as he handed me a red envelope. My fingers were trembling by the time I finally extracted the first article.

It was a color photograph of four people, all of them a little older than me, standing in front of a building called Blackthorn Hall. There was a boy with sandy blond hair; a younger boy whose skin shone like Minho's; a girl with wavy hair, like Isabelle's; and finally...

My voice came out in a choke. "Maman."

I flipped over the photograph. On the back, in Maman's scribbled handwriting, were the following words:

The Keepers, 14 July 1894

"The Keepers?" Fox echoed, peering over my shoulder. "What does that mean?"

"And what were they keeping?" Isabelle tacked on.

I exchanged a significant look with Minho. We had heard that word before—Les Voyants had uttered it like a secret. Burning with questions, I studied the print. I had never seen this picture before—this small window into Maman's past, a past she'd always kept so hidden from me.

Fox shifted at my side, his eyes zeroing in on the sandy-haired boy.

"You know him?" I asked.

His lips tilted into a half smile. "How well does one actually know their own father?"

My eyes shot back to the photograph. Indeed, I saw an echo of Fox's grin in the boy's smile. He had an arm draped over my mother's shoulders, as if the two had known each other for a long while.

At least Fox could recognize him. I didn't know my father at all.

For a moment, there was a consuming silence. Then Isabelle stepped forward. "I would recognize Mama anywhere."

"Which just leaves me." Minho studied the picture. "That's my uncle, Hyunwoo."

An image flashed through my mind. I fished for the pamphlet I had taken from Maman's boudoir, now hidden in my dress pocket, and lifted it so it was level with the photograph.

"The university," I realized. "It looks exactly the same."

Fox bent a brow. "Which means..."

My mouth went dry. "Our parents—or in Minho's case, his uncle—all attended the same academy during the summer of 1894... *together*. The Botanical Academy of Paris."

"They knew each other, all of them," Isabelle whispered.

"I suppose we can't have all the answers—not yet, anyway." Minho took out what was left in the envelope and held it so we could all read it together.

Congratulations, contestants.

You have solved my first task. Now use my musical offering to complete your next.

Beware—the path ahead is not always forward.

With care,

Tara Gupta

" 'Musical offering'?" Isabelle repeated quizzically.

But I was too focused on the *with care* part to answer. If Maman had actually cared, wouldn't she have left the house for *me* to inherit? Wouldn't she have trusted her own daughter with what was rightfully hers? The idea refused to leave my brain, like a stain that took no liking to soap and water.

"I think she meant this." Minho flipped over Maman's note to find a piece of sheet music: *The Magic Flute* by Mozart.

With all of us hot on Minho's heels, he carved a path to the piano in the parlor. My feet moved with a kind of electricity I'd never experienced before. When we burst into the room, I threw myself onto the piano's bench.

My fingers hovered over the keys as Minho placed the sheet music on the holder. "Take it away."

As I began to play *The Magic Flute*, a flood of memories hit me. The insects buzzing in the garden, harmonizing with Maman's stories... Maman and I in the grass, the moon beckoning from above... Maman holding a finger to her lips, telling me to be brave as blood dripped from my knee...

Come out, come out, her voice echoed in my head.

My fingers hit a sharp note when they weren't supposed to. The others winced.

"I'm guessing that wasn't right?" Fox asked.

My fingers were shaking now, and Minho sat next to me, gently removing my hands from the keys. "Allow me."

He played through the piece with ease. All the while, I couldn't stop thinking of that image of Maman: the blood on her lips, on my knee. The coffee-eyed figure in the garden.

By the time Minho finished, I was breathless. But not because of his flawless playing skills, or his technique.

Was Maman truly back?

"Nothing happened," Isabelle noted. "Are you sure you played all the keys correctly?"

"I followed each note, each beat, precisely."

I bit my lip. "Perhaps we should reframe the clue. Does anyone know what *The Magic Flute* might signify?"

"A key part of the opera is banishing evil spirits," Fox commented. "Given all the rumors about this estate..."

"Maybe Sana's mother was trying to tell us something," Minho finished, eyes flickering sidelong to meet mine.

It seemed more than one person was beginning to think that there was a ghost haunting the property of Razorthorn Manor.

THIRTEEN

Night brought a seemingly unbreakable gloam.

My restless mind couldn't part with today's discoveries. Paired with the figure I'd observed behind Minho in the garden yesterday, I was too rattled to leave well enough alone.

I tucked into my slippers and tiptoed into the hallway. My neighbor, Fox, was snoring louder than a horse, and I'd heard Misha's rumbles after a long day of riding. Fox, somehow, put that to shame.

Down at the front door, I slid on a jacket, slipped outside, and meandered past the garden gate.

A chill peppered the air. The branches of the bare trees, which in the daylight resembled patterns of lace, now appeared like tines of a pitchfork. The flowers I once called friends turned toward me, weed-choked and half-dead, opening their petaled mouths to cry in low, eerie tones, *Why did you leave us, Sana? Why did you go?*

A punishing wind snatched the voices away, and I exhaled a shaky breath as quiet settled around me once more. My imagination was running like a new engine, and I desperately needed to pull the brake.

I began searching the grounds with haste. Once, a squirrel giving chase made my heart rate tick up expediently, but otherwise the garden was calm. What was I doing here?

I needed to go back to the safety of my bed.

I needed to forget about the thing in the shadows.

A prickling feeling gave me pause. *Someone was watching me.*

The thought was only confirmed when I spun around, eyes locking on my target: a human form, deep in the shadows.

The figure darted from one tree to the next, merely a blur in the darkness. When it passed into a shaft of pearlescent moonlight, the body appeared to glow, its hands nearly translucent. It turned for only a moment to look back at me, and I swore I saw those coffee-colored eyes again, bright with fear.

"Maman?" I reached out, but the figure only shrank back. Was it afraid of me—or something else? I needed to follow her. To confirm that she wasn't a result of an unfettered fantasy.

So I did. Every time I neared close enough to touch her, something stopped me: a stray vine curling around my ankle, pulling me back, or a branch swinging with force toward me, as if conspiring to give me a concussion. It was like the garden didn't want me to touch her—to find my mother.

I wasn't going to let it stop me.

But at the edge of the Wildwood, in a sea of endless trees, I lost track of the woman. I wasn't sure exactly where I was; I must have been in the north quadrant of the garden, judging from the angle of the manor in the distance.

"Come out, come out," a voice beckoned from within a thicket.

The words pulsed through my veins, and I bent onto all fours to follow the sound. Small branches and thorns cut into my skin, but I didn't wince. What began as small bushes grew into tall hedges, opening up to me like a welcome breeze. I stood, dusting myself off. I had arrived at a gate I had never seen before.

A secret waiting to be revealed.

I pressed a hand against the gate, but not a second later my hand sizzled with heat and I drew it back sharply. By the gods' teeth, what *was* this place? I glanced down, marveling at the hot sensation. It was the same sensation I'd felt yesterday when I'd touched Flora's insignia.

A blink later, I noticed a thorn had lodged itself into my thumb, surrounded by golden, glowing light. How did that get there? I pried at the pesky thing with a pinch of my thumb and forefinger, but it was no use. It felt like it was lodged there . . . permanently.

Out, damned spot. I scrubbed at my skin—nay, scratched—until the flesh beaded with blood. The thorn was growing now, a painful thing that seemed to come from *within* my skin rather than *outside* of it. My finger throbbed angrily as the thorn grew and grew and grew, a knifelike slice bursting out of my skin, writhing and squirming.

Soon, it was no thorn at all. Instead, it took the shape of a thin, rising vine.

The pain showed no signs of ebbing, and soon I was numb from my temples to my lips, my head lolling back. Still, the vine shot skyward, forming a stalk that housed a hundred thorns, and now, red flowers that slowly unfurled. Painful, bloody flowers.

The last thing I saw before I collapsed was my mother's face hovering in front of me.

He found me the next morning, entwined with the roots of a gnarled tree.

"Sana, what are you doing out here?"

I blinked awake. The blurry contours of a body slowly became sharper, more refined. A robin soared by overhead, and freshly turned autumn leaves brushed the boy's cheeks. I tried to disguise how well I'd come to know that face.

Minho wore an apprehensive look. "You're hurt."

Vaguely, the sensation of pain returned, and I lifted my left hand, blocking out Minho's face. There was a gash on my left thumb in the shape of a lightning bolt, exactly where it had been last night.

I groaned. I must have succumbed to a nightmare. It made my head pound just remembering it. It all felt so *real.* The gash on my thumb was proof enough.

And the sight of Maman. But that stalk of flowers sounded like a laughable fairy tale. Was it real or false? Memory or myth?

I grumbled something, slightly delirious, and Minho laughed. What did I say?

"Let's get you washed up."

I dutifully followed Minho, my brain too foggy to fully process the way he helped me to the house, one hand on my waist, the other holding up my injured hand.

We stopped by the sink of the nearest lavatory. He rolled the sleeves of his thin white shirt up to the elbows. Now that he wasn't sporting a jacket, I noticed the straps and buckles of his suspenders glinting in the light. My eyes roamed to his sturdy forearms, where veins canvased his skin like azure rivers.

Minho let the water run while he found a basket of supplies. Upon his return, he checked the temperature, found it suitably warm, and then twisted the knobs back into place. I didn't oppose as he began to wash the wound with careful, precise movements, turning the water a rosy pink. All the while, I studied his face in the mirror. The way his lips scrunched in concentration. This felt so different from the boy who'd thrown quips at me yesterday.

When he was done, he let out a satisfied hum. Alarmingly, I realized his hand was practically closed over mine, just as it had been yesterday, like the branches of a tree linked together, entwined there under the slowly rippling water. Our fingers, drawn together like magnets.

Sleeping in the gardens must have done a number on my usually pragmatic sensibilities.

Dispelling any romantic notions, I pulled our hands apart. Minho was only caring for me the way he would a horse, no matter how tenderly he approached his work. I would not misconstrue his attention to detail for affection.

Minho moved to the tub and filled it with clean water. "I've set up the bath. I'll return in ten minutes to dress the wound." And with that, he departed.

I begrudgingly undressed, realizing the dirt from the ground had somehow snuck into the strands of my hair, under my fingernails. I scrubbed myself clean with a small bar of soap. The smell reminded me of home. Of Maman.

Triumphantly clean, I emerged from the tub and dried myself with a towel. My clothes had been laid on the counter, and I slipped into a day gown, a dress with sheer sleeves and a heart-shaped neckline that enhanced the sharpness of my clavicle.

When Minho returned, knocking thrice on the door, I let him in. He paused to evaluate me.

"You look..."

"Cleaner? Not crusted in dirt like a girl born from the garden?"

"I was going to say divine," he finished.

His candor struck me with unexpected force. For once, I had no retort.

"Your bandage?" He held up gauze, and I let him apply it expertly around my wound.

"You told me you take care of animals. Are you always this good with humans, too?"

"Humans are much more temperamental. Animals are kinder. Better, they can't talk back."

I let out a surprisingly warm laugh as Minho finished dressing the wound.

"Care to tell me how you ended up sleeping among the trees last night?" Minho asked.

"Oh." There was still the large matter of assessing what I'd seen in the gardens. I could have sworn I'd smelled a lingering lavender perfume. *Maman's* perfume.

But I wasn't at liberty to say all of that, even though Minho had just cared for me in a way I hadn't been cared for in a long time.

"Just reminding myself of my roots. Now come on—we have a game to play."

Come midmorning, Fox, Isabelle, Minho, and I were all gathered at the grand piano in the sitting room. We'd excused ourselves from breakfast; we couldn't very well focus on a meal when all we wanted was a taste of our next clue.

"Let's take a closer look." My eyes roved over the paper until I saw it. Indeed, the treble clef had stuck out as strange to me before, but I wasn't entirely certain why. Now that I was looking closely, I could see that the clef had been drawn backward.

I thought over my mother's warning in her note. "'The path ahead is not always forward,'" I recited. "Meaning..."

"We need to go backward!" Isabelle finished my thought.

Minho began playing the piece over, from end to start. The rest of us listened in stark anticipation.

Finally, he hit the last note. And the room filled with silence.

We all held our breaths as a *click* emanated from the piano.

"The lid...," I began. I spun around to the back of the grand piano and found it had lifted slightly—as if some inner mechanism had unlocked it. "Help me raise this." My voice was urgent enough that the others peeled from their positions.

"On three," Minho said, the lid unbearably heavy in our hands. "One..."

"*Three!*" Fox cried out.

With a grunt, we heaved the lid open. I peered down into the cavity, countless silver hammers connecting taut strings to the soundboard. How Maman had come up with this, I wasn't sure. But the precise set of keys needed to unlock the piano would never be played at random, ensuring that whatever we found today would be for our eyes alone.

Isabelle reached into a small, empty corner of the piano, where a velvet bag was tied with a ribbon. She opened and upended it, letting a heavy coin drop into the palm of her hand.

One side depicted an image of the Botanical Academy with the label ESTD. 1863 underneath. Isabelle flipped over the coin, and Flora's profile beamed up at me, embossed in deep copper.

"*That's* our next clue?" Fox aimed to take it from Isabelle's hand, but she turned away.

"Not all of it." Isabelle reached back into the bag and pulled out a piece of ripped paper. Her eyes flew over the words. "There's another message, from your mother."

I pried the letter from Isabelle's grip and read:

Another clue solved, just as I hoped.

My next challenge requires travel to the place that keeps your mind sharp.

Do not leave your fellow competitors behind—

for this, all four must be combined.

"Combined?" echoed Isabelle. "I thought the level of collaboration was up to us now."

"I suppose not just yet," Minho said, failing to smooth over the irritation in his voice. "The clue mentions travel, and combined with this coin..."

"The Botanical Academy," I whispered.

Maman, in the gardens. Maman, hiding in plain sight...

"The academy awaits!" Fox whooped. "Imagine us entering the grounds like a group of students—nay, cohorts—nay, *colleagues*—"

Isabelle's gaze hardened, and I had the sense she wasn't feeling the same camaraderie as Fox. She wore a mask of determination. Determined enough to win my rightful inheritance.

But I didn't dwell too long on that. With Fox's aid, I wouldn't need to rely on her help—or Minho's.

I'd been solving riddles since I was a babe. Even if I couldn't always admit it, I was my mother's daughter.

TARA'S RIDDLE

For Sana's sixth birthday:

I buzz like a bee, but I cannot fly

I speak with no mouth and listen with no ears

Who am I?

FOURTEEN

We prepared arrangements for a ride to l'École Botanique first thing that afternoon. It was our first group outing since arriving at the manor, marking it as a sort of adventure. There was no chaperone, either, which felt incredibly liberating.

Before we left, I wrote up a letter to my aunt Neena with a bit of spare ink and parchment to ask her if she might be coming to the manor, as she had promised. The envelope from her was still here in my trunk, and I copied the return address on an envelope of my own.

All of this was becoming quite confusing. My missing aunt. Maman's riddles, so much harder than I remembered. I recalled the one she'd offered the morning of my sixth birthday.

I buzz like a bee but I cannot fly…

I speak with no mouth and listen with no ears…

I had trailed all over the house for an answer before I'd come upon the wireless in the sitting room, running a hand over the knobs until it crackled, buzzing to life. Maman had tried to trick me, making me think it was a *who* instead of a *what*. That was her way of saying that anything could live, in its own way. Anything could flourish, and consequently, anything could wither.

"Fox," I asked once we were in the carriage and well on our way, "what do you know about ghosts, anyhow?"

Beside me, Fox's face pinched. "That they might haunt you for eternity if you don't help them move on to the paradise of Elysium. Or the *other* less savory option."

Across from me, Minho and Isabelle were each focused on their reading material: *Le Petit Journal* for Isabelle, *A Crystal Age* for Minho. I raised my own magazine to hide my face from them. "I think I saw one in the garden."

His eyes darkened with recognition. "Are you saying what I think you're saying?"

"Yes," I breathed. "Maman."

His face paled. "Are you certain?"

"Positive." Positively certain I was sounding more delusional by the day. But I couldn't ignore the lingering scent of lavender clinging to my hair.

We hit a bump in the road. When I drew back the curtains, I saw we were almost at our destination. Fox said nothing, looking lost in thought.

We turned onto the grand avenue that connected the Arc de Triomphe with Place de la Concorde. Shops flanked the street, and vendors hawked their wares on the cobblestones. Parisians perused the goods with eyes that shone like newly minted coins.

I felt like a tourist myself, seeing the city for the first time in almost a decade.

Much like flowers, people blossomed along the streets of Paris, bringing the city to life: a woman strolling by, parasol in hand, her plum coat matching her thick leather gloves. A man exiting a Renault taxi and adjusting his gilded moon-phase watch, his gray mustache twitching as he spoke in rapid French to the driver. A boy hanging firmly onto his father, who was busy tucking the morning edition of *The Paris Gazette* into his double-breasted coat pocket. FEAST OF THE GODS: CELEBRATIONS TO TAKE PLACE ACROSS PARIS.

I'd become a serial avoider of newspapers after my mother's disappearance. I didn't enjoy the way they wrote about her, how they exploited her. That was probably what had angered me most about the reporters on my doorstep: their gall. And I'd completely forgotten today was the Feast of the Gods. The celebration, marked by grand devotional feasts—not to mention the heavy foot traffic all over Paris—was created by Louis XIV to commemorate the abundance offered to mortals by the hands of gods: a good seasonal harvest from Ceres, large catches of fish thanks to Neptune, and so on. It was widely understood that offerings made at ritual sites today would be well worth the cost of your token of gratitude. Parades would run through the streets tonight, a night of revelries as sumptuous as a plate of coq au vin.

After Fox handed a few coins to our driver, we filed out of the carriage. I inhaled as much of the cool, misty afternoon air into my lungs as I could. The birds trilled with gossip.

"How stunning!" Isabelle gaped at the grand feat of architecture before us—the Arc de Triomphe. Her face shone with good spirits now that we were out of the stuffy carriage. "The relief work is—"

"Very typical of neoclassicism?" Fox interjected.

"I was going to say *ethereal*."

I had to agree. There were scenes of soldiers valiantly fighting, and above them, the gods peering down at the world. I shuddered under their gazes—particularly Flora's, who seemed to be watching me from behind her polished marble eyes, a crown of flowers frozen on her head.

Instinctively, I reached for the back of my neck, where fine hairs stood on end.

We proceeded on foot to the academy, making several turns onto narrow side streets, remnants of the medieval city. The shops' inviting storefronts greeted us: one displayed hats of all shapes and sizes, some with feathers attached neatly above their brims; another all manner of capes that stopped neatly above the dress dummies' elbows; and finally, a dressmaker's latest ladies' fashion collection.

The next window was quite different. It was filled with all sorts of offerings for the gods, from rose-scented incense sticks to sacred herbs and honeyed wines.

I didn't know why I felt a sudden pull to enter the shop. Did I think making an offering to Flora on the Feast of the Gods would win me the elusive razorthorn seed? How could I? I hardly believed in the gods' beneficence at all.

I had to stop myself from going inside. Instead, I continued along with my competitors, passing through a park with a copse of trees. Beyond it was the hidden jewel of Paris: l'École Botanique.

The academy was a seamless and stunning piece of architecture. Myriad windows covered stone turrets that rose like fists into the air, as if they were fingertips that wished to brush the heavenly threshold that the gods so deftly hid from us.

I wanted to trace the path Maman had walked, find where she had sat, sit on the lawns with my back to the grass and face soaking in the sun. I wanted to see the brilliant spots beneath my eyelids as I shut them, hear the birds' chirps and feel the flowers kiss my skin.

I shrugged my bag closer to my body, hoping it helped me blend in with the other students. My outfit had been carefully selected from Maman's boudoir, a long plaid skirt and tweed jacket that still held her scent. Not lavender this time, but almond oil, which she often slid through the strands of my hair before bed. The ritual was one of the few times I felt my mother's love. Her magic.

Today, I'd tied a black ribbon in my hair to keep it out of my face. We would be poring over books, not puzzles. Or so I hoped.

Fox, Minho, and Isabelle were dressed in a similar fashion. Minho tucked his fiddler hat over his eyes, while Isabelle donned a black cape jacket and matching beret. Fox opted for a deerstalker, and I imagined he had a traveling set of five such hats to cycle through depending on his mood.

Once we entered the grounds, we passed droves of students poring over texts. Some were lazily strewn under trees, others frantically searching through material like they had a test to prepare for. The busy yet warm nature of the campus wrapped around me like a wool scarf. It was almost enough to make me forget the strange happenings of the last two nights—the sentient thorn in my hand, the ghosts that filled my mind with more questions than answers, the assault in the alleyway.

We followed signs to the library, ducking under archways connecting the stone-bricked buildings. A couple walked by, hands clasped, and I looked away, a sharp blush rising to my cheeks when I recalled the way Minho's hand fit into mine.

"A distracted mind does not make a lady," my governess once berated me, her voice like the whistle of a steaming kettle. "Proper etiquette, posture, and attention—now *those* are the fine qualities a person requires for dignity."

I despised knowing that Minho possessed all three of those qualities, while mine were abysmal, if not entirely absent. I swung my hair back as we passed through the threshold of the library building.

A trio of smells welcomed me: dusty tomes, fresh ink, and sheaths of luxurious paper. The library was a garden, except the flowers were made of booklets and dictionaries, pages and pens.

The pages of books are sharp, but the words even sharper, Maman once told me. Only now did I realize that similar words were written on the academy pamphlet. I knew her clue must have been leading us to the academy library today. I just needed to find Flora's insignia, left behind by Maman, to confirm it.

"Let's split up to find Flora's symbol," I suggested. There were no protestations. We separated, then stalked around the half-filled tables and the bookshelves, the volumes upon them stacked in a near religious manner of cleanliness. Monsieur Champlain would approve. But Maman's puzzles were often concealed in an unusual manner. I needed to see the library from a new angle.

"Find anything?"

I nearly jumped when I found Fox shadowing me. "What are you doing?"

Fox removed his pipe from his coat pocket and stuck it between his teeth. "We're working together, remember, Sana Gupta?"

There was something strange about the way he said my last name. Like he wanted to test it on his tongue, understand it.

"Right. Then give me a boost."

"Er... well, my back isn't exactly the most *toned*—"

"It'll just be a moment."

Fox clumsily tucked away his pipe and got down on all fours. I gently propped one foot on his back, then stepped with the other onto a shelf to divide my weight. From this vantage, I was near enough to see the tops of all the bookshelves on the main floor. And just past them, hovering over a bookshelf tucked in an alcove against the eastern wall—there it was!

Flora's insignia.

Once I was safely on the ground, Fox got up with an overdramatic stretch of his limbs. "That carpet needs a thorough cleaning."

I was about to make a comment when I noticed Fox's favorite plaything—ahem, *prop*—had toppled to the ground. I retrieved his father's pipe, finding a small groove where the two halves of the pipe joined. Hadn't Fox said he kept matches inside? It felt too light for that.

"You're quite attached to this thing, aren't you?" I stepped closer to him, rattling the pipe close to my ear. "What do you think I might find inside?"

Fox inched back. "I'm not sure what you're talking about." His eyes were so brown, so wide.

"Don't be coy with me, Richard. We're working together, aren't we?"

Fox swallowed. "We are, Sana. I swear on my mother's life."

"I swear on my mother's, too," I said, before realizing how dim and empty that promise was. Time was trickling out of my fingers.

"All right, if you insist. Open it."

At Fox's words, I twisted each side, watching as they spiraled farther and farther away from each other until the two halves popped free. From inside, I retrieved a small stash of paper. A typed note, old and crumpled.

10 September 1894

Dear Percy,

I will not forget what you told me among stolen kisses. Soul meets soul, and ours is a story that will not be forgotten.

But there is something of great urgency we must discuss. Please tell me when you are available to meet.

Sincerely,

Mary

"Percy and Mary," I said. "As in . . . the Shelleys?"

"I think so," Fox said. "But I believe them to be code names. Secret names, for secret love notes."

"What would someone else's love notes be doing in your father's pipe?" I asked, brain churning until the thought struck me. "Unless . . ."

"My father is Percy?" Fox finished for me. "It's been my theory, ever since I found this note a few months ago. In fact, Percy is my middle name, and Father practically *dotes* over anything written by the Shelleys. I believe this Mary might be related to the game." Then, under his breath: "And the question I've been seeking an answer to . . ."

"What question?" What was Fox rambling on about?

He recollected his thoughts. "Ah. You know what? It's nothing. I'm sure it's nothing. Merely ordinary romantic slog." He snatched the paper back, rolling it back into his father's pipe. "The clue, Sana. What did you find?"

I didn't bother pressing him for more, knowing our time was running short. Instead I dragged Fox across the library, careful not to look too harried or out of place, and wound up at the alcove. It was hidden from students' prying eyes. "Flora's symbol was left above this shelf for a reason."

"Then we've found the right place," Fox agreed, eyes twinkling.

"Let's try pulling out certain books—maybe it'll work like it did in the study." The encyclopedic journal concerning Jupiter had helped lead us to the parlor, after all.

We tried, but to no avail. Once we reached the last book, Fox uttered, "What you said about ghosts earlier—there are a few things I've gleaned from studying Romantic poetry. Ghosts will continue to haunt us whether we see them or not. They live not in the shadows, but in our souls."

"That's *highly* comforting," I retorted. "But also . . . that might just be the wisest thing you've ever said to me, Professor Fox."

"Then allow me to be shrewd once more. I believe I know how to handle your *spectral* conundrum."

"How so?"

Fox only held up a finger. "Give me some time this evening to gather my supplies, and then we'll rendezvous in the manor's library. We'll be discreet."

"Why—" I started, already having a bad feeling about this. "Fine. We'll meet tonight."

"What's tonight?" Minho came up behind us, and I nearly jumped out of my skin again.

"Nothing." I cleared my throat, avoiding his crisp gaze. "Any idea how this bookshelf might pertain to the game?" I pointed up at the symbol hidden in the wall.

"No, but the clue did say *all four must be combined*." Isabelle joined us, tapping her fingers against her crossed arms. "Take a look at the sconces on the wall."

There were four sconces, each at an equal distance to the bookshelf. Perhaps, like the levers, if we turned them just right...

Minho seemed to have the same idea. At once, we each turned the sconces, then hissed.

"My finger." I bit back a curse at the bead of blood on my right thumb. Some sort of sharp protrusion, nearly invisible to the eye, had been attached to the sconce. I glanced at my bandaged thumb, recalling the thorn that would not go away. A nightmare...or an indelible piece of reality?

But the sconce had done more than prick my finger. The blood it extracted now traveled through it, hissing against the cold stone of the wall. Within seconds, the bookshelf clicked as it slid aside, revealing a hidden cavity.

Blood had been spilled once before, when we signed the contracts. It shouldn't have surprised me that our blood, when combined, might be the key to unlocking Maman's current clue.

"I'm not going in there," Fox said, sucking on his bloody finger.

"Be brave, Sherlock," Isabelle encouraged, giving him a gentle squeeze on the shoulder. Fox pouted, acting like a dog with its tail between its legs as he followed her into the passage. Minho and I exchanged a look before trailing them.

Another hidden passage. My mother certainly had a liking for them.

Inside, Fox pulled on the nearest chain, and a light bulb flickered to life. We found what appeared to be a workspace of some sort, holding tables full of books on all matters of botany, trays of specimen slides for microscopes, and beakers upon beakers, like those one might find in a chemistry laboratory.

"This place looks like it hasn't been touched in years." A fine layer of dust coated a nearby journal, and I swiped it with my finger for good measure. A pot held a fiddle-leaf fig tree that was now so dry, it would certainly wither into nothingness with the smallest breeze.

"This journal has the same symbol above the doorway. And look—it's full of drawings." Isabelle opened the journal, landing on depictions of crossbred plants. Noted underneath a black-eyed Susan was the implementation of resistance to certain fungi. On the next page, someone had feathered out a hybrid of roses with daylilies.

Isabelle flipped through the journal. I stopped her when I spotted a familiar stamp. I eased the book into my hands, feeling my heart flutter.

Maman's journal.

STAMP:
FROM THE DESK OF TARA GUPTA

Trial Number	*Date*	*Experiment Results*
1	*4 July 1894*	*No power detected*
2	*16 July 1894*	*Petal combinations improper*
3	*9 August 1894*	*Erratic and unstable. Add a final ingredient from a more powerful source*

"How cryptic," Minho gritted out.

"What does it mean by *trial*?" Isabelle's voice shook. "What was your mother doing?"

"I believe Tara wanted us to find her workstation. She was clearly pursuing more than basic botany here." Fox twirled his pipe for good measure, pointing at the other chairs and desks in the workspace, each labeled with a name: HYUNWOO, MARIA, RICHARD, and TARA. "And she wasn't alone."

My mind trailed back to the photograph we'd found in the music box. Maman had been friends with three other students at the academy. The Keepers, they'd called themselves. But keepers of what? And how had Les Voyants known the name?

"I think you should all see this."

Minho gathered us by the back wall, where Maman seemed to have hung pictures of her and her friends. But there was more than that—there were clippings of flowers and hybrids, each labeled accordingly, and depictions of the goddess Flora, snipped from newspapers and books and scholarly articles about the gods themselves. It was like Maman was making some sort of collage, and in the center was a diagram of the anatomy of the flower.

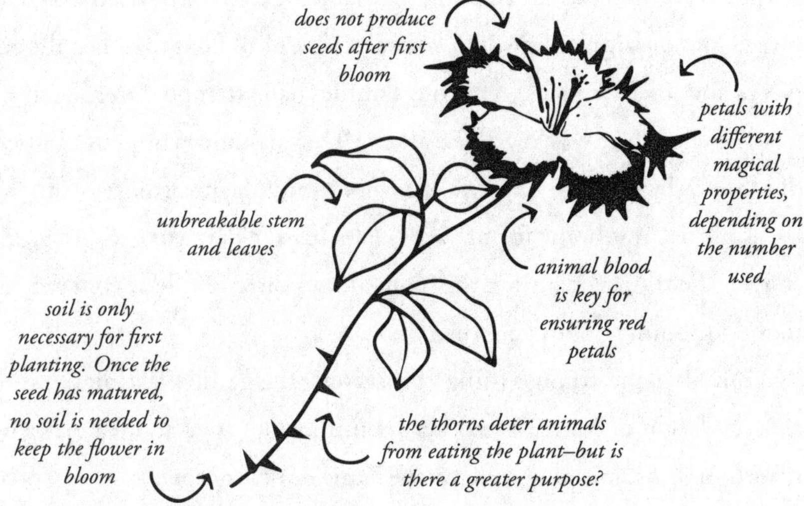

Beneath the diagram were captions written in bloodred ink.

Bloody flower with bloody past.

How to attain the blood of the gods?

Assumption incorrect—blood of gods not needed, but blood of divine provenance might suffice.

The realization of what Maman was doing hit me with sudden clarity. "Maman was trying to make a new razorthorn."

"Is such a thing even possible? There were only four seeds!" Minho exclaimed.

"Which is why my mother—and your family members—were all conspiring to create a new one. They were studying Flora herself, trying to emulate whatever she'd done to create it in the first place!"

"So your mother led us here... to show us that *she* crafted a new razorthorn? Is *that* the seed we'll find at the end of the game?" Isabelle asked, aghast.

My head pounded from all the questions. Maman was a woman of mystery, and I was knitted into her fabric. I didn't know how to cut myself loose. I didn't know if I *wanted* to. Not until I put together all the pieces and uncovered just what our families had attempted to conceive.

Isabelle's voice was low as she asked, "Do you know why your mother did this? Why she's offering up the manor... and the razorthorn seed?"

I racked my brain for answers. Perhaps she'd started to get sick. Maybe she didn't mean for this game to go on at all. It was merely a night's insomnia put to good use.

But after the strange things I'd seen in the garden last night, and this revelation of Maman and her friends having tried to create a new razorthorn... something told me the game ran far deeper.

I flipped through her journal and landed on a page with several names and addresses. *Professors to meet*, Maman had written, including each of their specialties, which all seemed to focus on areas of study surrounding the gods themselves. Some of them had check marks next to their names, indicating that perhaps Maman had already spoken to them. Was this our next clue—tracking down scholars who could help us delve into the properties of the razorthorn? What about it did we need to uncover?

"Let's head outside. We can go over our next course of action with some fresh air."

I led the charge, holding the journal close to my chest, still shaken up by what I'd discovered in Maman's secret room behind the bookshelf.

There were even more invisible strings knotting together my, Fox, Isabelle, and Minho's existence.

And I would untie them all.

FIFTEEN

We gathered under one of the stone archways outside the library. Evening approached with the steadiness of a legionnaire's march, but all of our discoveries made my blood run hot.

"Maman left a list of professors in her journal. That can't be a coincidence. They all appear to hold scholarly information about the gods. Perhaps even about the origins of the razorthorn."

The razorthorn. That word was as precious as a prayer, something that couldn't be held but only cherished. Soon, however, one of us *would* be holding that elusive seed—if, in fact, my mother had succeeded in producing it. I pressed down the sweltering resentment in my stomach, the wish that this seed and this game never existed, and that my mother had never left me for whatever lay beyond the confines of our house.

There had to be more...something else Maman wanted us to know—something about her summer at the academy, about the experiments that took place.

Fox's face pruned. His eyes were full of untold secrets as he thumbed his pipe. He might have been thinking of our alliance, but I wondered, briefly, if there was something else on his mind. That note in his father's pipe?

"It would take weeks to reach out to each and every one of them," Minho reasoned. "We don't even know if they're still working at the academy, or at other universities. If your mother intended this to be part of the game, it wouldn't work within the time constraints."

"So we've hit an impasse." Isabelle suppressed a groan.

"Not necessarily. Some more time in the library might enlighten us," Minho argued.

Fox scoffed. "My bloody finger begs to differ. I think it's swollen to the size of a peanut shell. Would you like to see—"

"No, thank you." I pulled Fox aside, away from Minho and Isabelle's attentive ears. "Are we still meeting tonight? You said you need to gather supplies. I can help with whatever you're planning."

"I'll handle all of that. Don't you worry," Fox said in a tone that had me utterly unconvinced. "I do need to peruse a few shops, if anyone would like to accompany me?" He turned to Isabelle, who looked like she'd rather not spend another second with him. "We can take the train home instead of that unwieldy weapon of a carriage, if that makes you feel any better."

Isabelle's face lit with enthusiasm at that promise, and she followed him. They rounded the corner, and I glanced up to find Minho and I were alone.

To my surprise, Minho lifted my hand, examining the dressing. "How's the pain?"

"Better," I said, even though my skin was now scorched from his touch. The air around us had shifted; the path under the archway felt too intimate, too quiet, like the darkening sky was conspiring against me.

He pulled away, although I hadn't made any objections.

"You're right," I said in the ensuing silence. "The library might have more answers. But..." I recalled the photograph of the Keepers. The building they had stood in front of.

Sensing Maman's academic spirit, I followed the crowd of students moving from building to building, until I found the one that called to me.

A sign identified it as Blackthorn Hall. Inside, a dim air of stuffiness and shuffling books greeted me. Students on benches and stairs pored over tomes of all kinds, from Dezobry to Quinet. I clung to my bag and peered through the ajar door of an ongoing lecture, listening to the *scritch* of fountain pens on paper.

I slunk closer to get a better look at the board behind the professor, limned in chalk. *La fête des dieux.* Today's lecture must be about the holy Feast of the Gods. I was struck with a strange urge to know more.

"If only we could get inside..."

"And pretend to be *students*? *Here?* I'm enrolled at the Sorbonne, if you've forgotten."

I pulled Minho by his tie out of view of the lecture hall. "Maman wanted us to come to the Academy. We've found her journal, but I sense there's more we need to discover. Clearly she was trying to mimic what the gods had done—to make a razorthorn flower."

"Still processing that fact," Minho said with a rub of his temple. "A lecture, then..." He glanced down to where my hand still held his tie. "I should like to take proper breaths, if you'll allow me."

"Oh." It seemed now I was the one holding onto Minho instead of the other way around. I let go of him, smoothing my hands over my skirt. "Shall we?"

Minho and I slipped into the lecture hall. It could boast a seating of a hundred students. The lecture itself had just reached a pause, and the students' chitter crescendoed, but the professor motioned for silence. With attentive ears, I leaned forward to catch a question from a keen student with a hand raised high in the air. The professor nodded at him.

"Professor, you don't think the Cycle of Light will come to an end one day, do you? That the gods will leave us? I heard Les Voyants are on the rise again..."

Whispers funneled throughout the classroom.

"I have heard such rumors, too," the professor replied. "It is true that the group was founded based on an old oracle's divinations that the Cycle of Light would end before the next millennia. But I'm sure Janus would not allow such a thing."

The name of the god of beginnings, gates, pathways, and doors allowed a memory to sharpen before me. On a hot spring day, Old Ben, the manor's landscaper, found shelter by the shed and sipped from a tall glass of tonic water. Belle and I were used to playing tricks on him. But that day, we were too tired for games, and appealed instead to the gardener for stories.

"Followers of Janus were the ones to open the gates between our world and that of the gods. The calendars began anew, ushering in the Cycle of Light. Since the day the gates opened, many believed that we have moved out of an age of darkness into one of enlightenment. The gods have since bestowed many gifts on humankind."

"Like the razorthorn!" nine-year-old me replied.

Old Ben wiped his sweat-beaded forehead with the back of his hand. "Yes, just like the flower. But not all gifts were permanent. The gods' power is often too volatile for this world."

Vol-a-tile. I had formed the word in my mouth, getting a taste of the consonants and vowels, strung together like beads on a wire. It was no wonder the flower didn't last forever.

"I believe they are much too engrained in our society to leave us now," the professor intoned before checking the clock. "Let us take a rest for ten minutes and resume after the intermission."

The wave of voices crashed over me as the intermission began. Minho and I glanced at one another askance as two students debated the need for the Feast.

"My mother thinks the Feast is more important than my birthday," a girl said with a swish of her well-trimmed hair.

"Wouldn't you rather pray to them than do nothing?" her friend replied. "We *are* in a time of upheaval. We need them to turn the tides of the weather, the trade of goods... even to determine our soulmates."

A few guffaws from the students, although some glanced at each other with lust, as if certain Cupid might pair them in some divine act.

"If they're so important, why haven't they been spotted in centuries?" countered one of their peers. "They abandon us for Olympus all the time. They're barely here at all."

"That may be so. Imagine if we could see the gods as they are in their true habitat."

"They're not animals," Minho muttered under his breath, although I couldn't tell if he meant it unkindly.

A student whirled around, noticing our eavesdropping. "Where are your uniforms? I don't recognize either of you."

"By Jupiter, I do! That's Tara Gupta's daughter, is she not?"

The name could silence nearly every conversation in Blackthorn

Hall. Pens dropped with dull thuds onto the desks. Necks turned like overly curious swans.

"I think we've gotten the hall mixed up, haven't we? Best we head back to the dormitories."

"Y-yes," Minho agreed with a sharp nod. "Best we do."

Minho and I made to cross the lecture hall, but in our haste, my bag flew open, spilling its contents onto the floor. Minho hurried to stuff the papers back in, and as I reached for Maman's journal, another hand found it first, turning it over to read the inscription: *Property of Tara Gupta.*

I glanced up. The professor had returned.

"Is it true?" she asked, her voice as thin as a reed, eyes sparkling with recognition. "Is Tara Gupta your mother? I had a colleague who taught her many years ago. Said she was always holed up somewhere, trying to learn everything she could about the razorthorn flower. How tragic that she fell into the Seine."

Ice flooded my spine as the professor returned the journal to me. "Yes. Tragic."

Minho handed the refilled bag back to me, and we gathered our bearings. "There's been a mistake, Professor. If you'll allow us to leave—"

"Some say she went in search of the gate," the professor said, eyes going cloudy with memories. "Many have drowned searching for it."

"Gate? What gate?"

Minho eased me out of the vicinity of Blackthorn Hall, but not before I caught the dregs of the professor's words, staining the air like stale cigar smoke.

"To Elysium."

❦

The lively greenery of Champ de Mars was like the remedy of sunlight after a long, dark night. Foggy streets unfolded by the esplanade, creating the arteries of Paris's beating heart.

Boats sluiced through the stunning waters of the Seine. To anyone else, the sight would be remarkable, but my stomach roiled at the thought of it. Of Maman, and the place where she disappeared.

No. Drowned. I'd spent countless nights in Canada trying to reason with myself, telling myself that she'd died peacefully. But all that water trapped in her lungs, burning her from the inside out, consuming her—that was no way to die.

I didn't know what had motivated me and Minho to take a coach to the Seine instead of going straight home, but we had, and now I was standing before the very river I'd once sworn to never see again. That I wished had never existed. Because if it didn't, Maman wouldn't be gone.

I approached the river and bent before it, my knees feeling the stone beneath through my skirt. It took me a second to realize Minho had joined me.

" 'L'énigme n'est pas une énigme,' " Minho recited, as if he, too, was thinking of Maman. *The riddle is not a riddle.*

I tried to decode his timbre in French—there was a smoky element to his voice I'd never heard before. "That's the first I've heard you speak French."

"I know a little," Minho replied in English, surprising me with his modesty. "The last thing my uncle would want is for me to appear barbaric in polite French society."

"Is that what you think you are?" I had heard people call Maman ghastly things when her back was turned, even as they shelled out money to see her perform. She was their circus animal, a sea lion balancing a precarious ball on its nose. I resented it so much that one day, I turned away a snobbish couple who had come from Belgium to see her. Their child left in a fitful of tears as I regaled the "oh-so-terrifying" hauntings of the manor.

"No," Minho answered. "But it's the picture people paint of me."

"Because they aren't painters," I said, turning to him. "They might hold the brush, but they use the wrong tools to color you in."

The truth was, I, myself, only knew him the way one understood a painting—interpreting what was on the surface but never quite reaching what the painter intended far underneath. Yet Minho appeared fascinated by my words.

Minho's eyes traced up the Tour Eiffel soaring into the sky. Its grandeur shocked me afresh. I'd seen it many times before, and yet now felt like a new experience altogether. Maybe because I was seeing it through Minho's eyes, eyes that were determined to soak in the beauty of an architectural experience like no other.

This city wasn't perfect. But it lured me in with its bright lights, its glitzy fanfare. I wasn't immune.

"*Wah*," he exclaimed in his mother tongue.

"What are you thinking?"

"It's beautiful," he said, a crack marring his voice. He wore a rueful smile. "Just the sort of structure that would make the Kim family gawk in amazement."

"Tell me about your mother."

As I hoped, his expression lifted almost instantly. "She makes the best kimchi jjigae in the province. She used to meet me every day after school, even though I knew my way back home. She scolded me when my hair grew too long and I didn't tie it at my nape."

There was something endearing about picturing him that way. Unrestricted, free, and entirely different from the stiff, well-maintained Minho I had first met.

"You said the Kim family would gawk in amazement, but I asked about *your* opinion."

Minho's eyes dawned back on mine.

"Beauty is in the eye of the beholder, n'est-ce pas?" Minho tucked an errant strand of hair behind my ear.

I couldn't help thinking that the look he'd given to the tower was nothing compared to the one he gave me now. Each memory of his touch burned brightly still, and I desperately needed to extinguish the flame.

"Should we head back?"

I wasn't sure if I imagined the flicker of disappointment in Minho's eyes. Why had I chosen to break such a beautiful moment?

"Unless you want to stay?" I pressed.

"I don't. I mean, I do, with you, yes. But I can't imagine how painful today has been. The professor in Blackthorn Hall... I'm sorry about how callously she spoke of your mother."

"I'm not sure what to believe anymore," I said. Did my mother truly drown in search of a gateway to Elysium, a destination of the afterlife? It was almost too absurd to believe.

I feared I couldn't rest until I discovered what Maman was doing the day she died.

My eyebrows knit together as the chill disappeared entirely around me. The world became windless, motionless. Boats sat frozen on the water, caps of froth forming a lace on the sterns. Minho was a statue, his hand still held out to tuck the hair behind my ear.

Something had been triggered, like a trap finding a mouse, closing with a menacing click. An iron key finding its lock.

Like time itself had been shackled.

The world remained in its frozen state as pain began to pinch me. First on my knee, and then on my thumb. I stared down at my hand, at where I'd seen the thorn grow like something from a folktale, reaching the clouds.

A voice spurred me out of my surroundings. I was no longer on the shore of the river. I glanced down at the enormity of the water, finding myself now standing knee-deep in the middle of the Seine. How did I get here?

"Sana," a voice called out, drawing my gaze to the left. *"Sana, I'm here."*

Maman's hair billowed in waves down her back. Her skin glowed with starlight, like she'd been plucked from the sky by the goddess Flora herself.

"Come." Maman's voice became more urgent as her face rippled, as if she was one with the Seine. *"Come."*

I reached for my mother, and as my hands connected with hers, cold and wet and lifeless, time's iron shackles broke loose.

With a jerk, I fell into the choppy waters, inhaling a lungful of Seine.

Where my mother had once stood, there was now only the menacing tug of the river. I whipped my head around, hands and legs wheeling for safety. In my peripheral vision, Minho dove in without a second thought.

The world grew black as water closed over me, dragging me down into its merciless depths. Dragging me to the same fate as my mother.

SIXTEEN

In a world of inky black, three voices bled into one another.

Maman's. *"Find me past the gate in the Seine, my daughter."*

Minho's. *"I might never forgive myself, Sana."*

My own. *Wake up. Wake up.*

I inched open my burning eyes, tasting the remnants of muddy river water. I was on a mattress in a wood-panelled room. I curled my frozen fingers and toes, trying to recollect what had happened. Maman, in the Seine; time, bound like a prisoner. And then, time was freed once more, and my mother the one in chains.

Without thought, I heaved out a mouthful of river water, my chest aching from the action. When I could finally take a clean breath, I became aware of Minho beside me, still soaked from the dive, his hand rubbing my back in gentle circles.

I wiped my mouth. "Where am I?"

"Fiddle and Fox Inn. You fell in the river and nearly clogged your lungs. That should be the last of it," he said. "The doctor has already been in to see you. Said you've no fever and are already en route to a miraculous recovery."

"I saw Maman. She was in the river— She was calling out to me— *I need her back—*"

"Shh." Minho's soothing motions resumed, and he slipped his other hand into mine, steadying me on the bed. "Remain still. Close your eyes and think of my voice. Focus on our hands. Tell me what you feel."

"But—" I stopped myself. I had no energy to dispute him, so I closed my eyes. Heard the soft drizzle now falling from the heavens. "I feel the grooves between your fingers."

"And?" Minho's voice carried just above a whisper.

"The impressions of your nails on my skin."

He chuckled breathily. "What else?"

I rubbed my thumb against him, felt the sheer size of his hand, somehow fitting well with my own. The texture—rugged in some parts, likely from days clutching a pencil or caring for a mare.

"Open your eyes," he said, drawing me to shore from the ocean of my thoughts.

I did. The tension in my chest had miraculously abated. With every rise and fall of my lungs, my dread extinguished.

"Thank you." I glanced down at our linked hands. "For saving me."

"I don't doubt you would have found your own way out, stubborn as you are," Minho said with a lightly teasing tone. "Wait here."

He brought me a cup of water to rinse my mouth, and I watched as he dragged a table closer to me. On it was a bowl of beef bourguignon, still steaming. Utterly in need of energy, I tucked into the stew. The floral red wine paired with sweet and roasted onions, carrots, and mushrooms was a symphony of flavor.

As I ate, Minho knelt to poke at the fireplace, stirring it awake. My eyes traced over his hair, damp and pushed back from his face. Next, the collar of shirt, unbuttoned. His jacket, clinging wetly to his skin.

The room had grown several degrees warmer, and the fire had nothing to do with it.

Needing to shed my inner thoughts, I set down my spoon and asked, "How did you get me a room?"

"Get *us*," he corrected, and I stiffened. "Don't worry. I've sent word to Madame LeBlanc of our situation and have covered the cost for the night. The inn will send up fresh linens and clothes."

The world spun as I absorbed Minho's boldness. *He merely wants one room so he won't have to pay for two*, I reasoned, even though I was fully capable of settling my own payment. Instead, I let myself revel in the idea of Minho Kim paying for my board, food, and clothing. Surprisingly, I was charmed by it.

A rapid knock at the door broke the spell. Our clothes were being delivered. "The cotton for you, and the gown for your fiancée."

A cough of disbelief escaped my throat. Minho quelled me with a look.

"Thank you, sir." Minho made to shut the door, but the deliverer stuck a foot in, halting his movements.

"Monsieur Kim, if you would like to stay past dawn or enjoy other comforts, there would be an ancillary fee—"

"Cela n'est pas nécessaire, monsieur. Correct, ma chérie?"

I somehow found the energy to nod. Some faculty of my brain was pleased with being called his darling, even if it was in jest. Minho offered a sour but somehow civil smile before shutting the door in the delivery man's face. Lumbering footsteps indicated he had retreated.

"And here I thought I might enjoy a few more precious years before I found a suitor."

A smile threatened to appear on Minho's face. He must have sensed my good spirits as he said, "So you think me suitable now? Does this mean I've been upgraded from George Wickham to Fitzwilliam Darcy?"

I recalled the way Minho had acted when he'd first come to the manor. His mannerisms had been curt and courteous, secretive and yet considerate. And then he'd begun to uncurl, like a flower accepting dewdrops in the morning chill. The moment he stood up for me in front of the reporters. The way he looked at me as he recited Shakespeare's sonnet. The gentle caress of his hand, the sound of my name on his lips.

"I've yet to make a decision." I set my food aside, stood, and stepped behind a trifold paper screen. Minho handed me the gown over the top. After I dressed, I emerged from the privacy screen to find Minho already changing in the corner, having traded his sodden trousers for fresh ones. Against my better judgment, I watched as he peeled back the layers of his jacket and shirt, revealing the supple skin underneath. My eyes wound their way down from the taut muscles of his arms to a scar in the shape of a crescent moon on the small of his back.

Instinctively, I moved closer, shuddering at the size of the scar. This was no small accident.

He pulled the smooth, clean linen shirt over himself before turning back around. If he was startled by my nearness, he didn't show it.

"You never said why you wound up in the river. One moment, you were close enough to . . ." He trailed off, his cheeks beetroot. "And the next, you were drowning. I haven't felt as scared as that since—" He inhaled sharply, like he'd been stung. "Since my accident."

I placed a hand on his arm. "You don't have to tell me anything if you don't want to."

"To speak of a memory is to relive it, but it is also to learn from it." The painful memory rippled over his face. "The last time I rode a horse, I fell. The horse had been spooked, and I had landed in her path. That's a hoofprint on my back. I haven't been able to ride since."

My mind shot back to Misha. "Minho, I had no idea."

"The pain ebbed in its own time, but the memory still feels fresh. And after what happened today, I felt like I'd been knocked down all over again as soon as you went below the water. I felt my heart stop beating."

As if the admission had taken a lot out of him, he shuddered. "I might not have the courage to ride, but I want to find courage in other ways."

I swore all the air was sucked out of my lungs when he gently placed a kiss on my cold knuckles, then another, tenderly, against my bandage. I glanced down bashfully. My eyes drank in his chest. He was shivering. I was, too.

But wasn't this all a charade? Minho didn't mean anything by calling me his fiancée. He didn't mean anything when he washed my wound, when he asked me if I was in pain, or when he asked me whether he was Wickham or Darcy...

For the last few days, I'd found it difficult to shut Minho out of my mind. I had thought it was because of his uncanny ability to get under my skin. But what if my body, traitorously, wanted something more?

I wanted to explore this. *Needed* to.

I let go of his hand, trailed my fingers over his shirt. Then, more boldly, slipped them underneath the collar, feeling the steady rhythm of his heart, now beating faster, faster.

In a time when I was so unsure about my life, about my mother and my future—Minho felt secure. Minho felt *real*.

But Maman had told me to keep my heart closed. Hadn't she?

Seeing the tension in my brow, Minho used a single finger to turn my chin back up to him, his touch searing against my skin.

"You're a terrible distraction, Kim Minho."

"You've managed to bewitch me, as well. *Il n'y a pas de fumée sans feu*," he told me. "What should we do about it?"

In the silent seconds that followed, I wondered why it had taken me so long to realize—he wasn't a lily of the valley, or any other toxic plant for that matter. He was a sturdy oak tree, and I wanted to cling to his branches as long as humanly possible.

"The only rational thing we can," I reasoned, my heart thumping so loud I was sure he could hear it. *Feel* it. "Dampen the flames."

There is no smoke without fire.

With a simple tilt of my head, my lips were on his.

There was nothing shy about it. I pressed myself firmly against him, and him against me. Our kiss burned inside me like a roaring hearth. None of this should have made any sense. We were oil and water, moonflowers and morning glories—but for this singular moment, we collapsed into one.

Minho's hands roved over the plane of my back, the same hands that had so assuredly brushed down Misha in the stables, that were still so sure and strong even now.

He moved behind me and peppered my skin with kiss after burning kiss. As he mapped a path up my neck and behind my ear, I shuddered, pressing as close to him as I could. Our lips met again when I turned my head, and this time I let my tongue guide him gently backward, until we were both tangled on the mattress, stealing kisses beneath the rain-pattered roof.

When we came up for air, I straightened my askew ribbon and pressed down my clothes. "I would say the flames are suitably extinguished," I managed, still panting.

"Indubitably snuffed," Minho agreed, trailing a finger across my cheek.

"Entirely quenched," I challenged.

"Completely suppressed."

We didn't move for a long second. And then, like magnets finding one another again, we reconnected, the flame rekindling to a blazing heat.

Another mind-melting kiss on my throat had me clumsily running my fingers over his chest. Could I find a way under his shirt? I desperately needed to feel the heat of his skin against mine.

My hands slid under the fabric, finding the planes of his chest. Then, around to the small of his back, where his scar lay—

He pulled back. Immediately, I realized my error. "I'm sorry. I shouldn't have—"

"It's not the scar." Minho's throat bobbed. "Before we go further, I must be plain. There's something I haven't told you."

My chest stilled.

"I tried to solve the first clue on my own."

"Didn't we all?" I said breathlessly, desperate to resume our kiss.

"I meant I tried to *stop* you all from seeing your mother's clue. I took a part of it, hoping I might be able to complete it myself."

He slid off the bed and retrieved a still-wet paper from his vest before handing it to me. I unfolded it and froze, completely and utterly baffled.

"What is this?" I whispered, even though I knew exactly what I was holding. A blueprint of the third floor of the manor. There was a small splatter of red ink where the ballroom was, and the surname *Kim* was signed at the bottom. My mind sprinted toward the obvious answer, ashamed I hadn't realized sooner.

My designs await you in the pages of this book.

Minho had ripped this from Maman's Poe collection.

Minho had hidden this from me. From *all* of us.

I yanked myself off the bed. My voice was clad in iron. "This was part of the Poe clue, wasn't it?"

Minho's cheeks were still flushed—from the kisses or sheer embarrassment, I wasn't sure.

"Yes. I snuck a look at the book once the reporters arrived and we were all distracted. I was trying to solve the clue alone before realizing it was impossible. I was wrong. I needed you—all of you."

"Don't try to enchant your way out of this with words," I bit out. "Do you think me a fool?"

"You're anything but," Minho exclaimed with a passion I had just recently discovered on his lips. "Please, allow me to explain."

I stilled, giving him permission.

"My father's father, my harabeoji, was the architect of Razorthorn Manor—or at least, his company was. Back home in Korea, my family built an architectural empire. They even designed the school I attended."

That answered the *influence* he'd previously mentioned, but questions still burned in my throat. Minho's grandfather designed the manor?

"So you want the manor for . . . what? Do you imagine it's rightfully yours? Just because your grandfather *designed* the house doesn't make it *his*." I gave him a withering look.

"What would it matter if you won the estate? It's only a house. To me—to me, it's a home." The admission should have surprised me, but it was one of the truest things I had ever uttered.

Minho gathered his thoughts. "You're right—to me, it's only a house. But it's not just about the building. When I found the blueprint, that old part of myself returned. I wanted to take matters into my own hands. To *prove* myself. I'm everything you blamed me to be. Hubristic. Brutish. And gods, do I hate myself for it. I hate that my uncle isn't proud of me. I hate that my mother is ashamed!"

Pain marred Minho's eyes, and he glanced away, biting back the emotions tugging at his lips. I echoed his earlier action, taking hold of his chin and turning his face back to meet mine.

"Don't hold it in. Be honest with me now, Minho," I entreated. "It's the least you can do to make up for your lies."

Minho blinked, his expression changing. He leaned in dangerously close. Eyes aflame. This time not with lust, but clarity.

"I've looked deep into myself, unlocked the worst parts and bared them for everyone to see. I've admitted my own faults. Have you done the same?"

I flinched. No one had dared ask me such a thing before. No one had dared wonder why I acted the way I did: bullish, closed-off. Instinctively, my nails dug deeper. "This isn't about me. You want to make your family proud, Minho? Then right your wrongs. But I surely won't be the one to help you." I collected my anger and directed it into my final words. "I won't allow you to betray me in the end."

The heat in my voice ended our argument. Minho carefully clasped his hand over my wrist, bringing it back down to my side. He didn't let go as he said, "I'll take the settee downstairs, unless you have any objections."

I snarled a laugh of disbelief.

"It's settled, then." Minho departed for the door, not looking over his shoulder as he exited the room. I fell onto the mattress in pure exhaustion—and humiliation.

Minho was right. I never dared to open myself up, to hollow out the cavity of my heart. Because I was afraid of what I might find inside.

SEVENTEEN

A distracted mind does not make a lady.

It also did not make for good gameplay, and I vowed that I would not let Minho distract me ever again.

By the time we reached the manor's stoop, the sun had begun its ascent, and so too had Marta's fussing. I quelled her worries by telling her I'd had a minor fainting spell and had been attended to by a doctor. Thankfully, she didn't pelt me with further questions and ushered me inside.

Minho clicked the door shut behind me.

"We should discuss last night," he said lowly once Marta had taken our soiled clothes to the laundry bin.

"There's nothing to be said. You broke my trust, Minho. I'm not sure the break can ever be repaired." I despised how hot-tempered and cantankerous I sounded. In truth, I was deflecting from the admissions I couldn't yet make.

It was easier this way, making his name sound like broken glass in my mouth. I didn't even know my voice could sound like that.

Minho Kim was an enigma in his own right. But I wasn't currently of the mind to solve him . . . or myself.

As promised, Fox was waiting for me in the library, but he had fallen asleep, presumably sometime last night. I shook him awake from his drooling stupor.

"Henry, you know how ticklish I am—"

"It's me."

Fox ran a hand over his face with sudden alertness. "Oh, good. You're here. I was beginning to think you wouldn't come. I've got the supplies."

"Thank you, Fox. Apologies for my delay. Minho and I got… sidetracked." I didn't elaborate, and luckily Fox didn't pry. "But what, exactly, are these supplies?"

"Let me show you." Fox wiggled his eyebrows. I joined him at the table, examining the things he'd gathered.

"A ladies' hand fan. A piece of chalk. A jar of jam."

"Not just any," Fox said as he unloaded the bags. "*Plum* jam. My favorite!"

"Were you shopping for personal supplies, Fox, or helping me with my *spectral conundrum*?" I echoed his diction through gritted teeth.

Fox merely ignored my quip and continued: "A feather duster. A bottle of almond oil."

"Almond oil? My mother loved almond oil."

"I know. That's why it's here."

"And how did *you* come by that knowledge?"

"You must have mentioned it before." Fox shrugged off my insistent stare and continued with the final items: a candlestick, a pair of knitting needles, and a die.

"For the gambling portion of the occasion," Fox deadpanned.

"Har har. Could we get on with this now? You haven't explained what we're doing."

"Séances don't just *happen*. Well, this one does, but I've had plenty of practice. An assortment of random but key supplies can help attract the spirit from the spirit realm. To draw a ghost near, we must entice them."

"A *séance*?" I laughed without mirth. This wasn't a good idea. "So we're going to trap my mother's spirit."

"Not trap—just call. I've spoken to the spirit of Dolly the cat once before. She was causing quite a fuss, wanting her old quilt that she slept on top of every night. And *poof*, once she got it, she was gone!"

"You saw this cat spirit with your own eyes?"

"Precisely!" Fox rubbed his hands together. "I believe we can call upon the spirit of your mother to commune with us properly. If she's seeking you out in the gardens, perhaps there's something that must be said."

If that was true, why was Maman running away from me in the garden? Why not simply speak with me? I was certain I'd seen her at the Seine, one second alive, the next a phantom captured by the waves.

Had my mother escaped to Elysium? Or had my mind conjured up her voice in the bleary dregs of sleep?

I shuttered away the negative thoughts and focused on Fox's voice, the way his hands slipped into mine. Except Fox's hands weren't the kind that made me dizzy with anticipation. They gripped me with the unexpected warmth of a friend, the bond of a brother.

"As Tara's daughter, you'll have a stronger connection with her than I." Fox's eyes settled on mine like hot coals. "Are you prepared? If so, close your eyes and concentrate."

I did as he told me, even though just a few days ago I would have scoffed at the idea of a séance altogether. And for Maman? A woman I'd sworn had left my life for good?

After the week I'd had, I wasn't certain of anything anymore.

"Dear Tara Gupta, Great Spirit of Razorthorn Manor," Fox began in a theatrical tone, "we ask that you kindly reveal yourself to your child!"

Silence. No sign of a specter in sight.

"Are you sure this is how it works—"

Fox shushed me and continued. "Gracious Spirit, we only wish for you to show yourself and unveil why you are haunting this place. Please, give us a sign!"

Before my very eyes, the curtains drew shut of their own accord. The candles lighting all four corners of the room snuffed out one by one until we were left in consuming darkness, smoke lingering like fingers of fog.

"Fox," I growled, although it came out rather pitiful as I squeezed his clammy hands, mine equally cold. "What did you do?"

Something hard fell to the ground from a nearby bookshelf. I couldn't see much in the darkness, but that only made my auditory senses stronger, and I released Fox's hands, rushing toward the fallen book. As if by magic, the candle perched directly above me flickered back to life, and I prayed Fox wasn't pulling some elaborate jest as I retrieved the fallen volume.

I propped the book back on the table and ran a hand over the foiled lettering. *Tales of Old*. An illuminated manuscript.

Of its own volition, the book flipped open, the pages rustling from a phantom wind. I glanced up at Fox, but he seemed just as amazed—or perhaps alarmed—by the scene before us. In seconds, the book seemed to have made up its mind and landed on a specific page. A flourished vine-work border in greens and reds surrounded an image of a two-faced god.

Janus, doorkeeper to the heavens, the top of the page read.

Another haunting wind flipped the page, and Fox came to my

side, reading the words aloud: " 'The god of doors and duality is often depicted with two faces, one to represent the present, one to represent the future,' " Fox read. He looked up at me. "Everyone knows that. Why did your mother want us to see this?"

When I was younger, the stories of the gods were something to savor, like taffy. They gave me an imagination that grew like wildflowers. But not every event in human history was an act of the divine—not to my mind—and I had lost interest in veneration years ago.

The book closed on its own, and the sound reverberated through the cold, dark space. "Wait— Maman, don't go! We need more."

Fox returned to his seat. "Valiant Spirit, thank you for communicating with us. Please, use this die to answer our questions," he encouraged. "Are you safe? If yes, roll odd. If no, roll even."

"Can a spirit even choose that?" I asked, then grew even more perturbed as the die levitated over the table, shaking in midair.

"Yes," Fox said, aghast, as if he, too, wasn't certain this would work. "Spirit of Tara, give us your answer!"

The die landed with a sharp, tinny melody. Four.

Even.

My skin iced over. "Maman, tell us how we can help."

The chill on my skin now seeped into my bones as the chalk lifted from the table and began hovering toward the back of the library. Entranced, I followed it, pausing at the large blackboard, and I cringed inwardly at the sound of the chalk scratching its surface.

Keep...

Playing...

"Playing what?" My voice broke with desperation. "The game?"

The chalk continued, nearly breaking in two from sheer pressure.

Ma…

Petite…

Papillon…

And one final, heart-wrenching phrase.

Je t'aime.

The chalk dropped and snapped into pieces on the ground, and I toppled to my knees with it.

Keep playing, my little butterfly.

Those words haunted my mind, each one pounding in my pulse like a mallet. When I was young, Maman's voice was like a gentle morning bell, summoning even the sleepiest of flowers awake. Yet as I imagined my mother voicing her coded message aloud, her voice changed: now, it echoed a siren's, luring sailors away from safe harbor and into choppy, unknowable waters.

Luring me into this game of hers.

Maman knew she would leave the manor, leave *me*…but did she know for how long? Did she know her death awaited, merely days or weeks later? That she would become a ghost, haunting the very grounds she claimed held a magic like no other?

I didn't know if it was understanding the truth that Maman was still, somehow, here on Razorthorn Manor's grounds, or rather whatever had transpired between me and Minho last night, but I was more determined than ever.

Maman was here. Maman loved me.

And most imperative of all: Maman needed help.

But what could I do to help her? What did she need? Would the razorthorn seed's power help her somehow?

There was only one way to find out—and that was to win.

Come breakfast, I had already gathered the group, including Marta and Monsieur Champlain, to reveal my idea to host a party. Everyone was agreeable, most especially Isabelle, who was already eagerly planning out the menu and hors d'oeuvres. Marta would hire help using what salary she had (paid from a trust), and we needed only a few days to prepare the manor for our guests: a list of Parisian scholars renowned in the studies of the gods and the gifts they've bestowed on humankind.

After our morning meal, I worked with Fox to craft letters while he sealed the envelopes with melted hot wax. I didn't know how to properly thank him for reconnecting me with Maman. It didn't answer why she was running from me in the garden—or what else she might have been running from—but it gave me solace for the first time in seven years.

"I'll deliver the invitations by hand. It'll be faster that way than by post. I'll be back before noon," Monsieur Champlain offered. I had a feeling he was desperate to get away from his tedious duties, and I didn't blame him.

Or perhaps . . . to meet with the mysterious Alain again?

Thankfully, Minho didn't attempt conversation with me, even as we brushed past each other several times to transform the manor. The newly hired domestic staff moved like a unified troupe in and out of rooms, carrying unneeded furniture with them.

I hurried toward the kitchens, a haunting aroma sweeping through the narrow corridors. I prepared myself to find Marta and whatever kitchen staff she'd hired, but the kitchen was surprisingly empty—save a girl whose face was focused on the tantalizingly sweet dough beneath her calloused hands.

"In need of a sous?" I asked, startling her, but she seemed to calm when she saw it was only me.

"Last I remember, Sana Gupta was terrified of knives."

"You needn't worry about that. I've been practicing my new magician's trick. Sword-swallowing."

Isabelle rewarded me with a laugh, but it broke off too soon. She sighed, relenting. "If you must, then help me knead the dough."

Isabelle showed me how to work the dough with care, twisting the brown-sugar-laden bread into a star-shaped pattern. The repetitive actions were calming as a lullaby, as was the rich smell of the sugar and butter. Isabelle moved like a painter, using a thick-bristled brush to dapple a broken egg yolk over the dough. "Ensures even coloring," she explained. I merely nodded, fascinated by her movements. I was not one to disrupt a maestro at work.

Finally, we finished by sprinkling coarse grains of sugar on top. Once it was prepared to perfection, Isabelle popped the tray into the brick-and-tile oven and brushed a flour-dusted hand on her apron.

"I've yet to admit something to you," she began, taking a seat at the long kitchen table. "Not long after your tenth birthday, your mother wrote a letter to my own."

I stood straighter. My tenth birthday. The day Isabelle fell in the river.

Isabelle glanced down at her apron. "Sana, do you remember what happened?"

"Vaguely," I replied, recalling the way Isabelle had been completely soaked. "We were playing hide-and-seek."

"*You* were playing. I had wandered off. It still stains my memory, the force of two hands on my back."

I started. "You were pushed?"

Isabelle nodded. "I didn't see my assailant."

My thoughts scrambled for purchase. It wasn't difficult to tell where she was going with this. "You think *I* pushed you? Belle, I would never try to harm you. I might have been jealous of your mother's affection for you—"

"Jealous?" Isabelle scoffed. She fisted her hands. I could read the pain in her eyes like a freshly bound book. "My mother doted on me so much I was smothered by it. I often wanted *your* mother's approach instead. And as for that day—I don't believe you pushed me. I may have believed it once, but now, hearing the honesty in your voice, I see how wrong I was."

"I thought you wanted nothing to do with me when you left. I never made another friend again. At least, not one like you," I admitted.

Isabelle and I remained in relative silence until the star bread had finished baking. When we pulled it out, we were too famished to wait for it to cool, and we both greedily tucked into the dessert. My tongue hissed in reproach, but my stomach would soon thank me.

"Cooking is like art," Isabelle said after swallowing a large chunk of bread. "It can be more than a means of survival. But not everyone appreciates food for what it can be—not simply a destination, but a journey."

"I'll remember that the next time I attempt to cook."

Isabelle grinned. "You're not so different from what I remember, Sana," she confessed. "A bit more stuck-up, but still the girl I called a friend."

I would gladly accept whatever Isabelle considered a compliment. "Having you back in my life reminds me of what's important." Seven years without friendship had left me feeling emptier than this house. "My only wish is that we start over."

"The bread?" Isabelle asked jokingly. I stared down, realizing we'd devoured nearly half the tray.

When our laughter abated, Isabelle pasted on a warm smile. "I think we can do that."

The sound of pounding footsteps erupted in the air. Fox and Minho arrived in the kitchen, out of breath.

"What's going on?" I demanded. Isabelle looked concerned; Fox's countenance was equally pale.

"I found this in the post," Minho explained once he'd caught his breath, handing a red envelope to me. I studied his hands. Hands that had both held me and hid something from me. I brushed away the thought and accepted the envelope clinically, ensuring no skin-to-skin contact.

I pulled the envelope toward me, unraveling it with shaking fingers to reveal a letter.

These past few puzzling days have been by no means easy, so allow me to assuage your worries.

Should you wish to exit the game, now is your chance. Meet me at midnight by the garden's water fountain, and I shall sign a cheque in the sum you wish. Once this is complete, you must leave Razorthorn Manor for good.

My heart felt like it'd been clutched by a skeleton's hand. Someone was *bribing* us to leave?

"Is this some sort of test?" Isabelle asked, while Fox implored, "Just what sum of money are we talking about here?"

"The note isn't in Maman's hand," I told the group. "But who else knows about the game besides us?"

"Madame LeBlanc, for one," Isabelle noted.

"Monsieur Champlain, for another," Fox tacked on warily.

Minho shook his head, moving to the opposite side of the counter. "It makes no sense. They've done nothing but bring us together."

"Nothing to deceive us," I agreed, hoping Minho picked up on the venom in my tone.

Yesterday's rueful smile returned to Minho's lips. "Indeed. From the time we've come to know them, I believe they would never intend to hurt us. To *betray* us in the end."

I fumed. It was only fair of Minho to return the barb, but that didn't make it sting any less.

I gripped the edge of the kitchen counter, and Minho did the same, neither of us backing down.

Fox's gaze volleyed between Minho and me as he spoke out of the corner of his mouth to Isabelle. "Should we . . . ?"

He pointed at the kitchen door. Isabelle nodded, and I had never been so grateful to be left alone. At least now, alone with Minho Kim again, I could speak plainly.

"Well?" I tapped my foot. "Are you going to take the offer?"

"You know I wouldn't accept defeat," Minho said. "You know what this means for me. For—" His earlier bravado faded. "For my family."

Minho's hands curled into fists on the counter, and I was struck with the sudden urge to ease the crease between his brows. Blast my addled brain. I needed to forget everything that once appealed to me about Minho. I needed to show him how serious I was about winning.

Rather than vinegar, this time, I opted for honey, if only to make the sting sweeter. "I may not have a traditional family, but I understand you, Minho. You did what you needed to do to get ahead in the game. I won't fault you for that."

"You won't?" Minho notched his brows closer together.

"No." I dared to step around the counter, our noses just inches away, and offered him my proudest look. "But you *do* know what this means, don't you?"

His gaze fell to my lips. Although he had been hiding a secret from me, my traitorous mind couldn't help thinking of the tender moments we'd shared last night. Moments so tender, they bruised.

"No," he admitted, closing the space between us. "Tell me, in great detail."

His sultry tone had returned, but this time I knew better than to fall for his tricks. The glances he threw my way were nothing more than attempts to unravel and decode me, as if I were one of my mother's riddles.

I wasn't so easily solvable.

"Someone is trying to stop me from playing the game. They find me a threat," I said, not daring to step back. "And when I win, that will make victory all the greater. Don't *you* want to win on fair grounds?"

Minho's eyes dimmed for the briefest moment, a crack in his carefully constructed façade, before his usual resolve returned twofold. "I wouldn't have it any other way."

The air grew sweltering in the kitchen, but I stood my ground, tucking the paper deeper into my grip. The envelope felt as heavy as the hand of death.

Minho squared his shoulders, easing around me to leave the kitchen. Or so I thought—his voice appeared just behind the crook of my ear, uttering a warning that sent small shocks of electricity down my back.

"Icarus flew too close to the sun. Don't burn those pretty wings of yours."

EIGHTEEN

Early afternoon passed as the staff continued their duties, transforming the manor from rusted to restored. I couldn't help wondering if my time here was the same for me as it was for the house. We were both peeling back our outer layers to find something unexpected hiding underneath. Except my stubborn habits weren't so easily scraped away.

This was what I wanted: to restore the manor. To bring a sense of peace to a place littered with painful memories.

But the game still took precedence. With each passing minute, I worried over the same thought: when would our teamwork end and the ruthlessness begin?

Perhaps I was stretching things out of proportion. As badly as the others needed the razorthorn, we hadn't turned on each other. And yet whoever it was who'd left the bribe clearly wanted everyone to stop playing—which logically made it seem like a competitor.

Fox needed the razorthorn for his mother's health. Isabelle needed it for her culinary dreams, and to restore her family's fortune.

And then there was Minho. Craving the razorthorn for his family's affection and acceptance.

Regardless, none of them seemed capable of setting this up; they surely hadn't the money. Which meant someone else in the house could be responsible.

Marta was out of the question, which left the butler.

I requested Monsieur Champlain's presence in the parlor at half past three. I stepped in right on time, finding the butler already seated on a wingback chair. The room had been dusted and polished to perfection, bringing life and vibrancy to a space I had thought of as stuffy. The staff had clearly done their job, and well.

The butler was situated just below a portrait of the goddess Flora captured within a grove of thistle and huckleberry, the gilded frame surrounding it the color of amber honey.

The caption beneath the portrait read:

ACCORDING TO LEGEND, FLORA FIRST SET FOOT ON EARTH IN THE MIDDLE OF GAUL, HARVESTING CROPS AND SPREADING SEEDS. HER MASTERY AND KNOWLEDGE OF FLOWERS EXCEEDED THOSE OF THE OTHER GODS', AND SHE OFTEN BROUGHT FLOWERS BACK TO MOUNT OLYMPUS TO SHOW THEM THE BEAUTY THAT LIVED BELOW.

I had read the caption a hundred times over, believing that Flora's magic was one of the reasons my family had thrived in India. When I was young, I often pictured Flora as Mother Nature herself, able to control the natural world with a whisper from her tongue.

I quashed all thoughts of the goddess and turned my attention to the butler. "How were your deliveries, monsieur?"

"Successful," the butler remarked, marking a page in the book he was holding. I noted the author—Honoré de Balzac.

"Doing some light reading?"

He settled the book down next to him and manufactured a smile. "It keeps my mind occupied."

"Then perhaps you can help me with what's occupying my mind." I sat squarely across from him. "Someone left a bribe—a cheque for a supposedly limitless sum of money—in exchange for me and my competitors' departure. Someone wants the game to end."

Monsieur Champlain did not stir. "Come again?"

"Were you the one who left that letter in the post?"

The butler's laughter was delayed. "What an inane assumption. Do you think me Janus-faced, mademoiselle? I assure you, I know nothing about a letter."

"All I ask is for your honesty. You know, monsieur, you never answered how you came to be in service of the manor. The old butler, Monsieur Boucher, wasn't exactly the most appealing man. Is that why Marta fired him?"

"Fired?" The butler gawked. "No, that's not what happened at all."

"Then tell me what did."

"According to your nanny, the previous butler disappeared without a trace shortly before your mother left."

Two disappearances in the span of weeks, if not days?

The butler continued. "I was recommended by my former employer, Donne, who was no longer in need of my services."

That was a lukewarm translation for *thrown out on the streets.*

"I prefer to live a quiet life. This job allows me all that and more. I can communicate with my family with ease. I can create my own schedule."

"Is that why you went to visit Alain? To communicate with family?"

Sweat beaded the butler's forehead. He used his handkerchief to blot it away. "I was merely settling some debts. Marta can confirm this."

"You mean Madame LeBlanc," I corrected. "Unless I've mistaken your familiarity with each other."

"No mistake. Madame LeBlanc is merely my colleague."

My lips tightened. "You said your former employer was no longer in need of your services. Why?"

Abruptly, the butler stood from his chair and smoothed both hands over his trousers. "Pardon my frankness, but I am a man of reclusion, and I would appreciate if you kept out of my business, mademoiselle. Now, I must prepare for the party."

I was too stunned to speak. A seed of embarrassment blossomed in my stomach. "Of course. I apologize, monsieur."

The butler nodded and left me alone in the parlor.

After uncivilly scarfing down tonight's meal—a hearty bouillabaisse paired with crusty bread slathered in a saffron-infused rouille—I waited in my chambers for night to fall. It took every ounce of strength to unearth the courage to enter the Wildwood again. Not because of what had occurred the last time, but because I was going to identify the traitor in our midst.

If Maman had taught me anything, it was that I couldn't wait for answers.

I had to find them myself.

The garden greeted me with its thorny embrace, the moon our only witness. Everywhere I stepped, the grass seemed to sway under the moonlight, as if trying to get a passing touch of my skin.

"I'm here," I called out sharply. I may have incorrectly assumed that the butler had left the bribe, but whoever I spoke to now would bear the brunt of my next words. "What sum of money do you think could possibly eject me from this game?"

No answer. I feared this might happen.

"You can't remain in the bushes long," I said. "Show yourself."

A beat later, a woman's voice rang through the silence. "You came, my girl."

Icy shock laced over me. That voice—a voice I hadn't heard in seven years.

"You're here." My breath caught in my throat. My feet couldn't move, couldn't rush toward Maman's voice. I glanced around wildly. "Where are you?"

"I cannot show myself yet, my little butterfly," the voice claimed, sounding like it was coming from a thick copse of trees ahead of me. "Did you receive my message?"

My heart thrashed in my chest. "The envelope?"

"No, that was not from me," my mother said, voice rough with disuse.

I exhaled in relief. "You mean the séance last night—I saw it. *Keep playing.*"

"Good girl. How I've missed you, Sana."

I nearly broke apart at the sound of my name on my mother's lips.

It was real. *She* was real. But was she a phantom? A poltergeist of some sort? Why couldn't she show herself when I'd already seen her at the Seine? Was she in a liminal state of in-between, not dead but simply asleep, ferried away by the hands of Death's second self?

I had to reach out, find her, touch her. I took a step toward the trees. "Tell me what happened to you."

Maman's voice grew hoarse, insistent. "It is too complicated to explain, but I promise the truth will come out. Heed my words, little butterfly. There is power inside you. You need only set it free."

"No, Maman—that was only my mind. The thorn wasn't real. Was it?"

"I think you know the answer to that question."

I clenched my hand into a fist.

"Yes," I realized belatedly, staring down at my hand and wondering what strangeness lurked there.

No. Not strangeness. There was only explanation for this. Something I hadn't admitted could be real in a long, long time.

Until now, magic and myth were an inseparable blur, impossible to parse through. Clarity struck deep in my heart. How was any of this true? Had my return triggered something? Was the magic of the gardens affecting me—or rather, permeating me?

"Then you mustn't waste time. One day, you shall discover how strong it truly is. You are a mighty flower, Sana, and you will not bend or break."

"I hear you, Maman." I swallowed through the thickness of oncoming tears. "Please don't go. Don't you see how the manor is changing? How we're bringing it back to life? Is that what you wanted—for the house to shine again as it used to?"

"Yes," came my mother's voice, but it was weak and brittle. "But I cannot stay long. Remember: the flower is the key to everything. Soon, this game will meet its end, and we shall be reunited."

"What does that mean? Can you return from the world of the dead?"

There was a rustle from the copse of trees. Maman was gone.

I sank to my knees. For the first time since I came to the manor, I let my unshed tears spill. And the truth with it.

"Maman, I miss you," I choked out. I might not have seen Maman, but I knew now that she was more than a memory. She was a ghost, an entity transcending time and space. And despite all the things she never did for me, I knew deep in my bones that I would do everything in my power to answer her call.

It took several minutes for me to find the strength to stand and hobble back to the manor. Seeing Maman—*hearing* Maman—was like a long-awaited revelation, the taste of a sweet dream I didn't want to end.

A scream knifed into my thoughts, ending my reverie. *"Help! Help me, please—"*

I sucked in a breath at the familiar voice. *Belle.*

The rest of the words were gurgled, like she had been plunged underwater.

The river.

My legs pumped automatically. My heart backflipped. There was no time to analyze the situation—no time for tears or what-ifs.

Closer. I needed to get closer.

I needed to save her.

The trees whirred past me. I didn't stop until she was in my line of sight. Not a girl, but a long, limp thing face down on the water, with black hair spread around her.

I disregarded all sense and leapt into the river. I was never a strong swimmer, but I fared well enough as a child that I was able to latch onto her body, clutching it against mine. I used one arm to row us to a rocky edge. My heart threatened to explode.

My calf muscles spasmed, and I cried out in pain. I was in five paces' reach of safety, and my body was already failing me.

Keep going, a voice said in my mind—but not my own. Maman's. *For Belle. For your friend.*

Her voice restored me like a second wind. When I hoisted Belle up onto the nearest craggy stone, my muscles screamed with relief.

I hauled myself up, felt Belle's pulse fluttering at her throat. She was alive—but only just.

Placing my hands on her chest, I pressed hard in pulsing spurts, nearly cracking bone. My experience with resuscitation was confined to classes with mannequins. I scrambled to put my full force into the actions, and to my greatest relief, Isabelle jerked up.

She spat up wicked fluid and sucked in cool, clean air. I suppose I *did* have time for tears, because they spilled forth furiously now.

"Sana?" Isabelle asked weakly, settling back on the ground.

I shivered against her cold body, tucking my head into the crook of her neck. "I thought I lost you, Belle."

She ran a soothing hand over my damp hair. "You came to save me."

"I would, over and over and over." I raised my head, wiping strands of hair off her face. "How did you end up in the river?" A terrible thought occurred to me. "You were pushed again, weren't you?"

"No. It was nothing like that. In fact, I was asleep, dreaming of that day—your birthday. It was like my mind moved my body subconsciously to this very place."

I had heard tales of such afflictions. "Somnambulism. *Sleepwalking.*"

I thought of that first morning here, when I'd found Isabelle in her room. Her nightgown had been wet. Only now did I understand why.

Isabelle shriveled like a raisin. "Yes. I've been walking in my sleep for years, but never have I nearly drowned because of it. The night of my arrival here, I found myself knee-deep in the river. I hoped it wouldn't continue. But it's like my mind can't let go of what happened that day eight years ago . . . and I remembered something."

"Yes?" My breath hitched.

"It was your mother. I'd seen her creeping around the garden, and I followed. Something was off. The next thing I knew . . . she pushed me."

"You must be misremembering, Belle." I checked her temperature, which was slowly returning to normal. "Are you certain *Maman* pushed you in?"

"I don't know what to think anymore. But I fell in . . ."

Just as Maman had fallen into the Seine. Just as *I* had fallen in.

"Shh," I calmed her, channeling warmth into my voice. "I'm here now."

"Thank you." Isabelle shivered, and I gathered her closer, hoping to transfer some of my heat through her sopping-wet nightgown.

For the first time in years, I was reminded of what it was like to have a friend. A friend like Isabelle, who had chased me in the garden until we were gasping for breath. Who shared spreads of chive scones and clotted cream and thick orange marmalades with me beneath the trees, with nothing but a rough blanket under our knees and laughter on our lips.

I'd feared our friendship had evaporated over the years we'd been separated. I now realized that a true friend was never completely gone. They were more like a seasonal snowfall, a promise to always return.

I didn't know how long I knelt there with Isabelle, staring out at the river and the gardens beyond with nothing but my tears—and my friend—to comfort me.

Decode the cryptogram

Each letter in the hidden phrase has been replaced by another letter.

Hint: always think in reverse.

A	B	C	D	E	F	G	H	I	J	K	L	M

N	O	P	Q	R	S	T	U	V	W	X	Y	Z

BLF ZIV Z NRTSGB
UOLDVI, ZMW BLF DROO
MLG YVMW LI YIVZP.

YOU ARE A MIGHTY
FLOWER, AND YOU WILL
NOT BEND OR BREAK

NINETEEN

By seven o'clock the following evening, the manor was bursting with activity. Everywhere I looked, women dawdled in gowns of fashionable vertical silhouettes. Gloved hands held fans despite autumn's chill. Men's leather shoes had been buffed to a shine, and their clipped, rapid French filled the estate. Wine flowed with the staccato sounds of stimulating conversation, coupled with gasps of awe at the furnishings of Razorthorn Manor. Our esteemed guests—including some of the scholars Maman had written on her list—had arrived right on time for hors d'oeuvres, and the cooks, led by a now-cheerful Isabelle, had executed the menu perfectly in her vision.

It was both my and Fox's collaborative idea to make the party a themed masquerade: "A night in Flora's magical garden."

The message regarding the night's attire had been well-received. Guests graced the manor with elegant floral and woodland-inspired masks, ranging from mischievous foxes to wise owls. Smartly dressed garçons greeted them with platters of Isabelle's delicate pistachio bonbons, hazelnut petit fours, and buttery pains aux chocolat.

Laughter spilled from beneath the main staircase where I stood. I curled over the railing, ensuring everything was being executed as planned, the way I'd seen Maman look over her parties. For but a second I was a child again, and a memory ripened before me:

For my ninth birthday, Maman had created an elaborate game of checkers in the hallway with chalk. Except only *one* box mattered, and I had to figure out which. I determined the correct one based on its size—it was slightly different from the others, a rectangle, technically, in width, rather than a square. When I bounced on it thrice, Maman declared me a winner, and pointed to a piece of carved wood on the stairwell, which she popped open.

I crouched and ran my hand over that piece now, admiring the craftsmanship. The artist had chiseled the face of a fox, the body of a lion, and the legs of a horse.

Keep your wits about you, Maman had reminded me. The fox. *Your strength at your core.* The lion. *And your speed.* The horse.

Inside it had been my present—a vast collection of caramel drops imported from Germany, which I sucked on for twenty days straight until my teeth winced with saccharine displeasure.

The memory melted away as I headed upstairs into my room. I needed to attach one final piece of jewelry to finish off my look: a glittering garnet attached to a satin ribbon tied around my neck. I'd also borrowed one of Maman's spectacle dresses tonight, a puffy-sleeved satin gown striped with red and white. As I swished it in front of the mirror, I swore the stars had been plucked from the sky and handsewn on the bodice by Juno herself.

"Are you ready?" Isabelle appeared at my door. Her attire, a gown of sage green, highlighted her delicate frame. Earlier today, we'd helped each other prepare for the evening, painting strokes of rouge on each other's lips and snickering after Marta scolded us. Isabelle didn't need any more rouge for her face; her cheeks were already magnificently pink. After what had occurred last night at the river, I had promised her that I would not let it happen again—that we could room together as we had when we were children. She had gladly accepted.

"I think we should be asking Fox that." As we left my room, I nudged my chin toward where he now stood in the corridor, looking like he was trying very hard not to trip over his own coattails.

"And *that's* how a butterfly emerges from its chrysalis," Fox stated, speaking over his shoulder to Minho. "Some say the miracle of childbirth rivals that of the butterfly's metamorphosis, but I say that's a load of poppycock. Not that I have experience with either matter."

"Fox . . . ," Isabelle warned wearily.

He continued obliviously. "Now, as for moth larvae—"

While Fox looked somewhat swallowed by his garb, Minho managed to pull his off quite gracefully. It was almost as if the suit was made for him, although I didn't admit the thought aloud. He didn't need to know what I was thinking, even if it was plain on my face.

"Let's discuss larvae later." Isabelle practically yanked Fox by the arm and down the staircase. Fox glanced back up at me with a curious smile. I twiddled my fingers in a wave.

"She'll be sick of him by the time the night ends," I said to no one in particular.

When I turned, I couldn't help noticing the apprehension on Minho's face.

"Let me guess. Clumsy dancer?" I didn't inject the words with as much malice as I'd intended. Instead, they appeared genuine, almost playful—like I truly wanted to observe the spectacle that was Minho dancing before me. What an illogical notion.

Minho responded simply. "We'll test that theory tonight, won't we?"

The gods had joined us for a night of revelry.

Or at least one had. Flora's larger-than-life figure, imported to the middle of the manor's parlor, was being loaned from the local museum. Monsieur Champlain certainly knew how to pull some strings; apparently the butler was owed a favor after he'd arranged a grand wedding for one of the families he'd formerly serviced.

I lifted a finger and grazed the tip of Flora's, feeling once again that tinge of warmth sizzling inside me. My thumb was now fully healed, and I had removed the bandage to reveal the smooth skin underneath.

I moved on from room to room, greeting guests with a performative smile. Flowers shone from all sides, supplied by Paris's most delightful flower shop: calming lavender, floral hibiscus, sweet magnolias. It felt like I was in the garden again. Every corner of Razorthorn Manor was brimming with laughter, champagne, and—for the first time in nearly a decade—the official reopening of the manor to the public.

Tonight, however, wasn't about what lingered on the surface; it was about uncovering Maman's clues.

I greeted several already inebriated guests before we landed on the one we wanted.

The man admired the books lining the shelves of the parlor while he sipped on an elderflower spritz. He wore a broad bear mask atop a slim nose, his perfectly coiffed hair giving off an air of academic professionalism.

"That's Professor DuPont. I've seen him at the Sorbonne," Minho confirmed.

The four of us approached the man collectively. "Welcome to Razorthorn Manor. I assume you know why you're here."

The man lifted his mask, his cheeks ruddy compared to his silver hair. "You must be Tara Gupta's daughter. I saw your picture in the newspaper."

I thought back to those frenzied reporters snapping photographs and winced.

DuPont continued. "Your mother came to speak with me once. She wanted all there was to know about the razorthorn flower. Particularly of its *inception.*"

"The flower was crafted from blood," I recalled, "hence its reddish appearance. Some even blame the blood of the guillotines for its coloration, but it was red to begin with."

"Is that all?" Professor DuPont slathered on a smile. "Your mother appeared to know more."

"You're right. She knew that blood of *divine* provenance was the most potent ingredient used to create the razorthorn."

The professor nodded, pleased. "Unfortunately, no one has been able to find a source for that final ingredient. But I will tell you what I told your mother. Flora crafted four seeds out of love and care for the four mortal families who prayed to her enduringly. But this gift could not last forever, just as the gods' power has its limits."

"I don't quite follow." Fox's brows frowned in contemplation.

"My old colleague Professor Lemieux studied texts found in Rome's temples. They spoke of the cyclical nature of the gods—how their rise and fall was inevitable, and how our Cycle of Light must someday end. A group of people have taken this narrative and twisted it for their own gains, hoping to sway others to their side. They call the end of the gods' reign *the Collapse.*"

"Les Voyants." I shuddered. "Supposedly they've seen what is unseen, heard what is unheard."

"Indeed. What's more, they blasphemously believed the gifts the gods bestowed could be turned into weapons to be used against them. To try to fell a god . . . it's absurd."

The four of us exchanged glances. Even Shelley had written about mighty kings falling in *Ozymandias*. Perhaps it wasn't so absurd at all.

"And?" I pressed. "Was the razorthorn one of those weapons?"

"Not much is known on the matter. It is true that no one knew the nature of its fifth and final power . . . but I wouldn't put much stock in it; these were only rumors from cults that haven't been heard from in years." The professor polished off his drink before replacing his mask. Then he linked arms with his newly arrived dance partner. The strings had picked up their tune, the pianoforte swelled to a gentle rhythm, and a cluster of well-to-do couples filled the parlor. "I'll be off to enjoy the evening, if you'll allow me."

"Of course." I filed away the information, turning to face the room. While the scholar had given us *some* new information, it wasn't enough to direct us forward in the game, as we originally suspected. Which meant Maman had left us a *different* clue in her journal. Could it be we had missed something?

"I don't think your mother's next clue will be found among the scholars," Fox said. "But I can feel my legs shaking—I can't turn down an opportunity to dance!"

"Dance—?"

I hadn't noticed the parlor was now full to the brim. Couples paired off around us as Fox and Isabelle slipped into the merrymaking. I was pushed farther and farther away from the exit as the parlor transformed into a dance floor. Everyone moved in unison, but Minho and I stood frozen, obviously unsure of ourselves as the music swelled like the waves of a tide.

"There is only one way to escape this parlor," Minho stated. "We must dance."

My cheeks bloomed red. "Consider my dance card full."

"I didn't say it had to be with *each other*." Minho chortled to himself mirthlessly. "We truly are an old, bickering couple."

He offered his arm to an unmarried lady awaiting a partner.

My stomach roiled in confusion. I didn't want to dance with Minho—but what if I did, if only to see just how clumsy a dancer he truly was? Although considering the way he'd kissed me two nights ago, I wasn't certain there was anything he could perform clumsily.

Wearing a smile slick with unease, I accepted a waiting scholar's hand. We parroted the other dancers, keeping our hands parallel with one another but never touching as we moved in slow circles. I glanced over my shoulder once, finding Minho's gaze flickering sideward to meet mine, and quickly cranked my head back into place. The piece crescendoed, and I bowed in unison with the stranger.

When I turned around to meet my next partner, my complexion grew florid. It was him.

Minho smirked. "It appears the Fates have other plans."

"I determine my own desires, thank you very much." All this squabbling, and we were no closer to the exit. This dance unfortunately required our hands to touch, and I was grateful I had on my kid gloves as protection for my performative sanctity. No one had to know what rules Minho and I had already broken in the heat of the moment.

Cascading light from the chandeliers warmed Minho's raven hair as he wrapped a loose arm around my waist. We joined the dance, moving like chess pieces—side to side, up and down—with the parlor as our black-and-white-tiled board.

How fitting. It often felt like we were pawns in Maman's game. That she was some omnipresent puppeteer, advancing us from one chess square to the next.

"Your first dance partner," I began. "Who was she? What is her area of study?"

"Your interest in her is staggering."

"I'm merely investigating as any Watson would."

"And?" His voice was a thorny flower, poking me in all the wrong places. "What have you discovered tonight?"

I answered with brutal honesty. "A clumsy dancer you are not."

"Thank the gods for that," Minho replied with a rough edge to his voice, and I blushed down to my toes as he dipped me fully in a move that would have tongues wagging. One of his hands was low on my back while the other cradled my neck. His gaze brewed with intensity, both a promise and a warning. My imagination became an unruly thicket, a thing I couldn't tame.

Minho's eyes traced a line over the room. "Have you and Sherlock kept up your agreement?"

"How did you—" The room spun as he brought me back up. I struggled to find my footing. "Have you been *spying* on us?"

"I keep an ear to the ground," he answered, nonplussed.

"You sound worried," I said, hoping to rattle his cage.

"Is that what you think?" he asked, angling toward me as we met, chest to chest, for the curtsy. Then, in a tone that only just carried over the din, he revealed, "It's not Fox I'm worried about."

If he moved an inch closer, our bodies would touch. I could practically hear my governess shouting for me to keep my distance.

Around us, couples had joined together for the quadrille. We were close enough to the doors to safely make an inconspicuous exit, but for some reason, Minho's hand found my hip, as if the rules of society were merely suggestion.

Warmth radiated through my belly.

I desperately needed to leave the suffocating heat of the room, mostly caused by Minho's eyes, his grip. It was as if he were tethered to my body—to me and me alone.

Minho broke the silence. "Remember when I found you lying on the ground in the garden?"

"Not my finest moment." But I'd never thought to wonder what he was doing outside that morning—or how he'd found me. "What of it?"

"Do you remember what you told me?"

I scanned my memory. The pain must have scrubbed spots of it away, leaving empty holes. "Afraid not. Perhaps you could do me the favor of filling in the blanks?"

He appeared to be considering the request, but a mercurial change in temperament made him drop his hand from my hip. "Never mind." He cleared his head with a shake and found our beacon—the exit—leaving me to follow hurriedly on his tail.

"Kim Minho, a man of many words, including *never mind*." I threw the words at his back.

He paused, glancing down at his shoes. "I found you by a locked gate. Where do you think it leads?"

"What does it matter to you—"

He turned to face me. "Aren't you the least bit curious? What if it's part of the"—he ushered himself closer to me to whisper—"the *game*? With or without your permission, I'm going to look beyond it. Right now."

Was that a challenge?

"But what about Fox and Isabelle?"

"They appear to be enjoying the quadrille too much to stop now."

I spun around to verify his statement, but when I turned back, Minho had already departed like a shadow at dusk. If he found a clue before I did, he would never let me live it down.

I made to exit the manor, but on my way out, hushed voices in the sitting room caught my attention. I grabbed onto my swishing skirts, silencing them so I could hear over the din.

"Our time is short..."

"Then be frank with yourself, Auguste. Do not hide."

Marta's voice. Auguste—Monsieur Champlain. I dared to glance inside, choking on my breath as I found the two clinging on to one another.

So their familiarity wasn't my imagination, after all.

The two of them were hiding something, and I needed the truth to be clearer than a misty morning in want of sun.

I ducked just as they exited the room to return to the party. While I was hungry for answers, I was even hungrier to stop Minho Kim from getting ahead in the game.

Without another thought, I plucked up my skirts and dashed into the courtyard, which burst with both wine and guests. My feet moved automatically, bringing me to the garden, then to the thicket where Minho stood. His back was facing me, hands tucked into his pockets, and the moonlight illuminated his broad shoulders. My footfall grew hushed as I neared, recalling how I'd observed him from afar before, observed the roped muscles of his back. Felt his skin, *touched* it, even the spot marked by a crescent-shaped scar.

Sensing me, Minho grinned over his shoulder. "I see you've changed your mind. Come to explore the rabbit hole, Alice?"

"I feel more like the Mad Hatter," I admitted. "Go on. Wonderland awaits."

Minho wore an amused look as he got down on his knees. I snuck down beside him, failing once again to ignore his intoxicating scent. The one I'd come to know so well—from his jacket, his skin; the one I'd kissed with a delirious passion.

I never would have wagered I would still be clinging to that memory.

Upon our arrival at the gate, I stood and brushed my skirts. "Maman must have locked this door long before she disappeared. But why?"

"Perhaps like our first clue, there is no key to unlock the gate," Minho realized.

"And like our third clue, we need to spill blood."

Blood from my thumb. Blood from the thorn. Blood on Maman's lips.

I removed my gloves, dropping them to the soil. Next, I tugged off my satin ribbon necklace, using the jagged edges around the garnet to cut the heel of my palm, and then Minho's. I bit my lip against the pain before we each pressed our hands against the gate, and it sizzled with acceptance, easing open.

I stared at the ajar door, hands shaking. Minho nodded, and I pushed it open.

Under a swath of moonlight, the garden unfurled before me. It didn't simply exist—it was *alive*, awash with hanging purple wisteria over a man-made waterfall and small brown toads croaking from a pond filled with lily pads. Moss-covered rocks and pebbles lined the cobblestone path ahead, inviting even the smallest of creatures to play and chase each other in the enclosure. Two grand trees stood on either side of us, their branches clasped like lovers' hands. It was as though someone had taken a photograph of this moment in time, long ago, and we had stepped inside.

Minho's voice was incredulous. "How—*how* is this possible? It's all flowering!"

I snuck closer to the waterfall, pressing my hand against the rock. Water flowed over my hand like it was part of the stone itself, warm to the touch.

It all reminded me of what Maman had said just last night: my *power*. Power that seemed to be born from nature itself. After all, Flora had created these gardens.

"Magic," I answered simply, despite my awe. Just a few days ago I would have scoffed at the simple word. But after everything I'd discovered here in these gardens, magic was beginning to seem closer than I'd ever thought possible.

I trudged deeper, seeking more, *feeling* more. The tickle of the grass on my ankles. The waxy petals of begonias and petunias, hanging from sturdy baskets. A field of red poppies, shivering in the slight breeze.

Minho must have been studying my face, because he said, "Maybe this isn't something to make sense of."

His look was too much to handle, even in the darkening night. "I've just realized something," I said. "Won't Marta realize we're gone?"

"I'd sooner risk her ire than listen to a lecture on moth larvae."

Laughter poured out of me unchecked, harmonizing with the croaks of the frogs and the chirps of the birds, the slowly trickling water a metronome. For one luxurious second, I allowed myself to forget the bickering, forget the party. This garden was tonight's true prize, and I wanted to explore every inch of it.

So I did.

Might I have a bit of earth? I'd asked Maman once as we toured the garden on the first day of spring. Maman was collecting information about all the flowers in her journal: how much sunlight they needed, how much watering.

Earth? My mother laughed, the sound warm and melodious. *And why would you need that?*

In case, I told her. *In case we need the garden to grow again.*

The garden will always flourish, somehow, some way. My mother made a point of showing me a once-dead rosebush, its crimson leaves wilted and shriveled. Deep within, a single bud still clung to life, preparing for spring's light to bring life anew. She kissed the flower, as if she had magic that might help it grow.

I reached toward the wisteria, wrapping it around my arms like satin sleeves. I glanced at my hand, staring at the point where there should have been a line of blood, a gash—some indicator of what I'd just done mere minutes ago. But now...

"It's gone." All that was left was a thinning scar on the heel of my palm, as if the garden willed me to heal, the same way four petals from the razorthorn could cure all wounds.

The scar pulsed, as if breathing, as it shrunk down to a single point. Only a faint golden light remained before it disappeared altogether, no trace of a wound to be seen.

Minho checked his hand. "Mine, too."

I glanced down at my hand again, as if certain I had missed it. I shuddered—or perhaps shivered—at the thought. *Magic of the gardens. Flora's magic.*

My voice took on an ethereal tone, like Maman's whenever she told me a story. "When I was a child, I played in the gardens, with each and every flower. They spoke to me. The garden was alive, just like this."

I hadn't admitted those words aloud in a long time. I knew there was true magic in the gardens back then—at the very least the magic of companionship, if nothing else.

Magic that could exist and regrow once more, if I let it.

"There's something about this house, these gardens, that keeps growing on me like a persistent weed. Maybe you're right. Maybe I need to stop doubting the world around me and start living in it."

Minho crept closer to me, his face ever serious as he said, "Was that a touch of self-reflection I heard?"

I rolled my eyes, shifting to hide the burn in my cheeks. Moving behind me, Minho reached around me to cup the wisteria in his palms. His hands shifted lower, tracing a careful path over my sleeve. Before he could continue, I clasped my right hand over his, turning around to face him wordlessly.

I brushed the feathers of his owl mask with my fingers. "What are we doing?"

"Enjoying the moment," he said, leaning down so close his forehead could touch mine.

"I meant with the game. Sooner or later, it will come to an end."

"Do you want that?" he asked, almost tenderly.

"Isn't that the point of the competition? For there to be a winner?" I sounded unconvinced even of my own words.

Minho stepped back, mind seemingly flitting elsewhere as he sat before a tree, removing his mask. "Then before it ends, I have to tell you something. About my scar. About what happened that day."

I joined him, crushing the poppies beneath my skirts. "You said the horse was spooked."

"I didn't explain why. I told you my uncle cares for all manner of animals, especially of the equine variety. They're strong creatures. That's why he picked them."

I held my breath. "Picked them for what, exactly?"

"His experiments."

Ice latched onto my skin. I thought of that chart we'd found written in Maman's hand back at the academy library. "I thought Maman and her friends' trials were about the flower, not animals."

"Remember that diagram we found? Animal blood is thought to be one of the ingredients in the original razorthorn seeds."

My mind caught up to his words. "He was attempting to make a new razorthorn."

Minho nodded. "He told me he was searching for radical cures for equine disease. But the closer I looked, the more I realized what my uncle was doing wasn't in the service of animals, but despite them. I grew so sick at the thought, I couldn't live under his roof any longer. Luckily, the term at the Sorbonne had just begun, and I moved away. But I haven't been able to ride a horse since." Minho fisted the poppies beneath him. "Does that make me a coward? I should have gone back to stop his unethical trials. But I fear he wouldn't listen to me, even if I were on my deathbed."

"Don't let your uncle's mistakes define you. You're more than that."

Back in the manor, I had thought him a thorny flower. But he was more than a competitor.

Even more than a friend.

I leaned toward him, our noses mere inches apart. I should have moved away—should have remembered everything my mind had told me. That Minho was a cheater. That Minho was as unwieldy as the very magic of these gardens. That Minho stood in the way of my future with this house, with this magic—with Maman.

But now, standing in a piece of nature I never thought could have existed again, the truth blossomed before me.

I would not yield when it came to matters of the heart.

"If only you could hear the thoughts running through my mind," Minho whispered, flexing a hand.

"That would be improper," I noted. "But..."

My breath hitched as he came closer. "But?"

My confession surprised even me. "There is no one I would rather be improper with."

The words were a silent invitation, and Minho took the bait. He took my face carefully in his hands, his gaze falling to my lips as he waited for my command. The night smelled of elderflower and sweets and fresh-cut roses. And then he lifted my mask—gazing at me so intently, so fully, I thought I might burst like a dying star.

"Minho," I whispered, his name a request, and without another moment to spare, he granted it.

The boy I'd once called a stranger kissed me as tenderly as Maman kissed the budding rose. His lips lingered on mine, as hot as Pluto's underworld. One taste of him was like ambrosia from the gods, a divine substance I needed to savor. I clung to him with every fiber of my being, wanting this moment to stretch into eternity.

"When we first met, I told you I was seeking perspective. I've since found some myself."

I took a heady breath. "And?"

Minho swallowed audibly. "That I've never felt about anyone the way I feel about you."

"And I, you." It was the most honest thing I'd uttered in a while.

He whispered my name as if it were his undoing, as if he were mine.

At this moment, I would gladly let Minho Kim be my undoing.

On the ground, Minho rediscovered the grooves of my neck, the hollow of my throat. My toes curled, and I glanced up at the stars. Except now, the sky wasn't visible. The garden had awoken, and vines of wisteria had formed a cage of soft violet around us. A cocoon of flowers, hiding us in plain sight.

Once, I wouldn't have entertained the thought of spending time in the garden again. That old Sana existed with the dead gardens. But today, I would become a new person. A changed person.

I promised that to myself, and so much more.

TWENTY

After nearly an hour away from the party, Minho and I corralled ourselves into a semblance of decorum and wended back to the manor.

The garden carved a path for us to the main gate. Lilies with their heads formerly bent in chatter parted; trees lifted their branches into the periphery; shrubs of hawthorn bowed in reverence. The plants became my subjects, and I their worthy queen.

Voices surprised me by the circular driveway. "Surely this party is merely for appearance's sake. Everyone knows Tara Gupta's acts hardly turned a few francs," a man said.

I paused a few paces before the gate, the hairs on the back of my neck stiffening.

"So gaudy," a spindly woman agreed. "Without the flower, they never could have afforded all this. I mean, they don't come from old lines, if you know what I mean."

No, my inner voice spat bitterly. *I do not.*

"And with the flower gone...I mean, I wouldn't blame Tara for choosing to depart this world. They say fame can do nasty things to one's mind."

"That's foul!" I gasped, grabbing hold of Minho's arm. My nails perforated his skin, and, too late, I realized I'd drawn blood. Minho didn't seem to care. He, too, was reddening with rage as he listened.

"She was a tawdry woman. A cheap tumbler and nothing better. *I* wouldn't make a spectacle of myself, especially in death. I mean, to require sensationalism beyond the *grave*—"

Something within me snapped.

Ivy slipped up from the ground and wrapped around the bars of the gate. The vines slithered like tentacles, heading for their target. The spindly woman had only a moment to see the onslaught before they attacked. The man emitted a pitiful cry for help as tendrils slipped over the wrinkled skin of her neck, creating a tight seal, squeezing until her face became a mottled purple.

"Sana—" Minho's voice sounded as if it were coming from underwater. "Sana, *what is happening*?"

I barely noticed as I drifted toward the gate and clutched the bars. A glow emitted from my palms, that same golden light I'd first seen in the gardens days ago. But all I could focus on was the scene unfurling before me. My heart hammered an erratic tune as I watched the woman with what I realized was pure need.

A pit of fire, once in slumber, had awoken. The flames had been stoked, and my body filled with the numbing sensation of adrenaline.

No, it was more than that. It was *glee.*

She deserves it, a voice hissed inside me. *She has to pay for what she said, doesn't she?*

Yes. She did.

The ivy squeezed tighter. Tighter. The woman's eyes lolled backward, and I could feel every inch of her giving up. Her body spasmed in a futile attempt to regain control, but it was too late.

Her legs twitched, and finally, she stopped moving.

I let go of the bars only when Minho's hand gripped my shoulder, pulling me away. The man finally freed the vines from the woman's throat. She was still alive, but she coughed and coughed, trying to seize air into her aching lungs. I tasted tangy, acidic blood in my throat, but I didn't care.

Minho's fear-flecked eyes traveled from mine up to the manor. More ivy had crept over the entire house, mummifying it. The pressure of it was too much, and each window cracked, the weaker ones shattering into infinitesimal pieces on the ground.

Guests poured out of the manor in pure havoc. I watched with glassy eyes as the house was purged of every guest, every hired member of staff. Screams of fright replaced the music that once filled every corner of my home.

"This house is cursed! Cursed, I tell you!" one man cried, fleeing the scene.

Pandemonium filled the air, and I could do nothing but stand and stare as the house emptied out. I felt empty myself, as if I were stripped of my own skin, my own heart.

I didn't remember crossing the threshold into the house. Marta's face blanched with terror, matching Fox's and Isabelle's countenance. But the only *true* witness to tonight's horrors, besides the victim and her friend, was Minho.

I didn't enjoy the way he looked at me. Like those vines were extensions of my own hands.

"It wasn't me," I explained to Minho when Fox, Isabelle, and Marta went outside to assess the damage. "I—I couldn't have done that."

The garden had moved of its own volition. It could give and it could take.

"I don't know what to believe," Minho answered coldly.

He'd seen the garden flower to life an hour ago—and seen our cuts heal. But were the garden's actions truly its own, or was there something else—*someone* else—guiding its magic?

Two flames lit the darkness burning deep in his eyes. "But I also wouldn't blame you."

Several emotions rose, sharp as needles. A pang of disquiet. A cool flash of embarrassment. And pure guilt, raw and red as the petals of a rose.

I raced up the stairs, locking myself in my room. Locking away the truth of what had transpired in my home tonight.

That night, I dreamed of a thousand things. Wishes whispered in the garden; kisses caressing my skin; wisteria creeping over me and Minho, protecting us from all witnesses, including the moon and the onlooking trees.

The dream shifted. The wisteria uncurled and grew teeth, sharp as silver. Their mouths opened in a roaring cry, widening with pure anguish. *Mother*, they screeched, twisting and bending until the wisteria grew as tall as the sky. *We need our mother.*

I gasped awake, hands fisting my soaked sheets.

It took a moment for my breathing to still, for the dream to ebb away and for my mind to find reality once more. My gaze found the arched window, where the first fingers of sunlight crept in.

Seconds later, a knock came at the door.

I bolted upward, cheeks pinkening at the thought of who could be behind that door. Was it Fox, finally come to divulge what he was keeping from me about the note in his pipe? Or Minho, like that first night here at the manor? I still recalled the way I'd bumped into his chest, utterly unladylike in every way, and then everything we had shared together after, before resolving to banish the memories from my head.

"It's me, Belle." My old friend let herself into my chambers, dressed in her morning gown. "You're awake. Did you sleep well? I stayed in my own room last night—I didn't want to disturb you."

"Well enough, thank you," I said, certain Isabelle would pick up on the fatigue in my voice. "How much did you . . . *see*?"

"I was preparing dessert when it happened. Thankfully the kitchen was left undisturbed—my apple rose tarts and diplomat-cream-filled éclairs are in sparkling condition."

"Well, that's the most important thing, isn't it?" I gestured for Isabelle to sit beside me. "Too bad we couldn't have a taste."

Isabelle knew the desserts weren't truly my area of concern. My friend eased onto my bed, curling her hands into mine. I squeezed them just to reassure myself she was real.

"Madame LeBlanc says the reporters will have a field day with this supposed *curse*, but both you and I know there isn't one. Perhaps the high winds from the recent storms played a role?"

Isabelle's soothing tone wasn't enough to ease the anxious thoughts burrowing in my mind. Was the garden cursed, or was I? "This house is in shambles. It was supposed to be restored. *I* was supposed to restore it, with my aunt." I still hadn't gotten a response to the letter I'd sent upon my return to the manor.

"I talked with Madame LeBlanc last night. Monsieur Champlain will board up the windows, but she said we shouldn't halt our game."

Complete Maman's game. Win my inheritance. Beat my competitors.

But how could I when I barely recognized myself?

Not after what happened to the house, what happened to that woman. Not after the way Minho had looked at me: one second like I was a goddess, the next like I was a monster.

There was so much that felt broken, moments fracturing like brittle bones.

Isabelle drew me out of bed and helped me get changed. Downstairs, staff were already boarding up the windows and tossing away glittering pieces of glass with Monsieur Champlain's aid. Considering I'd caused the mess, I joined their efforts while Isabelle insisted on preparing breakfast so that Marta had the morning clear of her duties. Apparently, she was unwell and staying in her room today to recover from yesterday's disturbances. I had not known Marta to ever be of a delicate constitution, but I did not pry.

I sought out the dining room, grateful breakfast was being served. I filled my stomach on Isabelle's Afritada—a heartwarming chicken and rice stew that she swore cured her mother's homesickness on nights when she missed the smells of Manila. It tasted warm, like what I imagined a breath-stealing hug from a mother to be.

"Something smells divine." Minho entered the kitchen, eyes falling on mine.

I don't know what to believe.

But I also wouldn't blame you.

I drew my own eyes sharply away from his.

He took a seat, his gaze emanating both confusion and attraction, two opposed magnetic poles.

A field of poppies. A secret garden. A cage of wisteria. A thousand kisses.

I couldn't stay in the dining room a second longer. I thanked Isabelle for the meal and avoided Minho's crisp gaze as I headed upstairs for an appointment.

Fox bounded into my room with the energy of a newborn pup. "You requested me, mademoiselle?" he said with an overexaggerated flourish of the note I'd slipped under his door this morning.

"Good, you got my message." I retrieved Maman's journal from my armoire. Maman had once told me this dresser was magicked. That a wood nymph had selected a tree and spent seven days cutting, adhering, and fashioning its very existence. The story went that, with the right key, one could unlock its door to a world belonging to the gods and the gods alone.

It is a tall tale, I reminded myself, opening the journal. "I believe we missed something upon our first examination of the journal. A vital clue."

"A glued-on piece of parchment? Another message written in invisible ink? Perhaps a drawing of the flower itself?" came Fox's encyclopedic list of questions. I needed to narrow our focus.

"The answers we found previously were hidden in the endpapers of the books. What if this book is no different?" I suggested.

"Journals often have hidden folders to manage loose papers." He flipped to the back of the journal and stabbed his finger down, finding the seam of an opening. I had merely thought this slot was empty, considering how flat it laid. How wrong I was.

I pried open the folder and plucked out what was inside—a red envelope, so thin you could miss it.

"Eureka!" cried Fox.

Equally elated, I latched onto the red envelope and flipped it over, removing the wax seal. I fished out Maman's letter, which read:

Next I offer a more puzzling trick.
For life isn't all easy, and death is much too quick.
Bind yourself to ideal bounds.
Go where time may only confound,
And then you shall discover my subsequent hint.

"It's a riddle." I recalled my birthday riddles, the ones Maman gave me like clockwork on that special day. But the riddle before me felt different from all the others. It wasn't as direct.

"*Bind yourself* could mean any manner of things, as could the place where time confounds," Fox said.

"Perhaps we need to go to a place where time passes by," I suggested.

"I don't think we'll be able to fit inside a grandfather clock..." Fox scrunched his face in rather serious contemplation.

"*Bind yourself*—like the binds of a book?" I wondered. A devout reader of Austen, Maman once spent a whole summer rebinding her collection with leather, adhesive, corner protectors, and a sharp needle and thread.

"But which book?" asked Fox.

The question left me stumped. I paced the length of my room, stopping at the undamaged window to peer over the circular drive.

"Is that *Marta*?"

I rubbed a spot on the window to get a better look. My eyes did not betray me. Marta was scurrying off the property, disappearing into a carriage she had likely summoned from a nearby service. The spurred horses departed at a gallop.

"I thought Madame LeBlanc was indisposed today?" Fox stroked his chin, assuming a Sherlockian air. "Unless your nanny has lied to us."

My eyes narrowed to slits. "There is only one way to be sure."

The temple of the goddess Clementia, deity of mercy and compassion, had been erected outside Montmartre with limestone and Pentelic marble. Deep within the temple, a single devotee lit a votive with a swish of a match. The candle flickered to life, casting long shadows on the temple walls. A statue of the goddess oversaw the offerings with watchful eyes, a scepter tucked in one hand, a branch in the other.

Marta's swift French—a prayer to the goddess gazing down on her—was lost on me from the distance Fox and I currently kept. Only one word slipped out from the altar: *salvation.*

My nanny retrieved a slip of paper from her coat, holding it up like an offering to the goddess. And then, using the still lit match, burned it.

I plastered myself against the walls, keeping tucked in the shadows, but my lack of proximity wouldn't do. I glanced up, finding a second level with a low barricade. If I crossed the temple quickly enough, Marta might not notice us escaping to a safer viewpoint.

I gestured across the way, and Fox nodded. While Marta knelt, we launched ahead, our shoes scuffing the stone floors. I kept my eyes trained forward, but in my peripheral vision, Marta whipped around. I grabbed onto Fox and pulled him into the shadows on the other end of the temple, my heart thumping in my throat.

"Who's there?" Marta held the dwindling match like a torchlight. "Show yourself."

Fox made to move forward, but I dug my nail into his palm, keeping him steady.

Marta took one step forward. Another. Then she let out a deep, uneasy sigh, blew out the match, and kissed the cameo necklace dangling from her throat.

"I'm sorry, Colin. I must be off."

"*Colin?*" started Fox, but I placed a hand over his mouth, silencing him. He frowned.

Marta flicked away a stray tear and departed the temple in haste. Fox and I pressed ourselves deeper against the limestone walls, expelling air only when Marta was out of range.

"*Now.*"

Fox obeyed, and we snuck to the front of the temple, mirroring Marta's path. I stopped at the altar where offerings had been given, finding the note Marta had written. I blew on it, stopping the final line from being burned away.

La mort n'est pas la mort, mais une évasion vers une nouvelle vie.

Gracieusement,

Marta LeBlanc

"Death is not death, but an escape to life anew," I translated. "Who is Colin? Was she praying for him—or for some sort of salvation?"

"Has she spoken of a Colin before?" Fox asked. "Perhaps a family member?"

"Never." At least, not that I could recall.

I didn't know all too much about Marta's personal life, past or present. But I did know that Marta was keenly loyal to my mother, and my mother to her. I pressed two fingers to my temple, thinking of how Marta had spent seven years in Maman's house, still being paid all the while. Maman had thought everything through, including the event of her death.

"Maybe it's the goddess Clementia's keen gaze, or the truth simply begging to be set free," Fox said, "but, Sana, can I tell you something? Extend an orange branch?"

"Isn't it olive?" I asked, glancing back at the stone branch Clementia held.

"Olives aren't as divine as oranges, wouldn't you agree?"

"Citrus is considered a sacred food of the gods," I agreed, hating that I remembered the smallest detail from my governess's lessons and not the exact features of my mother's face when she smiled, whether her eyes creased or her lips wrinkled.

"Either way, you're right. I think it's time we built some trust between us. It's time I put Sherlock away and let Richard Fox do the talking."

"What do you mean?"

Fox found a nearby bench, and I eased myself into the empty space beside him.

"I'm always putting one persona on after another," he revealed. "If it isn't Sherlock today, it's Auguste Dupin tomorrow. What I mean to say is . . ."

“Sometimes you don’t know how to just be yourself,” I finished for him.

He nodded. “My father wants me to be one person—a businessman like him. But he’s the antithesis of everything I am, everything I do, everything I *read*. It’s easier to slip into someone else’s shoes, to live life like a game of mystery and puzzles and riddles. It’s what drew me to this house. The air of enigma, the question mark hanging in the air. We are constantly questioning this game, this manor—more than we interrogate our own lives. It’s like a reprieve from the real world—from the world I’ll one day have to live in.”

Surprising myself, I rested a hand on his arm. “Because it’s not easy to face the truth.”

Fox nodded, and I could see the relief in his dropped shoulders. “It isn’t. Not at all.”

With a somber air, he dug a hand into his pocket and retrieved his father’s pipe.

“I haven’t exactly been open with you, Sana,” he began.

“You’ve opened up to me today,” I said.

He twisted the pipe and handed over the note hidden inside. “Not about *this*.”

I unfurled the lovers’ note and focused on the rough texture of the paper in my hands. “We’ve already discussed this. Percy is your father, presumably.”

Fox nodded. “But I haven’t conveyed the rest of my theory. I don’t believe Mary to be my mother.”

“Yes . . . ?”

"This love note was written in the summer of 1894. Doesn't that ring a bell?"

I pictured the photo of the Keepers. Maman and Fox's father at l'École Botanique, his arm slung around her shoulder. Friendly, especially for my mother, who had almost no close associations I could remember, aside from Marta.

Or perhaps more than friendly.

"You can't be serious." I crumpled the note on instinct. If Maman and Fox's father knew each other at the academy, who was to say how *well*?

Fox's features held no guile. "I have never been more honest with you than I am being right now."

My blood fizzled with this new information. "So you think our parents were—what? *Courting* one another in secret?"

Fox shrugged. "It's one possibility. But if they were, what happened? Did they have a falling-out? They were once close, according to the photograph from 1894. Perhaps it was the flower that ripped them apart."

I crammed the note back into the pipe, feeling like I'd violated someone's privacy: my own mother's. And while she spoke nary a word about my father, I assumed it was because he was inconsequential to our family, merely a blip in the grand play of our lives. Frankly, I didn't want to know who he was, how he was, or where he was.

"Whether or not our parents were romantically involved, time is slipping away," Fox said at last, standing. He offered me a hand. "Are we still allies?"

I gripped my hand in his, wondering why Fox would question my judgment. Fox was my friend. He was, surprisingly enough, beginning to feel like family. "Of course."

"Good." Fox appeared to grow a few centimeters as he said, "Once we solve the last clue, I propose we take the seed together. That way we're *both* winners."

"Is such a thing possible?" For all I knew, Maman had made sure the razorthorn seed could only be in a single person's possession.

"Perhaps. We won't know until we get there, but I think your mother fashioned this game as more than a competition. It's very clear we're all becoming friends. Maybe *more* than that, from the time you've spent with Minho."

It was no use hiding the truth from Fox, nor the blush crawling up my neck. "You've noticed?"

"Marta did. Said you both came back into the house last night with dirt in your hair." Fox grumbled a laugh. "Very subtle."

I hid a burgeoning smile, thankful Fox, Marta, and Isabelle hadn't noticed what *else* had happened last night. Because if any of them knew, I was certain none of them would label me fit to be their ally.

"Thank you, Fox, for being honest with me." I closed my hands around the pipe, around his own fingers, recalling the way they had grasped mine at the séance. "We're in this together."

Fox's voice was an unbreakable oath. "Together."

TWENTY-ONE

Upon our return to the manor that evening, Fox and I snuck into the library.

Fox claimed to have had an epiphany during the ride back and practically shot out of the carriage for our destination. A chill came over me as I remembered the last time I'd stepped inside this place, the words I'd seen on the chalkboard. *Je t'aime.*

"I studied Shelley's *Frankenstein* extensively back in England," said Fox, finding a dust-laden copy on the shelf. "The story emphasizes the blurring of the lines between life and death, how Victor's ambition resulted in the monstrous and the sublime—"

"This isn't a book club," I chided lightly, although my mind was roiling as I took the book from his hands. *Mary and Percy.* "What is this realization you've had?"

"I realized," said Fox slowly, "that the words *ideal bounds* sounded familiar. They're from this book. The place where time confounds hints at the library. I don't think it's a coincidence she chose this book, given the names on the love note."

Ignoring the growing proof of our parents' entanglement, I flipped to the middle.

There was a hollowed-out circle, harboring a trinket. A secret hiding spot.

I withdrew what lay within, peering at it with an inquisitive eye.

"Looks like a small magnifying glass," Fox noted. "Without the handle, of course. A monocle of sorts."

"Perhaps it's meant to help us discover something else within the pages?" I reasoned. Maman loved to hide secret notes, even journal entries, within the pages of her favorite books. I raised the monocle to my eye, studying the page we were on, but no writing leapt out at me.

I closed the book, inspecting the leather-bound binding.

The riddle had pointed us to the *binds*, had it not? Maman often re-bound her books herself, careful to keep them in pristine condition. I rubbed a finger over the brown leather, feeling for any worn spots.

There was something off—an odd texture, like someone had written on the leather with a special paint and rubbed it away.

"I think there's a message here!"

I pulled the monocle back up to my eye and inspected the leather, seeing the fine veins and punctures in the hide. I stopped over a collection of letters—no, *words*—that brightened themselves beneath the dim light of the library:

Look for my letters where flower and wood meet.

"This glass can illuminate the letters on the book. Look!"

Fox took a turn reading the inscription. It must have been written in special ink, sealed so it wouldn't fade over time.

"While this is all very exciting," Fox began, "what kind of letters does your mother want us to find? Alphabetical ones, or sentimental ones?"

"It could be either. Let's start with wood and flower. That has to mean the garden, doesn't it?" I glanced out the library's moon-shaped window. "We'd better hurry."

Propelled by the exorbitant elation of our discoveries, we tumbled out of the manor, hoping the first threads of moonlight would illuminate the answer to this mystery. I had a feeling we were getting close to its end, close to unraveling all these threads once and for all.

Unraveling Maman's greatest mystery yet.

Strange to think that just one day ago, we'd been among the banter of scholars and well-to-do men and women of Paris. Cold bit into my skin, and I silently cursed myself for not putting on a jacket and gloves. The point of my nose became cold as ice as I roamed the garden, eyes raking the trees and shrubs I had passed an inordinate number of times since my arrival.

A memory pulsed to the forefront of my mind, but instead of looking blurred, the edges were jagged and sharp, like remembering was a painful, torturous thing.

"Come out, come out," calls my mother from the edge of the garden.

I giggle softly to myself, hugging my knees to my chest, from behind the garden shed.

"I can hear you," my mother continues. Taunts. "I can sense you, too."

My laughter abruptly stops. I tuck my shoes tighter to my frame, digging my nails into my palms. Maman doesn't like it when I keep my nails unkempt and unfiled. How odd; just a few minutes ago, she told me it was all the better to keep them sharp and long, to stave off attackers.

"Be wary. Be vigilant," she said. I thought she meant for the game of cache-cache.

So I tell the daisies to keep my location quiet. They hear.

They listen.

"Any ideas?" Fox's deep voice broke me from my trance, and I dipped back into reality.

Flower and wood. I knew exactly where to go.

"North. We have to go north." In seconds, we were off, navigating the paths of the garden like Daedalus's labyrinth. I found a familiar line of birdhouses, then stumbled on a dead patch of grass. If I closed my eyes, I could remember my game of hide-and-seek with Maman, where I hid myself in a field of daisies, propped up against the wood of—

"Here." I pointed at it. The potting shed was covered in vines and leaves that snaked upward to the roof like the tributaries of a river. It stood exactly where I remembered it, now blocked by a dead tree trunk and a bramble of branches.

Together, Fox and I worked to unload the branches and clear the vines.

"Look for my letters where flower and wood meet." There *were* once flowers here, before Maman's passing, meaning the shed could theoretically be our answer. "Search around the shed. Perhaps my mother buried something."

We dug through the dirt until our nails and clothes were coated in soil, until it became increasingly apparent there was nothing hidden here.

"Maybe she didn't want to hide something like letters in the dirt—they could have decayed, after all," came Fox. I agreed with his logic. Which meant sentimental letters were out of the question.

"Perhaps we need the monocle to find our answers."

All too eager, Fox pulled the monocle from his jacket vest. It, too, was now coated in slimy soil, and I rubbed it away as I held the glass to my eye.

There.

Letters had been painted on the side of the shed, in the same ink I'd found on the leatherbound copy of *Frankenstein*.

"*S*," I began. "*U*...*E*..."

Fox pulled the pencil from his lapel and wrote on a spare pad of paper. If I had to give him credit for anything, it was preparedness.

"*H, T, E, M, O, R, P*," I finished, lowering the glass. "What does that spell?"

"Rubbish," Fox said, tapping the pencil against his lip.

"Rubbish *backward*," I agreed. "Remember what my mother did in the previous clue? We had to play the piano backward."

We unscrambled the letters from end to beginning. My eyes lit up. "Prometheus."

"He stole fire from the gods," Fox stated. "What does this have to do with anything?"

"Maybe it's not just about the gods," I said. "Maybe it's a confirmation." I held up the copy of *Frankenstein*, flipping past the frontispiece to the title page. There, written under the new title, was the original one: *The Modern Prometheus.*

"Then then shed itself is the answer? Or perhaps it contains the next clue?" Fox asked, returning the pencil to his pocket. "*I* for one am not a fan of strange sheds. Who knows how stable this is?"

"We won't know until we go inside."

As one, we entered the dark shed. A small table and a stack of books were all that occupied the front, but I could see something farther back. A large planter box, as long as a coffin, full of soil but no flowers.

But I could barely focus on the contents of the shed with that horrid stench.

"What... *is* that?" I coughed out.

The stench attacked each of my senses, stinging my eyes and assaulting my nose. Fox held up an arm to his face, peering past his elbow to seek Maman's next clue.

"We'd better find whatever we need to and get out of here, *fast*," I said while pinching the bridge of my nose.

"I think I already did," Fox pointed out. He trudged to the far corner of the shed, where the stench was more bearable, and pointed at something tucked into the beams of the walls. A weathered envelope.

I practically flew to his side and ripped it open, my eyes skimming Maman's congratulations:

I will keep this brief and say, good work
One last puzzle awaits
End where you began
The finale is right around the corner

"What does it mean, *end where you began*?" Fox asked, baffled.

Maman's message was curt—and evidently, this was the final envelope of our game. I stashed it in my bodice. We would have time, and a clearer mind, to decipher it back in the manor, away from the stale air of the potting shed.

Just as we were about to leave, I pointed to the corner where Fox had found the envelope tucked away. "Wait. There's something jammed in there."

"How can you tell?"

"That beam, by the back wall…that shouldn't be there. There's already enough to support the roof," I explained. I'd never seen this beam as a child. I approached it, eyes searching for something to pry it back with.

"This might help." Fox offered me a crowbar he'd found by the toolbox.

We immediately set to work, using the crowbar to pry apart the board. It gave way after a few tugs, and something hard fell to the ground.

Upon closer inspection, I gasped, realizing what I was looking at.

A pair of bloodied gardening shears.

"What in Flora's—" Fox withheld the rest of his statement. The blood was dry and crusted. I had seen Maman use these shears a hundred times—but they were always spotless.

Bile rose in my throat. Someone *else* could have handled the shears, theoretically. Accidentally nicked themselves as they pruned the hedges. Maybe the blood was Old Ben's.

"Do you think this is another part of your mother's game?" Fox asked, even as disbelief coated his voice.

"I don't." But I had a feeling it meant something, something I didn't currently have the information to figure out. "We should return to the manor. Now."

No one needed to be told twice. We turned away from the scene, ready to move on with the contest. But something in the back of my mind prickled, a sixth sense drawing my eyes toward that largest planter, the wood sagging beneath the weight of the soil. I sifted through the soil, for a moment believing I might find the razorthorn seed within.

A folly. The dirt turned up nothing but broken wishes in the form of dank soil, and something else, curiously, tucked away in the corner of the planter.

A grooved, gold-plated ring. I had seen this band before—someone had been wearing it, not long before I'd left the manor…

I watch the man pass by me with a cool stomp, the glint of his ring ricocheting sunlight.

I watch his hardened scowl as he approaches my mother, who clutches a pair of gardening shears…

"Are you coming?" called Fox from the front of the shed.

I lowered the ring, feeling a tickle in my throat from the growing stench. On instinct, my empty hand reached out, digging until I found something dry and brittle. I yanked it up, and the soil parted across the planter, as if what I had discovered was large enough to hold a—

"*Body*," I gasped, falling back. The ring clattered to the ground as I stared at the curve of a human skull before me.

I retched.

PART III:
THE REUNION

Scholars have theorized why it is that the gods only set foot on mortal lands for so long. Many believe Earth is a world of material pleasures, and to belong to it will damage the divine nature of godly flesh. While some are sorrowed by the gods' lack of presence, there are a dubious few who rejoice in a world where the gods do not often meddle.

—from *The Book of the Gods* by Professor Lemieux, specialist in studies of the goddess Flora, Botanical Academy of Paris

TWENTY-TWO

Dark blue uniforms. Brass buttons. Matching caps.

The Parisian gendarmerie had arrived.

They swarmed like a horde of bees, ready to sting with their probing questions. Razorthorn Manor, now swamped in suspicion.

Everywhere I looked, I caught sight of them, their narrowed eyes, their daunting presence. My home had once been mine, but now, it seemed, strangers would not stop appearing within it. First, the competitors. Second, the reporters. Third, the partygoers. And now, these men who wished for secrets to spill past our lips, as if we knew all the answers we so desperately wished to have.

"Remind me," the officer before me said, seated on an ivory divan. His voice warbled, like I was hearing him from underwater. "How exactly did you find the body?"

More voices, words hushed in the corners of rooms, scrawled in the pads of notebooks.

Skeleton suggests adult male…

Six to eight years since the time of death, based on bone decomposition and soil quality…

Cause of death unknown…

I wasn't breathing. I was on the bottom of the ocean floor, trying to claw my way up.

It had been an hour since the police's arrival, but I'd kept silent most of the time, shock welling inside my veins at the simple thought of the skeleton in that planter—in that *shed*. Bile rose in my throat again, but I swallowed it down, careful not to let my hands shake as the officers peered over the only object they'd found with the body.

The object *I* had found.

After my stomach had emptied, Fox had guided me back into the manor. I was too frazzled to speak, hearing only snippets of Fox's shaky tone as he gathered everyone in the parlor and relayed what we had uncovered: the clue in the journal; the book in the library; and finally, the body in the shed. Monsieur Champlain had called the police shortly after.

It hadn't taken long for that terrible memory to come back to me again. The man entering the shed—there was only one possibility. One man who had been at the manor for years until his sudden disappearance, just like Maman's.

The ring could only belong to one person. My old butler, Monsieur Boucher.

The officer repeated his question.

"It's as I said," I reminded the officer, my voice foreign even to my own ears. My throat burned as I spoke. "We've been exploring the house over the past few weeks. We were taking a turn about the gardens when we found the shed."

Minho, Isabelle, and Fox listened rigidly. It was a small lie, but nothing in the grand scheme of today's shocking discovery.

"This manor hasn't been open to the public in years," the officer remarked. "How did the four of you come to stay at this estate?"

My gaze drew down to the nameplate secured to his breast pocket. "Officer . . . Dubois," I began carefully, "may I ask what all the questions are for? We've just discovered a corpse on the property—I don't think any of us is in the state of mind to answer such inquiries."

The officer did not divulge any answer with his gaze. "We're just going over all the facts. A man has been found dead, and only you and one other person can identify who this ring belongs to."

"Whom?" I asked before understanding dawned on me. There was only one other person who lived at the manor with me and the butler, aside from Maman.

Marta.

Right on time, my former nanny entered the parlor, blowing her nose. I had already heard her speak with a different officer earlier, even though my ears felt like they'd gone numb from frostbite.

I must have been the last person to see Monsieur Boucher alive seven years ago, she'd said tearfully. *He disappeared from the manor in a hurry with his suitcase without explanation. I had no idea he was—* Her voice broke like a dam, and she shook her head, unable to finish the thought.

But how could Marta be telling the truth, if my memory served me correctly? I'd seen Monsieur Boucher when I was eleven, sans suitcase, by the potting shed where he was now discovered dead. And my mother, right across from him, with what was likely the murder weapon in hand.

The bloodied shears, the body in the planter, the riddle hidden in the shed.

None of it was an accident.

A terrible thought took root in my mind, like a rotten plant festering in soil. *Was Maman a killer?*

I covered my mouth, hoping not to retch again.

"I need to use the lavatory," I told the officer, not waiting for his response as I escaped the parlor.

Once I found the toilet, I locked the door behind me and let my body rest against it. Finding a decomposing skeleton on the grounds of my once-home was nowhere near what I thought I'd be doing today.

I washed my face and glanced up in the mirror, hardly recognizing my pasty reflection. Was I the daughter of a killer? Did the apple not fall far from the tree?

Wiping beads of sweat from my forehead, I exited the bathroom—only to bump face-first into a rock-hard chest.

I held my stinging nose, and when I gazed up at him, my heart shot into my throat.

"We should stop meeting like this," I groaned.

"Trying to hide from the police, too?"

Minho didn't wait for me to answer. Instead, he aimed a crooked finger toward himself, drawing me forth. "Come with me. I have a better hiding spot."

Confusion warping my senses, I followed Minho's lead. Eventually, we reached one of the many rooms on the first floor and lifted a painting from the wall, revealing yet another hidden passageway.

The two of us clambered inside before Minho replaced the painting back to its original spot, shrouding us in darkness. The passage was small, likely used as an old cellar of sorts, so that we had to crouch down to fit together. It didn't matter. I needed a reprieve from the world I was drowning in, from the horrors I'd seen that made my heart hammer in my chest.

Even in this passageway, where shadows reigned, Minho's eyes were bright. "You're shivering."

I nodded before realizing he likely couldn't see me. "That was my old butler." The words brought tears to my eyes, an ache forming in my throat. I despised the man when I was younger, but speaking ill of the dead would only make me afraid—as if his ghost would haunt me for the rest of my days. "What if his death wasn't an accident? Why would Maman *want* us to see that?"

"Maybe she didn't know." I heard Minho scoot closer to me.

Every inch of this competition was ludicrous, down to the bribes and the hidden notes. Now, a dead body, another riddle we had to solve.

I knew what I saw that day—my mother holding those spotless shears. Maybe she *did* intend for us to find them. Maybe she wanted us to know the truth.

Her *Frankenstein* clue had been pointing us to life and death, the perilous line we cross from man to monster.

My memory had been spotty of late, dreams melding with reality. I couldn't trust my own brain to tell me what happened to Monsieur Boucher, not when I was still processing his death, his body hidden in a planter like he'd been inhumanely disposed of.

All I could see was Monsieur Boucher's skeleton every time I shut my eyes.

"We should hold a funeral. I'll pay for flowers, arrange a grave—"

"Sana." Minho took my hands in his, the warmth of them a shock to my ice-cold skin. "You're allowed time to grieve. I know you knew him well."

I squeezed my eyes closed, choking back a sob. The thing was, I didn't know him well at all. I didn't even know his first name.

"I wish there were no more secrets," I said, more to myself than anyone else. I glanced up, finding the shine of Minho's eyes, a steady reassurance in the darkness. "I wish this game was over. That I could go home. *Be* home."

Razorthorn Manor was nothing like I remembered it: broken, empty, just like my heart had been after Maman's disappearance. But those blooming plants we found in the gardens told me differently. There was some magic here, in both the plants and the people.

"What those people said outside the manor yesterday..." Minho appeared to grit his teeth. "It wasn't right. I wish I had done something."

A wall of tension slowly built between us. Neither of us had addressed what happened last night: the broken windows, the vines slithering like snakes. The pure, raw emotions I'd felt, and what they had done to me.

Magic, I finally admitted to myself, spurred from pure, unadulterated anger.

"It was an accident." My voice was a fragile thing. "I swear it."

"But was it?" he whispered.

Silence thickened between us. Finally, I revealed, "I don't know how I did it. One moment I was angry, and the next, I simply...surrendered."

And it felt good, a voice claimed—a voice that sounded rather like my own.

"There are more secrets here than either of us know," Minho commented vaguely. He released hold of me. It was hard to believe just yesterday, we'd been in the poppy fields, carefree, untroubled.

I wondered how long it would take for that memory to become tainted, too.

Sensing Minho was holding something back, I asked, "Like what?"

Minho looked like he was bracing himself. "My uncle saw my invitation to the manor."

My muscles tensed. "Hyunwoo." I thought of that photo of the four of our guardians standing in front of the Botanical Academy together.

Minho nodded infinitesimally. "He somehow knew you would be here, so he asked me to do something for him. Something I haven't been able to forgive myself for since."

I had a feeling he was holding his breath, and so was I.

"Tell me."

Minho blew out a breath. All or nothing. "My uncle asked me to . . . *charm* you upon my arrival. To distract you."

At first, I couldn't speak. Then that familiar sense of ire took hold. "So what happened last night—it was all false. An act."

"No, it wasn't. I swear it. Only on that first day at the manor was I heeding my uncle's orders."

I thought back to the way his hand brushed mine in the garden. Then that night, when he'd offered me a bottle of champagne.

A gracious gift, I'd thought. That might as well have been a lifetime ago.

"You lied to me! You said you ran away from him, but you're nothing but his pawn!" My tongue could hardly force out the words. "Is this what you call yourself? *Charming?* You are a foul young man, Kim Minho."

"Sana," he whispered. I expected him to be loud, cross, the way men always were with Maman when arguing. Instead, his voice was gentle, a raindrop in the sea. "I promise you, all of what I've said and done here after that first day has been of my own volition."

"Has it?" I argued. "Have you ever thought to ask yourself *why* your uncle wished for you to charm me?"

Resignedly, Minho sighed. "I deserve your distrust. And I apologize. But my feelings then—and now—are real. Please tell me what happened last night wasn't a mistake."

Kissing me under the wisteria. His breath on my skin. *Nothing was a mistake*, I wanted to tell him, but the words wouldn't escape my lips.

"I can't," was all I could manage.

I pried off the painting and climbed out of the passage, eyes smarting to adjust with the light. I didn't bother looking back. Whatever was between me and Minho had spoiled like curdled milk.

Maman never let men stay in her life for long. Perhaps I was destined to be the same.

TWENTY-THREE

Time moved sluggishly as the police continued their investigation. No one would be allowed near the crime scene over the next few hours, which meant no traversing the north end of the garden. While the planter suggested foul play, there wasn't much more evidence to go on, aside from the ring.

I thought of the bloody shears. Had they found those, too?

Would they pin this on the new butler? Marta? My mother, her final act before she disappeared forever?

Every thought muddled together as I retreated to the lavatory next to Fox's room to undress. I let out my first sigh of relief all evening as I lowered my body into the steaming claw-footed tub. I took my chance to finally wash away everything I'd seen and heard, using the soap bar to scrub off every last inch of the day's events. Marta's furtive prayers at the temple. The stench from the shed. The decaying remains of a body.

I couldn't fathom how just yesterday I had discovered that growing part of the garden where Minho had kissed me with abandon. A small world that belonged to only us.

I took a huge, gulping breath and then sank my head into the water.

Bubbles escaped my mouth, and I opened my eyes, staring at the ceiling as it wavered, like a tide was cresting over me. Everything below felt still, peaceful. More bubbles released from my mouth and reached the surface, popping one by one until they disappeared. I relaxed my limbs and fingers, pressing myself down against the porcelain tub.

A face appeared above the water, rippling and frowning. I gasped, and my nose stung like it was aflame. Needles pricked my chest as I inhaled water. I couldn't see who it was. It could be someone in the house. Maybe an officer. Or maybe—

The killer.

I crashed back up to the surface and spluttered out a series of coughs, each paining my lungs. I grabbed the sides of the bathtub and hacked until I could inhale a full breath, the air as sweet as gardenias. I wiped my hair out of my face and tried to see, but my eyes were still adjusting from the change, bleary with water and tears.

"Hello, Sana."

Marta's voice immediately calmed me. "Marta," I heaved, "what are you doing here during my *private bath*?"

"Hush now," Marta scolded, "it's not like I haven't seen you naked before. Here," she said, handing me a washcloth. I used it to cover myself as best I could, but in truth, Marta wasn't wrong.

"You still haven't answered my question," I chattered out.

"I was checking on you. The tub isn't an ocean, Sana. You shouldn't be holding your breath that long."

"I wasn't," I said, but from the way my chest had tightened, I supposed I had been. "Are the officers still here?"

"They're going to transport the skeleton for an inspection," Marta said clinically, but her face betrayed her true sentiments. Tears rose to her eyes. "They already found a mark on his skull. Monsieur Boucher . . . was murdered."

While I already suspected it, the confirmation felt like the blow of his death all over again, but tenfold. "The police will find out who did this, won't they?"

Marta rubbed her frail hands together as she sat on the edge of the tub. "I don't know. It's been seven years. Seven years of solitude. Seven years to relive the horrors of my past..."

I glanced at my old nanny's hands. They were shaking violently now. I reached out from the tub and grabbed on, stilling her. "Is there something you're not telling me, Marta?"

My nanny steeled herself. "I'm sure I've told you before, Sana, how most of my family members died of cholera?"

"That was many years ago," I remembered. What did that have to do with Monsieur Boucher?

"I have few living relatives left in the country. And I just got word by post yesterday that two more have passed on from other ailments. As far as I'm aware, I have just one person left to call family."

She glanced at our hands, settled over one another, and I realized with startling clarity what she meant.

Me.

Marta had been a second mother to me. Unlike Maman, she had always been there to clean, feed, and bathe me. And while that was her duty, Marta had never treated it as drudgery.

"You stayed for the game," I said numbly. "But after it's over..."

"I'll be gone." She wrinkled her lips, and I realized belatedly she was trying not to cry. "You're growing up, Sana. You don't need me anymore."

"That's not true." I clasped my hand with hers. I needed to express just how much I appreciated everything she'd done for me. "I need you more than ever."

Marta's eyes went glassy. "I never told you this, but I had a child of my own seven years ago."

I blinked in surprise as the moving pieces fell into place. Marta standing before Clementia's altar. Marta writing about life and death.

"Colin," I whispered.

"How did you—" Understanding dawned on her face. "You were my shadow earlier today. I should have known."

"And I should have known better than to follow you. Can you tell me more about Colin? What happened to him?"

"He passed when he was only two. It seems death follows me wherever I go. But one thing that kept me comfort was knowing that one day, you would return to this house. You would make it feel full again."

"I don't think I have. All I've done is play the game and whine about Maman," I said, though realization of who Colin truly was scorched me like this hot bathwater. "You said you had a child seven years ago. Which means..." I calculated. "You were expecting when I left. Did Monsieur Champlain sire your child?"

Marta's face flushed—but not from the revelation. From repugnance.

"Monsieur Champlain? You're sorely mistaken, Sana. He only just arrived a few months ago."

"So you have no romantic relationship?" Had I been reading their interactions wrong the entire time?

"Heavens, no!" Marta curled her lip. "Wherever did you get such an idea?"

"I simply thought... the father..."

Time heals all things, Marta had told me. *Even heartbreak.*

"The old butler." I reeled back, removing my hands from hers. How had I not pieced it together sooner? *Monsieur Boucher* was the only person who spent time with Marta besides me.

Marta nodded. "Monsieur Boucher was my true love. Or so I believed. His reaction to my pregnancy was not mild-mannered."

"He didn't want to be a father?"

"No." Marta finally sobbed. "I wasn't aware he was already married to another woman. He didn't wear his ring while he worked. He kept it in his pocket—except the day he died. The day he told me the truth of our affair."

Realization dropped in my gut like a stone. The ring—not just a ring.

A wedding band.

"I knew I was going to be shunned by society after I bore a child out of wedlock." She planted a hand on her belly. "But Colin was my miracle, the one good thing that came from that relationship. Only your mother knew the truth. I was pregnant." She sighed. "For that to ever happen again would require an act of the goddess Flora herself..."

"You think Flora could make you fertile again? With child?" I balked.

Marta shook her head. "No, no. It is not something I've prayed for in many years. One does not need a biological child to feel complete, dear Sana."

"It's a brave thing, being a mother. Even braver of you to hide that from the world. You shouldn't have had to."

"Your mother helped keep my secret—but she did more than that. She made me executor of this estate, and she gave me a music box and invitations to use on your eighteenth birthday. This game was more than my duty to her. It was the least I could do to say thank you."

Marta reached over the rim of the tub to tip up my chin. I observed her two startling blue eyes, as deep as the Atlantic. There was something haunting about them.

"The police could be wrong," I said, hoping to console her. "Perhaps it was an accident."

"And someone *accidentally* put him in the planter, too?" Marta asked, voice shrill. She rose from the edge of the tub abruptly. "I'm sorry, Sana. I shouldn't be speaking so freely in front of you."

"We all had a hard time today. Please rest, Marta."

"No, I will stay up as long as the police require. It would not do well to look meek in their presence."

I knew one thing for certain: my nanny bore the coat of a lamb and the fury of a lion. If anything, it was the police who should be meek in *her* presence.

TWENTY-FOUR

An air of gloom hung over the manor, thick and heavy as storm clouds. It was only fitting that the sky began to spit rain the following morning, drenching a delivery of fresh-cut crimson roses. They signified mourning, Maman told me once. A crossing from life to death.

We gathered at a creek that flowed beneath a small footbridge just under the main road of the twenty-first arrondissement. Each of us wore our sharpest and darkest outfits—the girls in long black dresses and the boys in fitted black suits. Marta allowed us to offer our condolences on paper to release into the stream.

When it was my turn, I faced the group, holding the slip up to my chest.

"Monsieur Boucher and I were never on good terms," I admitted. "But he brought me to this stream once, to teach me how to fish. I failed miserably, but he kept trying. Maybe he was stubborn, a bit like me."

Marta fought back tears. I understood why. It hurt, like a thousand little cuts, losing someone you thought you'd once loved. Cuts that might never heal.

I turned around and tossed the paper into the stream.

Minho and Isabelle followed next, offering polite words and embraces for Marta.

Marta approached the creek last, holding a small velvet box, but at the final moment she turned and handed it to me. "Open it, Sana. And then give it to the water."

Inside was a cravat, a pair of cuff links, and a letter Marta herself must have written. I closed the box quickly, feeling I'd seen something private. I dropped the entire box into the rushing stream. It bobbed off with the current, then disappeared around the bend.

"He won't hold anything over me ever again," she whispered—to me or the gods above, I wasn't sure. But for once, she seemed at peace.

With that, Marta retreated to the manor. Isabelle promised to make the luncheon. She still looked unwell from everything we discovered yesterday, but Minho tried his best to comfort her. I could feel the weight of his gaze on me as they left.

Then it was just Fox and me, the sound of churning water overpowering any thoughts.

Fox broke the silence first. "My father loves to fish, too. I fear I've let him down in every way imaginable. He even called my hats ridiculous." He paused, looking to me. "Do you find me ridiculous?"

"Eccentric, yes. But ridiculous? Never."

"My father has always been...how do I put it? *Fearless.* In every sense of the word. I want to live like that, but instead of being brave, I've merely affected bravery. I pretend to be a hawkshaw, but I'm no detective, and certainly no hero. Pretending is all I know."

I thought of how I first viewed Fox when I came to the manor. A false detective wearing a false persona. But there was more to him than I'd ever thought possible—bravery in his admissions, honor in his loyalty, and conviction in his beliefs. He was as multifaceted as a rose. And I knew he was holding on to who he truly was, whether his father approved or not.

"I've never met a single person like you, Fox."

"Nor you, Sana. You're a real brick."

"Pardon me?" I wasn't sure whether to be offended.

"A brick. A reliable friend." He gave me a half smile.

"Well, Richard Fox," I said, "you're not such a bad friend yourself." In fact, I was coming to realize that Fox was more than the layers of his clothes, the tilt of his cap.

"Maybe more than a friend?"

Before I could ask what he meant, he withdrew a yellowed letter from his pocket and handed it to me.

7 October 1894

My dearest Mary,

This summer was one of the best and worst of my life, and what you revealed to me is proof of that.

I wish to atone for what I said in the depths of my displeasure. Let me mend things.

With sincerest regrets,
Percy

"Where did you get this note? Your pipe?"

Fox gingerly retrieved the letter. "No. I found a chest of letters in the library. Your *mother's* library. It's time we look deeper into this affair."

"There was no *affair*," I said. "My mother wasn't— She's not—"

"Pardon my poor choice of words. I only meant this *state of affairs.* It happened when they were at school, after all."

If this letter was truly written by Maman, just how many had she exchanged with Fox's father? Why would she keep them?

"We need to accept the truth," Fox continued. "I told you that we could be more than friends, Sana. I think you know what I mean by that."

Fox's words echoed deep in my eardrums. He reached into the inner lining of his jacket, withdrawing another faded letter.

"I found this in my father's study. Read it."

I could barely contain my shaking hands as I accepted it. This letter was written in a finer, neater scrawl—my mother's.

15 March 1895

Dear Percy,

I sense the baby will arrive soon. There is no changing the past now.

Perhaps it's best that the child stays with you.

Mary

"Child?" I echoed, throat dry. Somehow, I knew this letter did not speak of me.

My pulse leapt to my throat; no breath passed through my airway. That one word thundered through me, answering every question and asking a thousand all at once.

I gazed up at Fox. His eyes gleamed, echoing my own.

"You," I whispered. "You're this . . . child."

Fox nodded. "Indeed, Sana. I truly believe that we became fast friends, because, well . . . because we're more than friends. We're family."

I blinked. "Family."

"We're related, Sana Gupta. I had a feeling the moment I stepped onto the estate. I wasn't *entirely* certain, of course—"

"You knew?" I nearly toppled over. "You mean we share a—a..." I clutched a hand to my chest, unable to say the word.

"*Mother*," Fox finished for me.

"W-what about the mother you were telling us about?" I shivered. "You said yourself your mother was ill! That your father needed the thorn to heal her!"

"She was indeed my mother," Fox said softly, "but not biologically, no. You see, my mother passed away a few months ago due to her illness." He paused a moment, swallowed. "After she left, I hoped to find out more about her—to heal the gaping hole in my heart from her loss. But I found something far different, hidden deep in the recesses of my father's study. A family tree. Only, where my mother's name should have been, I found a name I didn't expect. Tara Gupta."

"You're wrong." My teeth chattered in protest.

"Please, Sana, let me finish. When I received the invitation to come to Razorthorn Manor, it felt like a sign. So I accepted. I didn't confront my father about Tara Gupta—instead, I decided I would do everything in my power to find out if this hidden family tree was true." He held a hand to his heart. "I think your mother invited me here for a very special reason. To this manor, to this home... because she had more than one child."

The ice inside me cracked, giving way to a frigid waterfall. "You're delirious, Fox. How can it be possible? We're the same age!"

"I was quite premature. Perhaps you were, too. Either way, maybe *I* am the rightful inheritor of this manor."

"Rightful inheritor?" I lashed out.

"I'm sorry to have to tell you like this, Sana. I hoped it would be a lot smoother."

"And you withheld this information from me? For the entire game?" I nearly choked on my words. This couldn't be true. After all this time, these weeks of believing that *I* was the sole inheritor of the Gupta fortune—

"I did," Fox said plainly. "I hoped that coming to the manor would help me confirm my parentage. And it has."

I looked at him as I never had before. The slight tan of his skin, hidden beneath the freckles and pinkness of his nose and ears. The reddish hair, a shade of brown that mimicked red in the sunlight. The deep brown of his eyes, mirroring my own.

Boiling rage filled me, from my toes up to the crown of my head.

"You're not my brother, Fox. But if you were, then I have something to say to you."

"You do?" Fox didn't conceal the hopefulness in his tone.

"Yes. Our deal is off." I stormed away from the creek and paused to look over my shoulder. "May the best Gupta win."

I stopped at the front hall to gather my breath. Every revelation pounded through my skull, threatening nausea. I turned to the table beside me to steady myself, then laid eyes on the received mail. Monsieur Champlain must have left it there, as he did daily on the marble-top table. I shuffled through it, hoping for an answer to the letter I'd sent to my aunt Neena. There was an envelope marked with a bright red stamp, but as I picked it up, I recognized my own handwriting on the envelope.

A dead letter.

How could the address have been wrong? This was where Neena Massi had written to me from, wasn't it?

I dropped the mail, hating how all these disparate puzzle pieces appeared to hold no sense. My unanswered letters; Fox being my half-brother; Minho claiming he'd kissed me of his own volition, instead of acting on his uncle's baffling orders; and most pressing of all, Maman's final clue to *end where you began*.

I forced myself to take a slow, calming inhale. The smell of our midday meal reached me, and my feet moved of their own accord to the dining room. My gaze fell on a mouthwatering plate of sole meuniere.

"Isabelle." I gaped. "This is..."

"Our last meal of the competition," she began, "to echo the first."

The smell of warm butter, tangy lemon, and minced parsley should have enticed me. But then Fox's voice reached my ears, and my queasiness increased. Much as I appreciated Isabelle's culinary concoction, I found I no longer had the stomach to eat, not with Fox and Minho currently seating themselves across from me.

It appeared the only person I was on even footing with anymore was Belle.

After the meal, the butler cleared the dishes as I opened the envelope and laid out the note. Fox had already shown Minho and Isabelle the envelope's contents this morning, and neither had had a clue what it meant. I needed to examine it one more time.

One last puzzle awaits...

The finale is right around the corner...

The note felt so *unfinished*, especially by my mother's standards. Ending where we began could mean any number of places. We started our test game in the puzzle room. Or perhaps she was referencing the parlor, where Marta first disclosed the nature of the game.

I rubbed my head, groaning.

"Maybe she kept the note intentionally vague for a reason," Fox said. "You know, in case someone waltzed into the shed and, I don't know... found a dead body next to it?"

"It was a skeleton," I corrected with a heaping spoonful of malice. "*Clearly*, no one's been in that shed for seven years."

"There must be another riddle in here somewhere," Minho said, tapping the paper. "I can feel it."

I scanned the now-empty envelope that Maman had hidden in the shed for us to find. Instinct driving me, I tore open and flattened the envelope itself, finding something splattered on the inside in bloodred ink.

Minho appeared to physically recoil, as if remembering the ink we'd used to sign our contracts.

"It isn't real blood," I said, mostly to quell my own worries. "I've seen this before."

"Have you?" Fox asked.

I snippily ignored him. "It was on the blueprint Minho hid from us. Yes, Minho hid a vital clue from *all* of us earlier in the game. Did I forget to mention that?"

Isabelle and Fox whirled on Minho for an explanation, their eyes darkening.

"You bastard," Fox spat. "Ungentlemanly, sir!"

Minho ground his teeth. "I was going to justify myself to Isabelle and Fox at the *appropriate time*."

"When?" I shot back. "As soon as we'd completed the game? Better yet, when you had your precious razorthorn seed, and my house, in your possession?"

"Enough!" Isabelle cried. "Sana, what does the bloody ink mean?"

The front bell cut the tense air.

I dashed to the front door to answer the summons, arriving ahead of the butler. Loud, masculine voices came from behind the frosted glass.

"What's happening?" I demanded, flinging the door open to find three Parisian policemen standing there. "Is this about the corpse? We've already spoken to you in great length."

The policemen exchanged looks. "We're not here for *you*." Their gaze trailed behind me.

Dressed in a black overcoat and felt hat that covered her graying hair, Marta approached. She brushed past me and onto the front stoop, allowing an officer to clasp her hands behind her back. All the while, she kept her head tilted toward the ground, as if uttering a prayer to the earth.

The letter fell from my hands as I marched outside. "Marta! What are they doing to you?"

"Sana." Marta looked back. Her mourning wear was the darkest black. The edge of her wide-brimmed hat, attached to her head with a feather fascinator, barely concealed her red-rimmed eyes. Those eyes reached the depths of the ocean floor.

"I've confessed to everything." She spoke it with an air of responsibility, like a lady charged with the care of a fussy child. Even in this moment of utter confusion, she managed to look and sound ten times the person I would ever be.

"To what?" My voice was brittle, strangled. I turned to the nearest officer. "Let her go this instant."

"That is impossible, mademoiselle," he said colorlessly. "She—"

"It's too late," Marta interjected, and her voice finally broke. "I know what crime I committed. It was time I spoke the truth." Her next word pounded like the blood in my eardrums: "Manslaughter."

My world shrank to the size of a pinpoint. The air seemed too difficult to breathe.

"Marta..."

"I wasn't honest with you, Sana. I know exactly what happened that night. I helped put his body in the planter."

"No... that can't be right. This is all a mistake—"

But Marta's face betrayed no uncertainty. I recalled the way her hands shook as she sat on the tub.

"I want you to understand something." Marta leveled her gaze with mine. "Colin might be gone, but you are also my child, Sana. Not by blood, but water. Now win. For your mother." She inhaled shakily. "And for me."

I nodded, tears on the rim of my waterline. "I will! I promise!"

The officer pushed her along, and Marta tried to control her weeping. Under a darkening sky, I watched them lock her inside a patrol wagon, the engine groaning to life.

I watched as they took her away.

TWENTY-FIVE

The shock of Marta's confession had the four of us in the sitting room, silent, until nightfall.

Another wrinkle in the game.

Another mystery that remained unresolved.

My heart told me there was something else, something *greater*, to be uncovered. Marta's admission to manslaughter didn't sit well with me.

Perhaps because I refused to believe my nanny could hide a dead body.

"If she admitted to it, then she must have done it," Minho said, breaking the silence at a quarter to ten. I knew, because my eyes were glued to the clock, obsessing over every second that passed without Marta's presence.

The cold that had entered my bones as soon as Marta left was beginning to splinter.

"She said that it was an *accident*," I said frostily.

"What about the bloodied shears?" Fox demanded. "That's some damning evidence."

I rounded on him. "Are you saying Marta *murdered* Monsieur Boucher?"

My three competitors exchanged a long look.

"No—no, of course not," Isabelle said finally. I sensed she was merely placating me.

Marta had said something last night, as I rested in the bath: that it was no accident the body had been placed in the planter. *She knew what she'd done.* This whole time. But if she said it was manslaughter, then I believed her . . . I simply had to.

I got up, paced. "Marta followed my mother's exact instructions to bring us here, and she gave us the opportunity of a lifetime. Not for a second did she try to solve the mystery for herself."

"I may be able to provide some clarity on this matter," a voice announced from the sitting room entrance.

I whirled.

It was Monsieur Champlain, who entered slowly and took a seat, hands white-knuckled on the armrests. "I see you children have heard the truth."

"You knew?" The hairs on my arm rose.

"Let me say this: she promised it was all an accident. I wasn't there, of course. But she called me in confidence, asking me to come to the manor in anticipation of your arrival. I was freshly out of a job, and we needed each other. Needed family."

Minho, Fox, and Isabelle gawked. "You mean . . ."

I do have a cousin nearby.

"Yes. I am Madame LeBlanc's first cousin."

No one said a word. When the butler spoke again, his words were faint, almost broken. "Marta said I could have a new job and keep her company at the same time. During my time here, she admitted what happened to the man who had my position before me. I never pried for the details. We haven't spoken of that . . . *incident* since. We simply decided to forget about it. Or try to."

My shoulders sagged as I sank back into my chair. Then Marta truly was to blame: for the hidden body, the fatal accident. She had felt she had no choice but to hide the death of Monsieur Boucher. What other secrets did she have? What other secrets did the people in this room have?

"I can see the questions writ on your face, mademoiselle, so allow me to finally be forthright. I believe you overheard my troubles with my old employer, Monsieur Donne. I fear you have mistaken my meeting with Alain as purely business-related."

"Have I?"

The butler's smile bloomed like a budding rose. I had seen that smile before. Had worn it myself around Minho.

My features softened with understanding. The butler's preferred books. His secretive meetings—not enterprise but amour.

He must have sensed my deductions, for he continued: "We met as colleagues, both in service of the Donnes. While he worked exclusively with upkeep of the immediate family, I was often relegated to the security of the western halls, where the family kept their most precious jewels. We would sneak away any chance we got to be just breaths away from one another. To feel love as we had never had as children but often read about in the pages of books.

"One night, we were caught in the stables together by a hand. Donne appeared to be understanding of our relationship, so long as it didn't interfere with work. Unfortunately, when he learned I had often left the jewels unattended..."

"You were let go," I filled in. "You love the stables, don't you? They remind you of Alain. That's why your toecaps were dirty all those days ago. From the mud."

"Indeed. It pains me to be so far from him. Alain's current employment and housing is temporary, which is why we have been trying to scrounge up the funds to find a quiet place to live."

That explained their talk of money.

Fox stood. "Thank you for being honest with us, Monsieur Champlain. This house doesn't just hold secrets. It holds truths. Futures. One's identity shouldn't have to be kept secret." His gaze flitted to mine knowingly.

"Nor should their true affections," Minho tacked on, glancing over at me.

While Auguste and Alain's hearts were pure and steady as the summer sun, mine was an unpredictable winter storm—one I hadn't yet learned how to weather.

"Where are you going?" the butler asked as I jolted to my feet.

I was already halfway out the door. "To finish this game once and for all."

I rushed blindly up the stairs to the third floor, the others on my heels. We had no time to waste.

I hurried down the hall, all the way to the ballroom. I flung open the doors to moonlight bathing the floors, the enormous windows shining. I traced back through my memory, recalling the splatter of ink right over the ballroom.

"*End where you began.* Maman meant the ballroom—where we signed the contracts."

Each of us turned to our respective tables, the ones that held those strange inkpots of blood. It finally dawned on me who the blood must have belonged to.

My mother. Who else?

We lifted the tablecloths—nothing—and then, at my direction, dragged the tables to the sides of the room. I had a hunch, and it turned out to be true: there was something odd about the flooring underneath each of them, with four strange square designs engraved into the wood.

A puzzle hidden in the floorboards. Maman's grand finale.

One of the wood pieces in each square stuck out to me, varnished lighter than the others.

A memory sprang to life. My mother, completing a puzzle in which she needed to slide the pieces around to get one piece out—and when she did, it lifted, rewarding her with a delicious-looking piece of chocolate.

"It's a slider puzzle," I told them. "One for each of us. Whoever slides out the lighter-colored piece wins."

"What happens then?" Fox asked.

"I'm not sure." The end of the game—the end of this web of puzzles and riddles, deceits and truths.

I needed to win. If not for my inheritance, then to prove to myself, completely, unequivocally, desperately, who I truly was. Who I finally accepted myself to be. Tara Gupta's daughter. Her blood, both the good and bad.

We each sat in front of our puzzles, unmoving.

I was *this* close to winning. This time we had spent together, all of it, would soon become as distant as a long-forgotten dream.

"Sana. Before we start, I need to say one thing." Isabelle turned to me. "We were each handpicked to play, but I've learned something in my time here. We're all greater than a flower, and we're greater than this game. Our choices make us who we are—not what is chosen for us."

I reached out for her hand and squeezed it. "Good luck," I said. And I meant it.

With that, the final challenge had begun.

Twenty-three minutes later, as we each stared at the wood with determined looks and nibbled lips, the answer came to me. I saw the sequence of moves required to solve my slider. I moved faster than I ever had before, sliding the topmost piece to the left, the rightmost piece down, opening up a slot—

I could hear Minho moving fiercely, sweat beading on his upper lip. His eyes caught on mine for a fraction of a second.

Focus, Sana.

Turn after turn, minute after minute. I was a piece on Maman's chess board, moving closer to knocking over the queen. But I wasn't going to finish this game as a player. As a contestant. As a pawn in a game.

I would finish as *me.*

Click.

The piece of lightened wood slid out of the parquette, loosening from the rest of the design. I grasped it in my hands, turning it over. There I saw the following words:

SIX NUMBERS, ONE LOCK.
OUR SPECIAL DAY.

"You did it," Isabelle said. She had barely moved any of her pieces. "You won."

"Not just yet." I stared down at the final riddle. *How did I know it wouldn't be this simple?* I glanced over at Minho, who had just finished, too. He had received the same riddle on the back of his piece.

Another race. This time, to decipher this elliptical statement.

I deduced this clue must lead to some sort of combination padlock. The lock could be anywhere in the house.

Could it be...?

"This will always be our special day, and our special place." Maman told me that every year on her birthday, sitting at her desk with me on her lap.

"I know where to go," I said, rising and running to the door. The others clattered after me, abandoning their own puzzles. When I reached my destination—the study—I began feeling along the walls, hands roving for anything out of place.

There!

A small doorknob was hidden behind Maman's desk. But my excitement was short-lived. The doorknob wouldn't budge. My thumb brushed over a tiny catalogue of buttons hidden just underneath. A safety mechanism. A padlock.

Our special day. Maman said it wasn't a cause of celebration to grow older, but rather to grow wiser. I twisted the numbers in the proper order: two, three, one, one, seven, four...

23. 11. 74.

The code triggered a release.

"It's open," I breathed. Maman's birthday worked.

I placed a hand on the knob, but froze with uncertainty. What lay beyond? The razorthorn? The seed that had eluded us for so long? The thing that might change all our lives?

I didn't wait to find out. Leading the group, I pushed the hidden door open—so well-disguised in the wall—and slipped around the desk into a dusty, unused passage. A staircase led us down, down, down—all the way to an outdoor exit.

We emerged on the estate grounds, though I'd no idea where. Moonlight glazed the earth before us, shimmering in puddles of rainwater. And there, before us, rose the tallest hedges I'd ever seen in my life.

"A maze," Minho murmured.

A labyrinth—*of course* this was where Maman would lead us for her grand finale. It must be the easternmost point of the gardens, where I'd never been allowed before.

"Come on." I steeled myself, entering the mouth of the maze. Hedges twice as tall as I loomed overhead, as if threatening to swallow us whole. What lay within?

I continued onward. Left, right, dead end. Back, right, left. The hedges squeezed in on us, pricking us with their thorns. Rain began to fall again. And then—a laugh.

A melodic sound that sounded exactly like my mother's.

"Come out, come out..."

I was hearing things. I was delusional.

I was close.

I crashed my way deeper into the maze, clearing my mind the way Maman had trained me to do. Riddles were best solved with a simple answer, not an overwrought one. This was just another puzzle. Just another game.

The labyrinthine hedges loomed over me, and each turn took me into yet another wall of green, onto yet another sodden path. Something about these hedges felt haunted by memories, soaked in them with a bitter chill. I paused as two indistinct blurs passed by me, and I knew instinctively I was watching a scene from the past. The blurs formed into two girls, chasing one another in the maze with laughter on their lips.

Behind me, Minho's labored breath caught my attention, breaking me away from a memory that was not my own.

I halted. "Where's Fox and Isabelle?" Somewhere within the maze, we'd lost them. Was Isabelle trying to get ahead of us? Was Fox?

Minho pushed damp hair out of his face, sipping thin breaths. "I think we're lost."

"We have to keep moving anyway."

I made to grab Minho's arm, but he held me in place instead.

"I have to admit something," he said, eyes on mine. His cheeks were flushed, and I could tell they weren't that way simply because of rushing through the hedges. "I never got the chance to apologize to you for what I did."

"You don't need to say another word about that—"

"But I do." His cheeks flushed deeper. "Tell me the truth, Sana. That it wasn't all a mistake."

I thought back to the night in the gardens two days ago, the beauty of the leaves, the beauty of Minho's face. The game was about to end. I didn't know when, or if, I would ever see him again.

So I told him the truth. "What happened—what you felt—it wasn't a mistake. Because I felt it, too."

As if by Saturn's hand, time slowed, the rain falling at half its usual speed. Minho curled his fingers into the small of my back. "Do you remember what you told me that day I found you in the garden?"

The words appeared in my mind, as clear as dewdrops. " 'The heart doesn't require as much time as the mind.' "

Minho's face softened. "Will you indulge me one final time?"

I heard the implication in his voice. For once, I didn't care what my mind told me. Didn't care what society might think, what my mother intended for me to gain from this game. Didn't care what Minho had arrived here *intending* to do, a design he had abandoned. Because I had discovered something else—something I had been unable to name, until now.

As soon as one of us had the seed, the prize, in our hands, there would be no going back. If I wanted to remember Minho as he was now—as my friend, as my confidante—I would allow my heart a precious, quick-fleeted moment.

"Yes."

Minho crushed his lips against mine, hands painting portraits over my skin. Minho was ravenous, and I pushed with equal fervor, feeling the hedges conspiring to press us closer together. To have our hearts beating side by side.

A boom of thunder broke us apart, and I gasped for air. A flash of lightning lit up the sky. The sharp light illuminated Minho's features, the shadows lining his face making him look gaunt.

"I'm sorry," he whispered, and then kissed me again.

When he finally pulled his lips away, he did so slowly, as if he needed to crystalize this moment in time.

"You've apologized enough," I told him.

"Not for that." I could've sworn a tear, or perhaps just the rain, slid down his cheek. "For this."

The air between us shifted.

Eyes hardening, he spun me around, one arm like iron around me—and then a cold, damp cloth smothered my mouth and nose, smelling poisonously of chloroform. I struggled as black spotted my vision. My body fell limp and lifeless as a rag doll.

And I became one with the dark.

TWENTY-SIX

I was underwater, tasting salt and sea foam. I was a shipwrecked girl, seeking the security of land.

And then I came up for air.

When my senses found me once more, my hands were wrapped with thorny vines, binding me like rope.

I curled my fingers one by one, regaining my senses. The feel of wet earth under my body. The sensation of light rain drizzling onto my face. And vaguely, a familiar scent of lavender perfume.

Groggily, I noticed a clearing before me. Someone had transferred my body to the middle of the maze. In the center of the clearing stood, incongruously, a wooden door outlined in light, glowing from within.

A figure stepped into my line of vision, taking the shape of a man I'd never seen before. His pale face was marked with wrinkles and fine frown lines, his eyebrows barely visible, his mouth permanently curled into a snarl. I could almost imagine his younger self—no, I could *picture* him.

Just as he was in that photograph of the Keepers.

I groaned when I recalled what Minho had said. What he had *done.*

Not a kiss of remembrance. A kiss goodbye.

"Did you follow through with my instructions, Minho?" the stranger—Hyunwoo—asked.

Minho appeared at his uncle's side. "Yes, samchon."

Only then did I notice the revolver in his uncle's hands, pointed directly at me.

"Not well enough," he spat. "Your charms couldn't finish the job, but my minor sedative should make her more amenable. Get her on her feet."

Minho's eyes were fixed on the laces of his shoes as he pulled me up from the earth and steadied me. My mind was still hazy.

His uncle kept the revolver trained on me.

"It was supposed to be simple," Hyunwoo grunted. "The girl finds the bribe and leaves the game. My accomplice stops and *handles* her on her way out. We get the flower for the two of us to share, and everything else we desired. But you've bungled it, *of course*."

I backtracked through his words. *Bribe.* The bribe *Minho* had supposedly found in the post... because *he* was the one who'd planted it.

"Uncle," Minho said quietly. "You promised no more bloodshed than necessary."

With a huff, Hyunwoo lowered the gun—but only by an inch or two. Now it was level with my chest.

"Minho." My voice came out in a broken whisper, all strength having fled my body from the sedative. A cold wind slithered up, wrapping around my wrists like manacles. "What are you doing? Why did you tell your uncle about the game? The rules..."

"I hadn't signed the contract at that point," said Minho tightly. "I went to the garden and spoke to my uncle on the first afternoon. Not long before you found me outside."

I couldn't fathom any of this. Had his uncle been here the entire time?

“You’re soft, boy,” Hyunwoo ground out. “No matter. We’ll get what we’re owed soon enough. Minho, convince her to give up her blood.”

Minho stood there, wordless, before his uncle growled.

“Must I do *everything* myself?” Hyunwoo shoved Minho aside and swapped the gun for a tapered, deadly knife. My heart jolted as he twisted my hand over, pressing the tip into my palm.

A voice in the dark fractured my thoughts.

“No more dramatics, Hyunwoo.” A woman—Hyunwoo’s accomplice, I presumed, out of my line of sight—didn’t bother to withhold a disgruntled sigh. “Your nephew clearly lost sight of getting Sana out of the game a long time ago. A pitiful attempt, really. But no matter. We both knew she was too determined—and I, personally, wanted to see just how far she would go.”

I loosed a breath, unable to focus on anything but the female voice, warped but familiar. “Show yourself.”

“As you wish.”

Out of the darkness came a woman with beautiful tawny skin, coffee-colored eyes, and black hair. Each of her features a perfect reflection of mine.

My throat tightened. “*Maman*.”

Maman looked just as she had before she disappeared, and yet… there were a few altered qualities. Her nose was slightly crooked, like it had been broken and hastily pushed back into place. Her eyes were narrower, sharp as a hawk’s and just as bloodthirsty.

Maman chuckled to herself, eyes creasing as she smiled. It was the kind of smile that belonged in her portrait upstairs—a smile that felt less like my mother and more an imitation.

"How I missed you, dear daughter," she purred. "Seven years it's been, and it feels like just yesterday that you reached my hip."

My fear was quickly replaced by an instinctive desire to be in the arms of the woman who'd occupied my every breath, my every waking dream. She was here—right in front of my eyes.

She was no ghost. She was *back*.

"Maman!"

Hyunwoo cut my restraints. I rushed forward to throw my freed arms around my mother, choking back a sob as I breathed in her signature lavender scent. Yet my mother did not embrace me; she simply smoothed a hand over my hair and placed a delicate kiss on the crown of my head.

"I'm sorry to have created so much confusion for you children." Maman hardly glanced at Minho. "But I promise you will all understand soon enough why I did this. First, however..." She produced something from behind her back.

"Is that—a *razorthorn seed*?" I gasped. There was a small thorny stem sticking out of the seed, as if it were halfway to becoming the magical razorthorn I'd fantasized about in my youth.

"Indeed it is. You see, I made this game as a *test*. A test to see who could help me bloom this seed into something spectacular. And you, Sana—you are clearly the winner." She grinned. "Would you like to claim your prize?"

It didn't matter that Maman hadn't thoroughly explained the purpose of the game, the *reason* she'd brought us four together. All that mattered was that she'd been here, waiting patiently, agonizingly, for us to finish our tasks—and to see me again.

"Do as I say," Maman said when I didn't answer. "Prick your finger on this thorny stem."

I studied my mother's face. The sallow of her cheeks, which were once full. The way her lips were pressed tight—not in disappointment, but in anticipation.

I inched my thumb toward the thorn.

"Almost there," she replied eagerly. "That's it..."

I froze just before my flesh pressed against the thorn. Because from the corner of my eye, Minho shook his head infinitesimally.

Maman cooed, "Sana, dear, don't you wish to claim your prize?"

I didn't need a prize. Didn't need the razorthorn—or this manor, even. All I needed was her. Why didn't she understand that? And why had Hyunwoo called her his *accomplice*?

"What is that?" I pointed at the mysterious door, then turned and approached it cautiously. Before it, on the ground, was a puzzle box. It looked like it could only be opened by a key.

"Nothing, Sana. Now return and help me—help *yourself*—win the game."

The words came from an ocean away.

I fingered the key necklace at my throat and pulled it over my head. I had the strangest out-of-body experience, like I was watching myself win the game.

I knelt and unlocked the box, twisting the key to the right with a satisfying *click*. Smoothing my fingers over the wood grain of the box, I opened it.

A thin, cylindrical vial filled with purplish liquid greeted me. I held it up, one finger on the stopper, noticing a small stack of papers in

Maman's scrawl underneath. But it was the vial that had all my attention, a small tag on the side addressed to me:

FOR SANA. DRINK ME.

Maman had never called me Alice, but I knew I must go down this rabbit hole. I moved to uncork the stopper.

Behind me, Maman inhaled loudly through her nose, gathering patience. "Give me that vial, dear daughter. You don't need it. You don't need anything in that box—I am here now."

But she wanted me to drink it, according to the tag—or had, once. Maman *never* abandoned a puzzle she had already organized. And right now, my mother was acting anything but herself.

"I'm sorry, Maman. I can't do that."

In a moment of defiance, I uncorked the stopper and held the vial to my lips. I could see the word my mother's mouth formed—*stop!*—just as I downed the liquid, and my brain puddled into nothingness.

I run barefoot in the garden against Marta's wishes.

It's not her fault I'm eager to please my aunt Neena. She wanted another round of Marbles and Riddles, and I couldn't refuse her, not again.

I find her just where she said she would be, hidden behind the grand bend of the oak tree. Her faint lavender perfume fills the air—a sharp difference from Maman's familiar almond scent.

"You came!" I jump up and down. The daisies nearby twiddle in the wind.

"Of course I did, sweet Sana," Neena Massi patiently answers. My

aunt grins down at me before planting a kiss on my cheek. "Now, I don't have much time until your maman returns home. Remember what we agreed on?"

I nod excitedly. "Never tell Maman you come to the gardens."

"That's right," Neena says, her face identical in every way to Maman's. I wonder what it would be like to have a twin, or even a sibling for that matter. But at least I have my plants. "It's our little secret. Now, I have a different game for you today. How about cache-cache?" She places her hands in front of her eyes. "Ten, nine..."

I race away as fast as I can, deep into a field of daisies. The flowers threaten to swallow me whole, and I find a spot by the garden shed. I ask the daisies to keep my location a secret, giggling softly to myself.

"Come out, come out..."

Neena Massi is close, too close. I need to find a new hiding spot.

I'm up and flying through the flowers. I move so fast I don't see the rock ahead—

I crash right into it and soar into the air. For a moment, I am lighter than a feather. I am dancing on the wind.

Then I hit the ground, and any notion of feathery lightness dissipates. Pain shoots through my knee as two stern-looking leather shoes greet me.

Monsieur Boucher's.

The beak-nosed man with wide, rheumy eyes looks down at me. "You! Why are you out here? Your mother gave you explicit instructions to stay out of the gardens! You insolent little brat—"

In one swift second, he has me seized by both arms. His nails dig crescents into my skin.

"No one speaks to my daughter that way."

Monsieur Boucher drops me. For a moment I wonder if he has swallowed a fly, for he starts to sputter. "Madame Gupta, what are you doing home so early?"

I rise, turning to find Neena Massi arriving in the clearing. Her eyes level with Monsieur Boucher's. Then, calmly, she draws her gaze away from the butler and toward me, smiling. "I was just helping Sana learn more about flowers."

"I thought you forbade Sana from playing outside unpermitted," Monsieur Boucher says, narrowing his eyes. "She spends too much time alone in the gardens already."

"Is that what I said?" Neena laughs to herself. I notice her reach for something in her pocket, then hide it behind her back.

A pair of garden shears.

Monsieur Boucher is watching her closely now. "Are you Madame Gupta?" He lengthens himself into a looming stance. "Or are you someone else, madame? I do not think I recall that dress."

"If I am? What are you going to do about it?" Neena inches closer, daring him.

"I will use whatever force necessary to get rid of you, if you are not the lady of this estate." Monsieur Boucher sneers. "You have a fiendish stare! The whole Gupta family is a wicked lot. All of you! I knew I shouldn't have taken a position here. This house is a stain on the name of my country and the goddess you claim to pray to! Flora would despise what this once-holy site has become." The butler rounds on me. "Go inside, child. Before you see something you will not easily forget."

"But—"

I yelp as Monsieur Boucher grabs me by my hair and tosses me aside.

My aunt throws up a protective arm. No—not protective. Reactive. The shears glint in the light from the setting sun before they come slashing down on the man's head.

The blow only affects him for a moment before he draws himself back up to full height, incensed. Blood pours over his brow, over his eyes, but he throws himself on my aunt and slaps a hand over her cheek, the sound as sharp as a gunshot.

Before I know what's happening, tendrils curl up from the ground behind me. They shoot forward like extensions of my own arms and seize Monsieur Boucher's neck, tightening, tightening.

Red paints my vision. I want this vile butler to stop talking. I want him to stop moving, so he might never harm me or my aunt again.

When he takes his final breath, we both collapse onto the ground, the sky fading to black.

I don't know how long I'm unconscious for. Minutes, perhaps nearly a half hour. The sky is a deep purple when I finally come to. I am alone.

Was it all a dream?

Red drips down to my ankle. I don't care. I limp through the field toward the sound of voices talking heatedly in the shed.

I use the sleeve of my shirt to rub some of the grime off the shed window. Inside, Monsieur Boucher lies still on the ground. I blink hard, wondering why there are bits of wood sticking out of his head, right by a clotted wound—a wound imparted by gardening shears.

I press my ear against the gaps in the wood slats, listening.

"What a horrible accident. Imagine the scandal... Marta, take care of him, please."

Marta's voice is indistinct. But I do hear one word: "How?"

How. How. How.

And then, Neena's voice, strong and stiff as titanium. "The police will blame you. You were in charge of the upkeep of this estate while I was gone. It was only a matter of time before that beam fell and hurt someone."

"No, Tara—" Marta lets out a howl of pain, one I'd never heard her utter before. It pierces my skin, my soul, so loud I pull myself away from the boards and fall onto my rear. I scramble back on my arms and legs, chest puffing, the air coming too fast, the sky blotching with black—

Something thumps.

They've moved the body. Or a beam.

I don't want to know which. I hear my aunt cursing. She's searching for something. I watch as she exits the shed in a huff, eyes roving over the grass, over the flowers, and landing, with a menacing, punishing gaze, on me.

"What's going on?" I ask, hearing Marta's sobs come faintly from the shed. "Is Monsieur—"

"Let me take a look at that," my aunt interrupts as she examines my exposed wound.

I choke on bile. "Is he—is he dead*? Did I..."*

Neena strokes back my hair. "Don't worry, my little butterfly. I know how to make this all better," she assures me.

I don't know when the tears start falling; I just know they do. And through the blurriness, I see the woman who looks like my mother kiss my knee and lift her head toward me, grinning. Her lips are stained with my blood.

"You are a mighty flower," she says, "and you will not bend or break."

I believe her. Oh, how I believe her.

TWENTY-SEVEN

My memories became as sharp as the coppery taste of blood.

"I was the reason for Monsieur Boucher's death. *I* hurt him."

With magic. *My* magic.

"Your power was strong even when you were a child," Neena said, her gravelly voice pulling me to the present. "Power only one person has, historically, been allowed to possess."

"What is she on about?" Minho asked, gaze volleying between the two of us.

"I suppose there's no use pretending anymore." My aunt straightened herself, grinning. "My name is Neena. I have no surname, for I have no family. Except my pathetic twin, Tara."

My mother's sister. I tried to rifle through all the memories I had of my aunt, other than the one I had just unlocked. Why hadn't I known Maman had a twin? Perhaps it was because I had already started to conflate them both long before I controlled the garden to kill Monsieur Boucher.

Tara and Neena. Neena and Tara.

Our special day.

Of course. *Our* because she shared her birthday, and always had, with her twin sister. Maman must have been hinting to the fact that she was a twin during the séance, when she'd flipped to the page about Janus and his two faces.

Was this why Maman hated to see herself in the mirror? Hated having her portrait commissioned? It wasn't just *her* face, after all. It was one she shared, a replica, like two busts of clay rendered by the same artist. Nearly identical.

I swallowed down my fear. "You've been here since the game started, haven't you? Watching us, using the secret passages."

Coffee-colored eyes in the bushes. A spy who'd leaked our whereabouts.

"You were always good at puzzles, Sana. I should have known you'd see me in the garden—which is why I pretended to be your mother's ghost. I think I played the part quite convincingly, given the circumstances."

The woman I'd seen in the garden: not Maman, but Neena.

"You see," Neena continued, "until this past summer, I've been in a magic-induced coma that turned me into a husk of a woman. Do you know who caused it?" She didn't wait for an answer. "Your mother. She used old medicine—an elixir meant to nullify me—after what happened to the butler. I was magically asleep for *years*. Oh, how I raged! The years I lost..." She broke herself from her spiral with a cold grin. "But then I woke and returned to the manor. I couldn't help but overhear Marta in the parlor... how *salacious* of your mother, creating a game where you could lose your inheritance! And yet all your mother appeared to leave behind was an ugly memory."

I gripped the vial, finding the dregs of the purplish liquid still inside. "Tell me how my memory of that day got here."

"A preserved memory elixir, forged from the razorthorn, of course.

Our ancestors were wise to keep stores of them before the flower died. After your mother had you speak the memory aloud, it could be extracted from your mind. But separated memories are physical things. They must be kept somewhere, bottled up, lest they return to the mind of their owner. It seems now that you're of age, your mother wanted you to learn the truth of the razorthorn's power."

A realization pained me, like a blade to the gut. "That's what this contest was about." Before a wave of dizziness could overtake me, I whispered, "Where is my mother? Is she truly dead?" Fox and I couldn't have made up what had happened during the séance.

Neena only rolled her eyes and laughed. "*That's* what you've been wondering for the past seven years? Let her go, Sana. She was a pitiful mother. *I* was a much better one to you, don't you think?"

"You'll *never* be my mother," I said, voice thick with oncoming tears.

But a sudden thought stabbed me in the heart: *Which woman from my childhood memories is my aunt?* The mother who always stayed away, or the one who held me close?

"That's where you're wrong, Sana. Your mother was so lost in her dreamworld of riddles and puzzles that she forgot about her own daughter. She spent days and nights locked in her study. Who came outside to be with you? To tend to the garden as you played with the soil, like a flower yourself?"

I shook my head, hating the fact that a small part of me knew it was true.

"No mother of mine would frame Marta. Because of you, she believes she is at fault for a crime she didn't commit."

"The poor woman's suffering is nothing compared to what I have had to endure!" Neena snapped. "That day, I wasn't expecting such a horrendous outcome. I lost those shears in the shuffle. Your mother must have found them, just like she found me later after I hid the butler's body. Thankfully, she knew I could pretend to be her at any moment—pretend I was *afraid of my terrible sister Neena* and blame the whole thing on *her*. She vowed not to tell the police."

"Clever, that Tara," tutted Hyunwoo. "But not quite clever enough."

Minho stepped away from his uncle. "You never told me you knew Sana's aunt."

"Did you think I followed you to this house for no reason?" Hyunwoo barked before regaining a façade of calm. "The game was child's play, but what we've been waiting for is within our grasp. It's time to finish what we started in 1894."

Neena circled me. "Hyunwoo has been arduously working to create a razorthorn for the past seven years. Alas—I would have helped him, if not for my slumber. Thankfully, all those years of waiting have paid off. For this. For *you*." Neena tipped my chin up, forcing my gaze onto hers. "This seed your mother worked on... all it needs is your blood to blossom. *You* are the last ingredient."

"I-I won't give it you," I stammered, still in a haze of confusion.

Hyunwoo wore an oily smile. "Not willingly, it seems."

He looked like he was about to grab onto Minho when a rustling sound came from the hedges. Behind Hyunwoo, Minho, and Neena, Fox crashed out of the verge and threw out a grasping hand for Hyunwoo's knife.

"Don't!" I cried, but it was too late.

Like bulls incensed by their riders, Hyunwoo and Fox clashed and bucked wildly. Fox struggled against him, still trying to grab the blade, but Hyunwoo twisted his wrist, and Fox released an anguished wail. In one smooth stroke, Minho's uncle had Fox in a chokehold, the knife applying pressure to Fox's throat. The edge glinted, as bright as the whites of Fox's eyes.

Horrified, Minho pleaded, "Uncle, *stop*—"

"Not *now*, you halfwit!" I didn't think Hyunwoo could look more crazed, but somehow, he did. "Give us your blood, Sana, and I will let him go."

"Don't do it," Fox choked out, fighting against Hyunwoo's grip. "Remember what you told me? We're in this together!"

Tears threatened to spill onto my cheeks. I glanced at the razorthorn seed, then back at Fox.

We *were* in this together. Which was exactly why I needed to save my brother.

"I know," I told him, approaching Neena and the thorny seed she held. "And I'm sorry."

I pressed my finger to the thorn, watching as a bead of blood traveled from my finger into the stem itself. In a heartbeat, the flower began to bloom, petal by petal. The flower was magnetic—it called to you like a siren song, drawing you close enough to prick you. Its red petals unfurled to their full size as the flower reached its mature form in an ethereal awakening of magic.

I had dreamed of this moment, of finally seeing this flower. And yet it felt nothing like a blessing. It was a curse.

I attempted to remove my finger, but it remained stuck in place. Panic rose within me as I saw that my blood had both entered the flower and flowed *out* of it through another thorn, this one pricking the pad of my aunt's finger.

I tried to pull away again, but Neena only grinned. "It's working. The transfer is *working*." The words were a whisper. A long-offered prayer, finally given answer.

The flower burned so bright, I worried it might be set aflame. My voice grew hoarse. "I—I can't move. Minho— Fox—"

"They can't hear you. Now stop struggling and look closely, Sana," my aunt ordered. "*Look.*"

I did. My eyes smarted at the brilliance of the flower. At the blood that wound its way from my thumb, into the thorn, and finally, up to its crimson petals. "Do you see what I see?" my aunt asked.

I nodded, but it felt like my head wasn't part of my body. Dimly, I grew aware of the ground moving lower—or perhaps my *body* was drifting up, like I had become as weightless as the flower hovering before us.

"Good. Your blood is divine, Sana, and I want you to know why."

The light grew too sharp, and I shut my eyes, feeling the burn against my eyelids. Only once the light dimmed did I open them, batting away the bleary tears.

I was no longer in the garden. Surrounded by a flash of hypnotizing red and white stripes, I found myself in a circus tent, spectator to a show.

The curtains pulled apart, revealing a magnificent and quite identical sister act, no older than eight. "Et voilà—the Juggling Jumelles!"

The twins began on opposite sides of a tightrope, moving to a staccato drumbeat. When they were close enough to touch, they each flipped backward, landing on soft mats. The crowd roared. Next, they balanced balls and plates on their heads and feet, and the applause turned deafening. They linked hands as their routine came to an end, night after night after night.

But just like the end of a magic trick, the crowds thinned before they altogether disappeared, and so too did the money being thrown at their feet.

The tent slipped away, melting into a more familiar picture. Neena wore her leotard while her sister had shed the suffocating suit for a comfortable day dress. They raced through the hedges, becoming one with the leaves.

But one girl tripped and fell . . . and the other girl did not wait. Knowing how Flora once gave her family their luck, she devoted her time to learning more about the goddess herself. And her sister watched on from a garret window, looking down at the world as it moved along without her. Without the Juggling Jumelles. Without the flower.

I found the world splintering, fracturing, into a new setting. I was standing behind an older version of Neena and Tara as they traversed the academy grounds. A newspaper unfurled at my feet, and I bent down to read the date.

July 1894.

A *whoosh* of smoke, and my feet were on new ground. My eyes adjusted to the light, and I found myself back in the academy library. Except now, I was seated at a table with my mother.

Tara studied alongside Richard Fox the First, a flush growing on her cheeks as their hands brushed. She pulled back and glanced down, resuming her work, as Richard stole a long glance at her, tapping a pencil against his lips. How similar he was to Fox, and yet how *bold*. It made my stomach turn.

My body lurched as time sped up, colors bleeding into one another to form a painter's palette. Neena, snapping a photograph of the others standing before Blackthorn Hall. Maman, stealing private moments with Richard beneath the arches of the academy's stone edifice.

Days passed, from the way the clock wound fast, abruptly stopping at a sharp angle that made the bell above the academy toll. It was time for bed.

But my mother and her friends were wide awake.

I stayed hot on their heels as they each pricked their fingers, offering blood to open the concealed laboratory behind the bookshelf. Inside, they pored over their journals, scratching their heads in contemplation for that *one final ingredient*.

"I know just what we're missing. The flower was forged with blood," Neena told her classmates. "And so blood is what we require."

Maria's voice quivered. "Are you certain about this?"

Neena quelled her with a hand on her shoulder. "We're Keepers of the flower, remember? It's time we live up to the name we've given ourselves."

The scene melted away, and I watched as Neena knocked a professor unconscious, dragging her into the laboratory. Within minutes, she had set up the professor's limp body in a chair, using a thin clear tube to extract blood from the lady's veins and pump it into the seedling itself. The flower appeared to accept the blood at first, growing fresh petals, before those same petals hunched over, withering until they were dry and black. Neena grunted, pushing away from the table with such force she toppled it over, and turned to her friend Hyunwoo.

More, that look said, and her classmate obeyed.

Producing a knife with stunning speed, Hyunwoo prepared to make a practiced cut. The wound left the professor bleeding out. Her pallor grew white as she slumped deeper in her chair, her sleeve turning red. But still the flower did not respond to the offering. Tara's horror grew as she tried to staunch the professor's wound, but it was becoming horribly clear it was too late for that.

"We killed Professor Lemieux!" Maria slapped a hand over her mouth, suppressing a howl. Tara fell back, her skirts covered in blood, and sobbed into Richard's collar.

Hyunwoo's eyes hardened. "Help me move the body. I know where we can bring it."

Time leapt forward again, glazing past a sorrowful memorial. Moons later, my mother fled to the private dorm's lavatory before she vomited, one hand on her abdomen, the curve of which she was having difficulty concealing beneath her day dress. She wiped her mouth hastily and found her desk to scribble a note on parchment. *Perhaps it's best that the child stays with you.*

And then, by no small miracle, a baby boy, passed from Maman's arms to Richard's. Leaving her with a heart that might never be whole again.

I fell to my knees at the same time my mother did. I reached out to touch the tear escaping down her cheek, and I could have sworn I felt its warmth on my skin. My mother saw me. *Truly* saw me, even though I wasn't there. And an idea bloomed.

Maman moved frantically in her room, tossing aside her bedsheets, every material thing cast aside. She pulled items from under her bed, items her family had used in India to create spaces of prayer. She barely ate, barely noticed herself take a breath as she completed her project days later: a worthy shrine for a worthy goddess. And when she was ready, she whispered her prayers—her fears—aloud.

"Please, Flora," my mother begged. "I worried what the world would make of me, an unmarried woman hoisting a child on her hip. Nor could I reconcile things with Richard after our disagreements about who should keep the baby. Eventually, I gave in, and Richard passed off the child as a product of a new marriage. But I made a mistake giving up my son. Please, help me rectify it."

At first, the shrine did not stir. The offerings did not take.

And then—smoke rose from the incense sticks, flashing vibrant colors: periwinkle blue, rose-petal red, marigold orange.

My mother had prayed . . . and the goddess had answered.

A voice boomed from the heavens, not gentle but not unkind. "This is not a simple offering. For this prayer to take root, I require an equal give-and-take. What will you offer me in exchange, Tara?"

Maman's next words were muffled, like a bargain with a god was not something one could overhear.

But the goddess must have accepted, for my mother planted a hand on her swelling belly as she felt something move within it. The telltale sign of feet kicking. She wept and laughed and wept again.

I fell back, back, back—out of the memory and into the consuming garden. My aunt wore a stinging smile.

"Do you understand who you are now, Sana?"

My breath hitched. "Yes."

I was not a girl of this world. I was a girl made of ivy and thorn, riddles and enigma. I was made of magic.

TWENTY-EIGHT

The last piece of my puzzle finally clicked into place.

Light from my hand; thorns growing from my fingers; my miraculous recovery at the inn.

The flower removed itself from me and Neena at once, still hovering in the air before us. Fox and Minho exchanged long looks with me; clearly, they had seen this memory, too.

The tent might have been gone, but I knew, instinctively, that Neena was the ringmaster and I the jongleur.

Neena was the first to speak. "The day Monsieur Boucher died, I discovered the truth of your power. As a child of Flora, someone with divine provenance, *you* were the final ingredient to bring this razorthorn to life. You were what we needed all along."

I stared at the razorthorn, glowing brightly from my blood.

"That doesn't absolve you from *killing* someone," I shrieked. And yet my own hands had killed, too—I had used this divine power to end a life.

"That professor's death was one small price to pay. She revered Flora until her dying breath. But did she know the truth?" Hyunwoo shouted, shoving Fox aside. "Flora didn't offer her devotees true power. She dropped the flower in front of her worshippers like a toy, *knowing* its magic would not last forever!"

Neena stepped in. "The flower disappeared when I was just a child. I began to resent Flora and the invocations my parents continued to offer. Prayers Flora never answered." She inhaled deeply. "Our family's healing business fell apart, and so too did our luck. We lost our livelihoods. We lost our home. We were forced to move to the one place where my parents owned land, in France. But like a plant placed in the wrong pot, I began to wither while Tara blossomed. It often felt like only I saw the cruel games the gods played."

"If their games are so cruel, why did you go to the academy? Why try to recreate Flora's gift?"

"To take fate into my own hands!" Neena inhaled a steadying breath. "*I* invited a member of each of the Four Families to the Botanical Academy. I knew it would take knowledge from each family to succeed in my attempts to create a *new* iteration of the razorthorn, one crafted by human hands. One that would never perish! Thankfully, Hyunwoo was aligned with my ideals."

Hyunwoo shared Neena's ambitious smile. "We found a group of likeminded people. People who understood that the gods do not bless us with gifts—they taunt us with shreds of their power, and once we are hooked on its taste, they take that power away."

"Les Voyants," I realized, remembering what they'd said about the Keepers. About a Great Sister—*Neena*. "They followed me. They're back, after decades."

"Faith always holds when you believe in your principles. Yes, the group has been in hiding for many years, but *I* have been the one to push their plans to fruition. I had a few of them scout you out to retrieve your blood, if only to test my theories, but you eluded them."

"You sent them?"

"Prometheus was ambitious enough to taste the gods' power. I am, too. Hyunwoo and I *knew* that we could taste that same might." Neena smiled. "Power is not born within us mortals. It must be taken, claimed, like a territory staked in battle."

"You mean *conquered*," I spat. "*Stolen*."

"So many people have conquered our land, Sana. Do not speak to me about what it is I can or cannot take."

The words were like a slap to my ears. I was too stunned to respond, because it was true. Just like conquerors, the gods had laid claim to this land. Did that make everyone who lived below just a pawn in their game?

Neena continued. "I poured everything into learning whatever I could from professors and scholars alike. To perfect creating a razorthorn. My conduit. My vessel to access a greater, unknowable energy. Because to defeat a god . . . you must become one."

"Let the blood transfer take hold. Let Flora's power fully awaken," Hyunwoo interrupted greedily after licking his lips, "so that we may destroy the goddess with her own power and end this Cycle of Light once and for all!"

Neena threw her hands forth, drawing on the magic of the garden. Nothing could control nature as I saw it now. The wind picked up with sudden fervor. The hedges grew taller, more fearsome, opening holes like the maw of a monster. Through them, vines as thick as pillars swarmed the grounds, pulling me, Fox, and Minho to our knees. Another score of vines lashed forth like snakes, binding our arms to our sides and pinning us to the ground. More slithered upward, forming a cage over us like a tidal wave and blotting out the moon.

We were trapped in a prison of leaves and barbs.

"Let us free!" Fox cried.

But Neena didn't appear to be listening. Her eyes turned into black holes. Dark, sweet venom filled her veins, turning them black and visible. Thorns grew through her flesh, piercing the corners of her mouth, making her skin tear and bleed as more and more points broke free, turning her from a woman to a monster.

No—a god.

Screams, rending the air. Skin, splitting apart.

Transformed by the sheer force of raw magic, Neena's obsidian eyes found mine. "The next step is within my grasp. Hyunwoo, the flower."

Hyunwoo pocketed his knife and grabbed the floating razorthorn before approaching the glowing door. He twisted the flower so it was perpendicular to his body, bracing it by its petals. The stem grew teeth, molding itself to the lock. It didn't look so different from the drawing in my mother's book, the thorns imitating the bits of a key.

Five petals, open and willing. A fifth and final power, waiting to be used...

The flower is the key to everything, came the haunting lilt of my aunt's voice.

Maman had been right all along. This power was the key that would connect us to the world of the gods, and not just metaphorically.

A portal to Olympus.

Hyunwoo's voice knifed into my thoughts. "The key is made. The door is ready." Before he could insert the makeshift key, Hyunwoo glanced over at his nephew. "It's not too late to join us, Minho. Romance is fleeting; dedication to a cause is forever."

"No," Minho declared. "*No,* samchon. I won't obey you any longer."

"I was afraid you would say that," Hyunwoo snarled. "I spent the better part of a year constructing this door, sourcing the right magicked wood, while Neena was in a fugue state. And yet you don't seem to appreciate at all what I've done for us—for *you*. For *mankind.*"

"I should never have listened to you. I believed you wanted the flower to restore our family's fortunes, not—*this*. You're unwell, Uncle."

Hyunwoo's chuckle appeared to confirm the statement. "Neena, why don't we just kill them now? That way, they can never divulge the truth of what's occurred."

"*Heel,*" she told him, as if he was a dog straining against his leash. "A goddess can handle her enemies alone. Now, open the door."

"As you wish."

With one smooth motion, Hyunwoo forced the flower forward into the keyhole and *turned*. The door eased open as white, shimmering light swept over us with its heavenly radiance.

He stood there, swaying on his feet. "We've done it," he said, fully entranced by the door and the balm of light shining within.

My eyes smarted. I, too, could barely stand its brilliance. Was I seeing the gods' realm with my own eyes?

Hyunwoo was spellbound. "L'égalité arrivera. Les Voyants verront."

Equality will arrive. The seers will see.

He held up a steady hand, and his skin sizzled as he slipped a finger across the threshold. He hissed, falling back. It was as though an uninvited guest could not enter such a realm, not without being doomed to burn for eternity.

"Neena, I cannot walk through the door. Your godly form must enter first, so I might follow—"

A vine slipped over his mouth, prohibiting him from speaking. His shouts grew muffled as another thorny rope of ivy shot up from the ground, tightening around his wrists. The ivy latched onto him like leeches, crawling up his thighs.

Hyunwoo fumbled back, falling squarely into the hedges. More vines clawed over him, dragging him deeper into the growth. "Neena," Hyunwoo gasped as the ivy claimed his face, his voice still muffled. "Neena, help me!"

But Neena remained unmoved as the hedges swallowed him whole. "There. Now he'll be quiet."

"*Uncle!*" Minho cried, fighting against his restraints.

My gaze grew molten. "Were you even planning on bringing Hyunwoo through the door? Your own *friend* worked diligently for your schemes all these years, and this is how you repay him?"

"I prefer not to owe debts," my aunt explained flatly. "Now, I have a trip to Olympus that will not be delayed. Not even my awful sister can stop me now."

The words shattered something inside me. Maman was gone. Her body, a captive of the Seine. But the truth was, she had been missing long before that fateful day. Missing from my life. And both Neena and I shared one haunting, terrible thing. Not her love, but the absence of it.

Perhaps to my own fault, I still loved Maman. Still loved my aunt. Because this world had not taken kindly to them.

I didn't know when the tears began to fall, but they did, hissing against the soil. And it occurred to me then that my aunt was wrong about one thing. Soil is soil, and no matter where we put down roots, our stories, our histories, our futures, will flourish.

As if sensing the gravity of my thoughts, the earth rumbled.

Neena made to turn on her heel, but stopped, startled, as the ground quaked beneath our feet. Cracks split the earth; vines scattered like rats sensing danger. Something was coming.

In answer, the roots of a tree slunk out from the cracks in the ground. The earth tremored harder as a tree exploded from the dirt, twisting into the air and swelling in size until it stood a hundred feet above us. I could barely fathom this thing of nature, mimicking the tallest of the Giants.

Another blast of roots knocked us all mercilessly onto our backs. I could only stare up, stars shining in my vision, at the monstrosity before me. A gnarled trunk, half-dead leaves—not a tree of life, but death.

When the ground stopped quaking, my aunt shakily got to her feet. Her eyes sought mine, holding both horror and wonder. We knew with equal understanding who had done this.

I glanced down at my now unbound hands, faintly luminescing.

"Gods' teeth," Neena swore as she absorbed the tree's grand height. With a hum of satisfaction, she offered her full attention to me. "You truly are a mighty flower."

She padded toward me. At first, the tree obstructed her path with a stern, thick branch, but I lifted a hand. The branch lowered its guard.

Stepping over it, my aunt found me and brushed my tears the same way she had seven years ago. "You possess an otherworldly might, my little butterfly. Imagine it. Just *imagine* the power we could hold, together, in Olympus."

"What are you saying?"

"Come with me. Through the door."

I glanced uneasily at the open doorway. Then I turned to my friends Minho and Fox, both looking awestruck in their bindings.

And I knew my answer.

My hands flared with heat as I placed my palms flush with the ground, letting the soil around the tree stir. Letting the earth recognize me. The tree shivered with understanding, meeting its mistress. It shook its branches so the crumbling leaves scattered around me like raindrops.

More, my power begged, as if waiting to be freed from its locked cage. I mentally opened the latch.

"I'm afraid I can't do that, Neena Massi. My mother might not be able to stop you . . . but I can."

The thorn that had once been lodged in my hand appeared, breaking out of my skin and growing and growing, creating a vine that coiled around my wrist, a bracelet of barbs and petals. It slithered up my arm like a snake. Not a snake I feared, but one I was learning I could control. More thorns grew from my skin, from the hollow of my throat, the corner of my lip.

I dug my hands deeper into the dirt. The roots of the tree slipped over my feet, like they were my companions and not my foes.

What was once fear of my power turned into anticipation.

Into acceptance.

I had spoken to the garden as a child. Become one with it. And now, we would work in tandem.

I rose to face Neena. She fumed, stumbling back.

"Flora's power exists in us both." I raised my chin. "How ironic, that you've become the very thing you're trying to destroy. Enjoy your time in the heavens—it won't last long."

Without warning, I threw my hands forward, drawing on the roots of the tree to mirror my actions. They slithered toward Neena, binding her feet. With a growl, Neena cast a burning light downward, and the roots shrank back in recoil. The garden roared as she sent a slew of retaliatory vines. They pierced skin, but instead of pain, all I felt was a trio of raw, unyielding emotions. And not my own.

Neena's sense of loss, from leaving her homeland. Her jealousy, from watching her sister abandon her. And finally, a deep well of grief. For a life she might have lived, with or without the flower. For a future not drawn by the Fates, but by her own hand.

As if sensing what I felt, Neena dropped her arms. "Don't you dare try to empathize with me, Sana. You cannot begin to understand my pain." She whipped a hand toward me. A new vine shot forward and wrapped, viselike, around my neck. I clawed at it with futile fingers, sinking to the ground.

My aunt loomed overhead, grinning. It wasn't so different from the day I had bruised my knee. She had loomed over me then, too, whispering false promises, licking my blood…

This is it. I've reached the end.

Tears stung my eyes from the pain. As my vision blurred, I thought I was looking at my own mother once again—a demonic, deadly version.

"If only you obeyed as easily as the flower—" Neena halted, noticing the flower was no longer in the keyhole. She spun with wide, frenzied eyes. "Where is it?" she spat.

"Looking for something?" a sweet voice asked.

In Neena's distraction, the vine around my neck loosened, and I gulped in breaths of air. "Belle!" I shouted over the roaring wind.

My friend was standing on a sturdy branch of the tree. It moved through the air, depositing her in front of me. She raised a hand, holding up the razorthorn.

Loosening the vine from my throat, I shot to my feet. Now more than ever, I was grateful for Belle's nimbleness, her bravery.

The vines around Fox and Minho grew slack as Neena balked, losing her grip on the garden. They wriggled out of their climbers to join me, Isabelle just behind.

Neena resumed a cool mask of displeasure as she reached out a delicate hand toward Isabelle. "Give it here, girl. That should only be kept in a goddess's hands."

For once, I agreed with her. This power, it was becoming clear, was too great for this world. It left her with an unsatiable greed, drove her to murder. I would not fall prey to its temptations.

"Four must be combined," I recited to my friends, understanding dawning on me. "With blood, the razorthorn was made. With blood, it can be *destroyed*."

It already had mine. What it needed to be unmade was theirs. The blood of the Keeper families.

Resolve settling on her features, Isabelle pricked her finger against the thorn, drawing blood. Next, Fox did the same, followed by Minho.

"No," Neena caught on. "*Stop!*"

Without warning, Isabelle flung the flower in the air.

The ringing sound in my ears grew to a dull roar as the razorthorn soared like a bird taking flight for the first time.

We each raised our hands, palms facing the flower, as if a magnetic force was propelling us to move closer to it. Cords of light threaded the air from the tips of our fingers, reaching the thorny stem.

"One petal for wisdom," Fox began.

"Two for the muses," said Isabelle.

"Three to affect the mind," added Minho.

"And four to heal all bruises!" I finished.

We needed no elixir, no drink, no potion to harness this ability. Our connection to the razorthorn required only the magic that was buried deep within each of us. Our blood. Our bond.

Obeying my command, the flower rose into the air, spinning faster, faster, a blur of thorn and shadow. Within moments, the petals began to singe and burn black. Acrid smoke and ash filled the air, mimicking the smell of death.

The flower burst into a hundred infinitesimal pieces.

"You *imbeciles—*" my aunt screamed, then flicked her arm out again. The garden stirred, but this time it was not in Neena's control.

It was in mine.

Vines twitched in the soil. The hedges loomed closer. The tree craned down.

The garden was displeased by the false god. And that simply wouldn't do.

The ground shifted beneath my feet. The ivy and vines latched onto Neena's wrists, scaling perilously up her body. The roots of the tree moved of their own accord, squirming with need. I understood immediately what the garden wanted—what it needed.

A sacrifice.

"What is going on?" Neena seethed. "*Obey* your master!"

You have proven yourself to be a charlatan, the garden whispered back. *We do not bow to those who play with the garden like a toy, but those who accept it like the blood in their veins. We obey only the goddess and her kin.*

I could feel the eyes of the garden turning on me. *I* needed to be the one to give restitution. To right this wrong.

My magic reignited, propelled by the garden's wrath. I let it consume me, turning me so numb, so absorbed by heat and fire and pure, unfiltered power, that I didn't feel the oncoming rain as it pelted my skin like rocks.

But my aunt had one last ace to play. She gathered the vines digging into her flesh and flung them forward, forcing them to attack me. I ducked, peering up to find I was not, in fact, the vines' target.

The ivy turned in a loop, setting its sights back around on Neena, and cast itself forward, throttling her neck.

Neena screamed as a cable of vines began to push down her throat.

Her veined skin transformed into a deep, scorched red. Welts appeared on her fingers, her neck, her mouth. And then even her eyes burned, so much that she clawed at them, leaving raw, red strokes of blood and skin and sinew.

I didn't want the garden to stop. I wanted everything to burn, fall, crumble. *Break.*

I was part flower, part girl.

I was what Maman had always wanted.

My aunt writhed on the ground, thrashed in the soil—and then she became still.

"Sana." Minho rushed over and eclipsed the horrifying image before me. My eyes dimmed as I found him—truly found him. Just as he had found me.

I collapsed into his arms, letting the power go.

Isabelle was panting on her knees. Fox hurled at the sight of our aunt—her lifeless body, covered in welts and burns. I crawled on hands and knees toward her, feeling her warm, warm hands. The place where her heartbeat should have been pulsing at her wrist, now silent.

Cold fog escaped her throat, swirling away like smoke on the wind, and I sobbed.

Vines from the soil below reached forward to claim Neena's body. They dragged her into the ground until she was swallowed by the earth, leaving nothing but upturned soil in her place.

TWENTY-NINE

Death had taken hold of Razorthorn Manor once again, and it had not been kind.

As if the gods had sensed a disturbance with the forged door, a frigid storm pummelled us. Snow fell in sheets, but I did not feel the cold. Did not sense anything but a dull, pounding dread, like the moment one wakes from a bad dream and isn't sure what was real and what was imagined.

Time passed in short vignettes.

Fox, grabbing the doorknob. The door, now closed, splintering into pieces. Its light, snuffed out like a candle.

And soon after: Monsieur Champlain, arriving with a ghostly pallor, finding us all covered in injuries.

After the ambulance attendants arrived to tend to our wounds, I remained on the stoop. The snow was like a reprieve from days of lightning storms. But the cold could not ice away the heat of the world beyond the door, out of reach once more.

Hours after the incident, when my body had begun to thaw from all the icy revelations I had unpacked, I sat by the candlelight and read the pages Maman had left for me in the puzzle box. I absorbed every line and stroke of ink, every word Maman had written specifically for me to find:

Dearest daughter,

I'm sorry to have deceived you and your friends into playing this game. I hope you see it not as a ruse, or a loss, but an opportunity gained. A way for me to shed some light, without putting you all in too much danger.

Allow me to start at the beginning.

I have been putting my final touches on this game for many weeks now. Based on the clues in the laboratory, I hope you children have divulged the truth—we tried, and failed, to create a razorthorn, risking the life of a teacher who was wrongfully sacrificed for our trials. I won't go too deep into the details, but I wish only to impart to you the dangers the razorthorn flower can bring. I hope you understand now why I have had to keep everything so tightly wound—the clues, the puzzles, the riddles, the contracts bound with my blood—all for you and the other children to decipher what has truly been going on these last few decades with the razorthorn flower.

My sister was ambitious to a fault. From the memory I left you, you have discovered just how much.

After what occurred in the garden, I knew I had to end Neena's unsettling charades—and her wish to bring about the Collapse—but I didn't anticipate my sister turning into a shell of herself. I often left our home to learn how to destroy the razorthorn flower, should I ever get my hands on the half-created seed again—and to visit Neena in her comatic state. She is still my sister, my mirror. It is both a fault and a gift to love.

I'm sorry to have siphoned your memory of that horrid day. I hope that you are old enough now to handle it, the terrible truth of what occurred, and that you might use that information to understand the power, the gift, inside you. This will shock you, but you are not born of this world. You are a gift donned to me by the goddess Flora herself—a seed that is born of my flesh and of nature itself. You have no father, Sana, and I must also admit that you have a half brother—Richard Fox the Second. But perhaps you've already learned that through your time spent together during this game.

I invited the other children here, offspring or close kin of the friends I once had at the Botanical Academy, to learn the harsh truths about the razorthorn as well. As I have taught you, four must be combined, and I hope one day, you four combined will be enough to destroy the flower should it ever be made again—for if it is, its allure will certainly be too great to resist.

Come nightfall in two weeks, when I have put the final touches on my puzzles, I will be escorted through the Seine, a portal to Elysium, to serve as Flora's apprentice. Most mortals cannot cross the gates to this other realm without having perished first, but I can. This is the bargain I made—when you began to exhibit powers that you are part goddess, I would be called to fulfill my duty.

I hope one day I will find you, and I will hold you in my arms once more.

I pray you will forgive me.

With deepest sympathy,
Your mother

P.S. The manor and subsequent inheritance are indeed yours and Richard Fox the Second's, split equally to do as you please. I have decided to offer the other two children generous amounts of money for playing this game. I know money does not heal wounds. I know it does not make up for my past or future actions. But neither does magic, and of that I am in short supply.

I reread the letter thrice over. It felt surreal, impossible, even, to hold my mother's last note to me in my hands. The explanations for her riddles, her game—her desire for us to learn the truth of the razorthorn's inimitable power . . . it all made sense.

And yet I couldn't find anything in my chest but heartbreak, confusion, and finally, some sense of repose. A small semblance of closure.

Closure, from knowing that my mother left on her own terms—from her own bargain—and that she wasn't truly dead at all. She was in the Elysian Fields, away from the child the goddess had gifted her, but still able to reach me, if summoned, like that day with Fox in the library.

But it still took me all night, turning sleeplessly, tears streaming down my face, to absorb the fact that my mother was never coming back. Not physically.

Knowing the clarity this letter would bring us, I handed it to my competitors to read in the morning. Isabelle was most shocked of all, realizing it was not my mother who had pushed her into the river on my tenth birthday, but a woman pretending to be her.

I pray you will forgive me.

I wasn't sure I felt forgiveness. A small voice inside me might call what my mother did selfish. I suppose she wasn't the perfect mother, nor I the perfect child. Maybe, one day, we could make up for that.

Despite that voice, I did feel something else—prepared. Ready to move on, to start afresh, and turn my home into the manor I always hoped it would be.

Soon after, Monsieur Champlain and I came to a decision on the state of the house. We would complete the final renovations together, so that when Marta eventually returned—and she would; she had only acted out of fear and played no true role in Monsieur Boucher's death—she would have a peaceful place to stay.

We moved outside as the cabs arrived to take Isabelle, Fox, and

Minho away. Fox would certainly return, as one of the blood heirs of the manor, but it still felt strange, saying farewell.

"Goodbye, Sana." Fox held out a stiff hand. He had borrowed a jacket from Monsieur Boucher, which made him look less like a paperboy and more like a man. Gazing at him this morning, in the cool fall light, I knew we were siblings, and I had come to accept the fact with my whole heart.

I crushed Fox in an embrace on the stoop, letting out a sigh as he hugged me back.

"I've made one last Sherlockian discovery," Fox said as he pulled away. "Except I think the term should be changed to *Fox*ian."

"Oh, most certainly," I agreed. "What is it?"

"The puzzles. Each one seemed to have a link to one of our families' traditional uses of the flower. For example, the Picasso clue must represent Isabelle—coming from a long line of artists. The parquette puzzle, clearly a connection to Minho's family's architectural empire."

"And us two," I said, "connected to the *Frankenstein* clue. Mary and Percy—your parents."

"Precisely. Now, I've got a long trip home with a copy of Monsieur Champlain's favorite book to accompany me." Fox held up the Oscar Wilde novel to his chest and waved goodbye.

Next, Isabelle stepped off the porch, her trunk in hand. Her lavender-colored ensemble looked chic enough to be sold at one of those shops we'd passed near the Champs-Élysées. Somehow, she managed to look thoroughly put together, despite the previous night's events.

"I'll be going for my next culinary school audition next week," she told me, wearing a slanted smile. "Wish me good luck?"

"You won't need it, but"—I pulled my key necklace over my head—"take it as a good luck charm."

"I couldn't—"

"Please, Belle." I wrapped my hands over hers, tucking the gift safely inside. Now that I knew where my mother was—or rather, why she had disappeared in the first place—I didn't need it.

"Maybe when we see each other again, you can return it to me."

"Will we?" Isabelle whispered. I saw tears blooming in the corners of her eyes. "See each other?"

In place of an answer, I wrapped my arms around her, squeezing tight. Isabelle gripped my arms with her hands before piling into the cab with Fox.

Monsieur Champlain ushered out the final houseguest. Minho wore a red-and-blue-striped scarf over his sweater. He approached me with shy steps. A sudden wind swept his hair back, like it was trying to give me one last opportunity to see him clearly before we were finished.

It was time.

"Give Marta my sincerest thanks," he said. "Will she return soon?"

"I believe so. Where will you go? Your uncle—"

"Is gone," he said, like he was still trying to learn how to mourn someone whose fate was unknown. "Whether the garden took him, or he disappeared, I might never learn the truth. I've already sent word by telegram to my mother about his . . . departure. And then, it'll be back to Korea."

"Is that what you want?" I asked, hating the way my voice cracked.

"No." The sole syllable was punctuated with genuine candor. "But I hope to resume my classes at the Sorbonne next term."

Those few words held a well of hope, and a well of questions. Did he mean he wished to return to Paris for school . . . or more?

I couldn't let myself dwell on it. Minho had lied, cheated, and worst of all, hurt. None of those things should have been forgiven.

But I'd also never done what I should. What was expected. We were all allowed to make mistakes; what mattered was how we learned from them.

Minho made no move to pick up his trunks. Seeing that our conversation wasn't over, the butler placed Minho's things into the cab that awaited to take him away.

"There's no reason to delay this."

My heart spiked. "Delay what?"

Minho straightened, looking me directly in the eyes, and guided me to a more private area of the stoop. "I don't resent your mother for what she did. In fact, I think she was courageous. I'm . . . glad I came here," he finally managed. "So that I could learn the truth."

"I'm glad you came here, too. I . . . I wish you well, Kim Minho."

I offered him my hand, expecting him to kiss it. Expecting it would be easier this way, to leave the past as nothing more than a collection of vows.

But as Minho eased closer, I realized what a fool I was. And how foolish, indeed, he was for me.

He held my hand fast as he spoke, tugging me closer. "I will not easily forget you, Sana. I . . ." The pause was not a hesitation, but a moment of clarity. "I admire you, most ardently."

"And I admire you, deeply." I pressed my other palm to his cheek, knowing what I said had come from the most inward part of my heart. "My Darcy."

Minho's eyes shone, and the events of the last week came rushing over me, unleashing a waterfall of emotion. Hot, salty tears fell down my cheeks. Minho kissed those tears away, pressing his lips gently around my mouth, like he needed to taste every bit of forgiveness I felt.

And when he'd finished, I kissed him with all the passion that I felt. Kissed him like it was a sealed promise. A kiss of forgiveness.

We broke apart just as the car honked, but Minho stayed rooted in place, his hands tangled with mine. "Go," I told him, for it was much easier to say than goodbye.

He squeezed my hands before retreating to the car, said farewell to Monsieur Champlain, and closed the car door.

I watched as the cabbie took my former competitors away, far into the depths of Paris, away from the game that had puzzled us.

If I'd learned anything this past week, it was that the garden was as much a friend as my three competitors. It wasn't simply a home, but a place to heal. A place to laugh. A place to live.

My mother had warned me to keep my mind open and my heart closed. But while Maman's heart had been broken, and mine fractured, I would not close my heart ever again.

I penned a letter to my family in Canada to let them know that I would be staying longer than intended. I wasn't sure how long, but I knew that this house was beginning to feel more and more like it belonged to me with each passing moment.

A real home.

It didn't matter that Maman wasn't here. Within the next several days after the game's end, the health of the garden appeared to be returning. This bit of earth—this hidden oasis—had magic within it. Not the kind that belonged to the gods, but the kind we could nurture and harvest, plant and grow.

I longed for the day Marta would return home to see the garden flourishing. Monsieur Champlain and I had already received a call from the bureau that she would be returning any day now. The lawyer I hired had told us a trial would await her in the winter, as she *had* technically hidden the body, with the help of Neena. Some might argue that it was coercion. Others might not believe her.

I had never believed so fiercely in my nanny all my life.

"Dinnertime," called Monsieur Champlain from the handrail. I trotted downstairs, tired from my day, but I wasn't hungry just yet.

"I'll be back in ten minutes, Monsieur. *Please*," I remembered myself.

Monsieur Champlain gave a half-hearted huff but indulged me. He already knew where I wanted to go.

The maze greeted me.

Except now, there was no fierce rain, no blast of thunder and lightning. In fact, the sun was setting over the hedges, casting a golden glow, and I retraced my steps back to the clearing at the center of the labyrinthine circle. To the tree, which now boasted a healthy coloring of red leaves. After all that had occurred, the tree had shrunk to a normal height, as though it had been planted decades ago rather than magically surging from the ground, an exhibit of my own uncanny ability.

I glanced at the ground. I still expected to find the razorthorn's divine petals scattered like disparate puzzle pieces on the grass. Instead, something new bloomed from the earth—just as I had hoped.

A sprig of lavender.

It was small but mighty, and as I glanced onward, I saw there was not one plant but a whole field of lavender, filling my nose with its overwhelmingly woodsy scent. Burying our loved ones was hard, and though the garden had taken my aunt for its own, I had tamed it into submission, enough to offer Neena one last parting gift.

"Goodbye," I told her, voice cracking, and turned on my heel to go back inside.

Welcome home, Sana, the manor said in greeting, and as I crossed the threshold, I tucked myself soundlessly into its sweet embrace.

The puzzle of this house—and of my heart—had finally been solved.

EPILOGUE

A chill November wind crept up on the house, wrapping the manor in a cold caress. Overgrown ivy clung to the porch step and rattled against the house's windows.

But the wind wasn't the only thing knocking on our door.

Monsieur Champlain greeted the visitor, letting him inside. A mane of tousled red hair; a set of warm brown eyes; and a pipe hanging from lips set in a familiar grin.

My brother removed his cap and scarf and strode in eagerly. "Did you miss me, Watson?"

"Fox!" I shot up from the sitting room couch, tossing my cross-stitch aside, and hugged my brother with the fierceness only a sister could possess. While I knew Fox would return one day to claim the manor as half his, I was not expecting it to be so soon.

"Sit," I offered, and he took the invitation. Monsieur Champlain poured two steaming cups of our most robust Darjeeling.

"I can't believe it's been a month! How are you? I hear Marta is conferring with a reputable lawyer. And you, monsieur? From Sana's letters, it appears you have found your own happy ending, n'est-ce pas?" Fox wiggled his eyebrows.

The butler wore a warm smile. "Indeed. In fact, I must be getting back to him. Our own tea is getting cold." He winked at me and turned on his heel for the parlor. Alain had visited several times over the past weeks, and while he hadn't accepted my offer of temporary residence as the pair searched for a shared home, he was growing more and more accustomed to the idea of staying at Razorthorn Manor.

Once Fox and I got past our niceties and drained half our cups, my brother hammered out a bone-chilling statement.

"I'm afraid this isn't a social visit."

"Oh?" Was this about his family? Did he tell them about the game—had he broken the truth to them about his biological mother? Were they going to excise him from the family and banish him from his English home?

"Remember what we discovered during the"—Fox lowered his voice—"*séance*? The dice had rolled even."

"Yes," I said. So vivid was the memory I had had trouble sleeping at night. "What about it?"

"*Even* spells danger. Tara wrote that she would be taken away to the godly realm, a servant of Flora's, correct? If I've made my assumptions accurately, I believe I know a way to help her come back."

"How so?" I asked him.

"This will clarify everything." Fox retrieved a pristine white envelope from the inside of his jacket, handing it over to me. The outside was postmarked from an academy in London. Beneath the crest was a Latin phrase that roughly translated to: *See as the gods see, and learn as the gods do.*

I had had my fill of the gods for the time being, but my curiosity burned too hot to ignore, and my thumb traced over the neatly scribed ink.

Was this truly a chance to save Maman, or another one of Fox's hunches?

I saved myself from spiraling by adding levity to the situation. "Is something afoot?"

"Why don't you take a look and see?"

I pulled out the letter with a feverish hand, then inspected the note thrice over. First to examine the letterhead; second to observe the sender's name; and third to fully absorb what the letter was saying. Only then did I look back up at Fox in awe.

"It's an invitation," I realized.

"Indeed." Fox leaned forward, a gleam in his eye like he'd just solved a jigsaw puzzle. "How about it, dear sister? Are you up for another game?"

ACKNOWLEDGMENTS

This book is an ode to *The Secret Garden,* one of our favorite and most beloved classics, and was born from the question *what if?* What if the story was told from a South Asian lens? What if the representation of India (and immigration as a whole) was differently portrayed? And, of course, how could we make this book a fun, edge-of-your-seat blend of our favorite genres: fantasy, historical, and mystery?

This undertaking would not have been possible without the following people:

Pete Knapp and Stuti Telidevara, thank you for seeing our vision for this story from the first emailed pages and sticking with it through mountains of rejections. You are both guiding lights in the sometimes-choppy waters that are the publishing business. Danielle Barthel, you are an email wizard and fierce advocate. Everyone at Park, Fine & Brower, you are literary champions!

Our editor, Mora Couch, your guidance and enthusiasm truly helped our characters and world leap off the page in ways we didn't expect. Thank you to our team at Holiday House and Penguin Random House, including Graciela Patron Colin for helping this book bloom in Canada, and Alison Tarnofsky for your marketing wisdom in the States. Enormous thank you to our copy editor and proofreader, Diane João and Stephanie Cohen Xu.

Our family, for encouraging us with every manuscript. From a young age, you fostered a love of reading and writing in us, and we are so grateful.

Thank you to June Hur and Judy I. Lin for the early reads and encouraging words. To Angela Montoya, Elle Tesch, and all the authors who took the time to share their kind blurbs, we thank you with buckets of flowers!

Thank you to all the readers who have shown up for this book with loads of excitement. Our community of friends, writing pals, educators, and librarians, you are all superstars at what you do.

Thank you to all the music that got us through draft after draft… I'm looking at you, Enhypen! (Did you catch the song references in the book?)

And lastly, to each other. This book was a lesson in perseverance. We did it!